"Leave my h
Leave my daughter out of this."

Sharon placed both palms on the table and stood. She leaned across the surface until her face was inches from Jackie's. "That nasty old spider never did anything but spread her poison and cause us heartache. If you keep at it, you'll end up just like her."

She left without another word. Stunned, Jackie sat in the silent room. Had she just been threatened? Reaching into her purse, she pulled out the recorder and saw that it was still running.

Good. If she turned up dead, at least Dennis...or rather, *Trooper* Walsh would have a record of the threat.

VIRGINIA SMITH

A lifelong lover of books, Virginia Smith has always enjoyed immersing herself in fiction. In her midtwenties she wrote her first story and discovered that writing well is harder than it looks; it took many years to produce a book worthy of publication. During the daylight hours she steadily climbed the corporate ladder and late at night after the kids had gone to bed stole time to write. With the publication of her first novel, she left her twenty-year corporate profession to devote her energy to her passion—writing stories that honor God and bring a smile to the faces of her readers. When she isn't writing, Ginny and her husband, Ted, enjoy exploring the extremes of nature—snow skiing in the mountains of Utah, motorcycle riding on the curvy roads of central Kentucky and scuba diving in the warm waters of the Caribbean. You can visit Virginia online at www.VirginiaSmith.org.

MURDER BY MUSHROOM

Virginia Smith

Steeple
Hill®

Published by Steeple Hill Books™

STEEPLE HILL BOOKS

Steeple
Hill®

ISBN-13: 978-0-373-44253-9
ISBN-10:   0-373-44253-X

MURDER BY MUSHROOM

Copyright © 2007 by Virginia Smith

www.SteepleHill.com

Printed in U.S.A.

For all have sinned and fall short of the glory of God, and are justified freely by his grace through the redemption that came by Christ Jesus.

—Romans 3:23–24

For my mother, Amy Barkman,
who loves mysteries and mushrooms.

Acknowledgments

I believe every good story comes from God, and He carefully selects the author of each. I'm thankful He gave me this one.

I'm also thankful to:

Ted, who supports me in so many ways, and who never thought when he married me that he'd end up becoming a "patron of the arts."

Maggie Tirey, Christy Leake, Beth Marlowe, Susie Smith and Amy Barkman, for their enthusiastic encouragement.

My dear friend, Tracy Ruckman, for critiques, support and prayers above and beyond the call of duty.

Trudy Kirk, my sister-of-the-heart, for helping me flesh out the details in her comfortable kitchen.

Susan J. Kroupa, Lisa Ludwig, Janelle Mowry, Sandra Robbins, Jess Ferguson and Tambra Rasmussen for expert critiques. And Chip Banks for patiently answering my banking questions.

Krista Stroever and all the folks at Steeple Hill Books for making my story so much stronger.

Wendy Lawton, for believing in me and handling all the yucky business stuff while I get to do the fun parts.

ONE

While the congregation of Heritage Community Church prayed, Jackie Hoffner fidgeted in her pew. Her backside had gone numb from a full torturous hour of sitting on the unyielding wooden surface.

For cryin' out loud, wrap up the prayer so we can get to the food!

She cracked open an eye and peeked toward the podium. From her seat near the center of the small sanctuary, she saw Pastor Earl Palmer standing with his eyes closed, his big black Bible clasped in his hands and his face alight with passion for the holy conversation in which he was engaged. As far as Jackie could tell, Pastor Palmer showed no sign of getting close to *Amen,* but instead seemed intent on reviewing in prayer every one of the finer points of his sermon. As if the Lord hadn't just heard it along with the rest of the congregation.

As on any potluck Sunday, the small sanctuary of the Kentucky church was practically full. Jackie doubted if anyone paid attention to the pastor's prayer. All around the sanctuary people shuffled in their pews, reaching for their purses or replacing their hymnals in anticipation of the moment of dismissal. Directly behind her, Justin Hart's stomach growled and his wife, Nancy, giggled. Jackie balled her hand and pushed a fist into her own stomach, which seemed determined to shout out an answering rumble.

And no wonder. The tangy odor of barbecued baked beans wafted from the fellowship hall where Lizzie Wallace had plugged in a Crock-Pot before the service. A variety of other smells had tantalized or tortured Jackie's nose through the service, as well. One row up, Mrs. Watkins sat with a casserole dish on the pew beside her, the telling odor of asparagus seeping from beneath the foil cover. Next to Jackie, Sarabeth Engelmann had set down a plate of foul-smelling deviled eggs that actually started to smell pretty good as Pastor Palmer's sermon lengthened and Jackie's stomach grew emptier.

With smug pride, Jackie thought of her own casserole on the floor of her car, wrapped in a thick layer of towels to keep the heat in. She had reason to feel good about it: at last month's potluck, Beverly Sanders had remarked, "At least we'll never lack potato chips as long as Jackie keeps coming to church."

Jackie's cheeks went hot at the memory of her snide tone and down-the-nose glance. Beverly, who was pushing fifty, presided over the monthly church-wide potluck like a queen. She assumed that a single female twenty-five years her junior couldn't produce an edible potluck offering. Well, Jackie had proved her wrong today.

Enough already! Say Amen!

A breath later, as though he heard Jackie's impatient thought, Pastor Palmer intoned, "Amen." The congregation's fiddling increased, as did the noise of bulletins shuffling and hymnals dropping with loud *thuds* into wooden slots. The jingle of Jackie's car keys added to the clamor as she fished them out of her purse.

At the front of the sanctuary, the pastor wasn't ready to let them go yet. "I have a couple of prayer requests for this week. Please continue to remember Mrs. Sawyer as she recovers from hip surgery. And this is our week to hold Bible study at the jail, so pray for that, too." His head turned in a sweeping motion as he scanned the congregation. "Are there any other announcements before we close?"

Lois Thatcher spoke up from halfway back on the left side of the sanctuary. "I need some men to carry tables out to the yard."

He nodded. "Okay, anyone who can help Lois, please go with her. Anything else?"

No one spoke. Pastor Palmer smiled and held his right hand high, palm toward the congregation. Jackie uncrossed her legs in preparation for her dash to the car the moment he pronounced the benediction.

As did everyone else. The instant the last word left the pastor's lips, the noise level rose considerably. Adults shouted orders here and there, and children called to one another in high-pitched voices as Jackie darted into the aisle and toward the exit. Pastor Palmer didn't even try to make it to the back of the sanctuary. No one would have shaken his hand anyway. They were too busy rushing to grab their covered dishes and get out to the yard.

Outside in her gray Toyota, Jackie uncovered her casserole dish and left a pile of towels in the passenger seat. She inhaled deeply of the spicy tomato sauce. Why had Beverly's comment bothered her so much? Maybe because it sounded like a stinging remark Aunt Betty had made several years ago, after tasting Jackie's first attempt at chili: "You'd better hope your looks help you snag a man, honey. Your cooking sure won't."

Well, she might not have a man yet, but she intended to prove today she could at least manage a decent casserole. Trying to keep the smirk off her face, she marched across the grass to where Beverly stood beside the buffet table. As Jackie approached, the woman's plucked eyebrows arched.

"Why, Jackie Hoffner, I thought you couldn't cook." Her voice dripped Southern charm, reminiscent of Scarlett O'Hara. Jackie suspected the inflection was fake, since the local accent around this part of central Kentucky sounded more hillbilly twang than Southern-belle drawl.

"I never said I *couldn't* cook. I just don't do it often." Jackie kept the sweetness in her smile as she placed her casserole dish on the table in front of Beverly. She removed the glass lid with a flourish.

Beverly's cherry-red lips formed an O. "Why, it looks simply divine! Is that cheese on top?"

Jackie inclined her head. "Mozzarella. It's spiral pasta in homemade tomato sauce with beef, peppers and mushrooms."

"Homemade? I declare, Jackie, you are the surprise of the day. You will share the recipe, won't you? It's not a family secret?"

Jackie didn't feel compelled to admit she'd Googled the recipe. Prior to yesterday, the only spaghetti sauce she had ever cooked—a total of twice in her life—had come from a jar. With a smile she promised to write down her special recipe and turned away so Beverly could continue organizing the food on the buffet table. She indulged in a moment of self-satisfied smirking. She'd sure shown Beverly Sanders who could cook. From now on, someone else could bring potato chips.

The sun shone brightly in a clear blue sky. The weather

had cooperated so they could hold their potluck outside for the first time since Jackie started attending the church. The white-plank building, erected back in the early 1900s, lay snug between the gentle swell of rolling hills on the outskirts of Versailles. Early-summer weeds poked through a meager layer of gravel in the parking lot that fronted the building, but the flat yard on the side boasted a thick lawn of true Kentucky bluegrass. Today the smell of freshly mowed grass almost overpowered the odor of the food. Across the lawn, filmy plastic tablecloths on the tables from the fellowship hall flapped in the slight June breeze, held down with rocks on the corners. HCC's five teenagers were busy unfolding metal chairs and setting them in place. Beneath the tables, the Dorsey twins energetically covered their Sunday clothes with grass stains.

The buffet table filled quickly. A smaller drink table held an assortment of two-liter bottles and plastic pitchers of sweet tea and lemonade. Jackie stepped out of the way as women bustled around her, rearranging the food at Beverly's direction so the salads, meats and casseroles were at one end and the desserts at the other. Several of the men had already staked their claims on seats, while a rapidly growing crowd lingered near the far end of the food table, ready to form a line.

Finally, Beverly clapped her hands for attention. "I think everything's about ready, y'all. Pastor Palmer, you want to ask a blessing?"

Jackie groaned. *Don't get him started on another prayer. We'll never get to eat!*

Pastor Palmer nodded, and a hush fell over the crowd as everyone bowed their heads. "Father, we thank You for the beautiful sunshine today. Thank You also for the freedom of gathering in fellowship with one another, when so many of our brothers and sisters in the world don't have that privilege. Bless the food we are about to eat, and all those who prepared it. In Jesus' Name, Amen."

At the last word, the feasting on the lawn of Heritage Community Church began.

Margaret Palmer speared a twisty pasta and a mushroom on a plastic fork. She stole a glance at her husband, whose single-minded attack on his plate of fried chicken, potato salad and green beans had her thinking she should feed him better at home. Of course, as pastor he felt he had a responsibility to taste and exclaim over every dish, but he actually went back for seconds on potato salad. She made a mental note to find out what spices Esther used, then directed her attention across the table when Alice Farmer's endless string of complaints turned to the UPS driver.

"Rude, that's what he was." The elderly lady gave a vicious nod that shook her tightly curled gray hair. "He wouldn't even help me with a few boxes. I told him I couldn't lift them. He left me standing on the porch without even a by-your-leave. And me a widow with a weak heart."

The creases around Alice's mouth deepened as her face settled into its habitual scowl.

Seated beside Alice, Jackie Hoffner stiffened and drew an outraged breath. "You mean he just dropped the boxes off on your porch and wouldn't bring them in for you?"

"Of course not," Alice snapped. "He was delivering a book I ordered off the television. I'm perfectly capable of carrying a book. The boxes are up in my attic, and he refused to go up there and get them down for me."

Margaret saw Earl hide a grin behind a chicken leg.

"But Mrs. Farmer," Jackie said, "UPS probably doesn't allow their drivers to go into people's houses. Maybe he was just following his company's rules."

Alice's lips pursed as her chin shot upward. "Then whoever told him that ought to be ashamed of himself. It's scandalous, I tell you. The Good Book says people should take care of widows, but do they? Of course not. This generation hasn't been taught proper respect. They don't respect their elders or widows or anyone else."

Margaret tried not to laugh at the expression on Jackie's face. The girl looked especially nice today in white slacks and a loose pink blouse that suited her creamy complexion and emphasized her slender figure. What a shame there were no single young men her age in the church. *Maybe… No.* Margaret mentally shook herself. Earl often accused her of obsessively trying to change the marital status of every single person over the age of twenty.

With a practiced gesture, Jackie tucked a lock of curly dark hair behind her ear and leaned back in her chair, her high forehead wrinkling as she searched for an appropriate defense for the UPS man. She was an earnest young woman who tended to consider a differing opinion from her own as a personal challenge. She'd started coming to the church six months ago, shortly after Earl replaced the previous pastor of HCC. Margaret often wondered how long she would be satisfied with the rather traditional small church when the area boasted plenty of bigger, more contemporary congregations with far more single men to choose from.

However, Jackie seemed perfectly happy at HCC. Odd that an attractive young woman would prefer the company of older people to those her own age. But look where she'd chosen to sit today—with a boring middle-aged couple and a complaining old woman.

Alice Farmer's eyes focused on something over Margaret's shoulder, and her scowl deepened. "No respect for the Bible, either, or the Ten Commandments. It's a crime, that's what it is. A crime."

Margaret turned her head, wondering what caused such venom in the old lady's voice. Behind her, people ate and chatted amicably. Several had returned for second helpings and hovered around the food. Richard Watson stood talking to Steve Townsend, while his wife, Laura, used a wet wipe on little Charlie Dorsey's sticky face. Kathy Dorsey had her arms around her second son, Jamie, holding him in place while she scrubbed at the spaghetti sauce on his hands. Esther Hodges stood close to Sylvia Graham, whispering rather intently in her ear.

Margaret turned back to Alice as Earl answered in his most soothing pastoral voice.

"We live in a fallen world, Mrs. Farmer, but we've been given a powerful weapon. Prayer. Our job as Christians is to pray for those who are struggling."

"Struggling is one thing." The old woman's gaze slid over to him. "Wallowing in sin is another."

Earl's eyebrows rose. "Those in sin need prayer as much as anyone. And that is every one of us. Remember, *All have sinned and fall short of the glory of God.*"

Margaret gave him a quick look. She couldn't remember easy-going Earl ever quoting Scripture to chastise someone.

Before Alice had a chance to flare at his reprimand, he pushed his plate away and stood. "I'm ready for dessert. Can I bring anything for you ladies?"

Jackie and Alice declined, but Margaret stood with him. "I want to see what choices I have."

As they walked away, Earl leaned toward her to whisper. "I don't know how Mr. Farmer died, but I'll bet he did it just to escape the complaining."

"Shh. Someone might hear you." Margaret aimed an elbow at his ribs, but he jumped away in the nick of time, grinning.

One end of the buffet table was a center of industrious activity. Several ladies busily dished leftovers into plastic containers, ready to send them home with anyone who wanted to take them. Margaret and Earl slipped into the line at the opposite end.

Dessert had always been Margaret's downfall. She loved homemade cakes and pies and had never met a cookie she could refuse. For years she fluctuated between a size fourteen and a sixteen, but lately those sixteens had felt a little snug. With a sigh, she took one of the small dessert plates and halved a slice of pecan pie. As she moved down the line, her resolve lessened and she cut a sliver of Mrs. Lewis's carrot cake and then added a moderate-sized spoonful of banana pudding. After only a second's hesitation, she picked up a chocolate-pecan cookie before scanning the tables for a seat not quite so near to Alice.

Jackie reached for another plastic bowl and scraped the last of the banana pudding into it. Seemed like she had packaged enough leftovers to feed the whole town. A quick glance down the length of the table confirmed that all the food was either eaten or covered. She didn't look the other way, toward the far table where a cluster of young women laughed over the latest episode of some stupid reality show on television. The girls at work talked about those shows all the time, but Jackie didn't join in there, either. What was the fascination in watching a group of people turn on each other week after week, voting to get rid of one of their own? Jackie didn't have time for nonsense like that.

Of course, she could have sat with the girls and listened. Maybe even pretended to be interested…

Impatient with the thought, she brushed it away. There was work to be done. Someone had to do the clean-up duty. Might as well be her.

She snapped on the lid and set the container near the edge of the table just as Mrs. Dressler walked up, leaning heavily on her cane with her right hand, a plastic grocery sack clutched in her left.

"Is this some of that good banana pudding?" the elderly lady asked.

"Yes ma'am, that's the last little bit."

"Oh, I hate to take the last."

"It's yours." Jackie picked up the bowl and held it out to her. "Enjoy!"

"Well, if you think so." Mrs. Dressler put it into the grocery sack along with at least half a dozen identical containers. "Thank you, honey."

Jackie followed Mrs. Dressler's progress down the table and hid a smile at the line of little old ladies flocking around the buffet with their sacks opened like trick-or-treaters. No HCC member past the age of seventy had to cook a meal for a full week after a church potluck.

She noted with satisfaction that none of the leftover containers of her casserole remained. Cooking would never be her claim to fame, but the sauce must not have turned out too badly.

* * *

Not far away, another pair of eyes studied the line of elderly ladies.

Old ladies liked to talk. But someone should remind them gossip was a sin.

A deadly sin.

TWO

"You know what I'm going to do, Linus?"

Linus the cat, seated in the center of the dinette table, paused his grooming long enough to give Jackie three seconds of undivided attention. Apparently deciding the interruption would not lead to food, he returned to the industrious licking of his left armpit.

"I'm going over to Mrs. Farmer's house to get those boxes down from her attic."

The elderly woman had been on her mind since the potluck. What if she tried to move the boxes herself? She might get hurt, and then Jackie would feel awful. Besides, after listening to Mrs. Farmer complain about how disrespectful young people were these days, Jackie figured she needed to see one doing something helpful.

She tossed the last bite of spring roll into her mouth and closed the lid on the remains of her chicken-fried rice. Not enough left for another meal, but if she added a slice of last night's leftover pizza she'd have a good lunch to take to work tomorrow. She put the cardboard container into the refrigerator then rinsed her fork at the kitchen sink.

Leaning against the counter, she faced the yellow tabby.

"After all, it's Tuesday. There's nothing good on television tonight anyway."

Completely uninterested, Linus thrust his left leg straight into the air and continued his bath. He didn't even look up as Jackie jotted down Mrs. Farmer's address from the church directory and let herself out of the tiny apartment.

The old gray Toyota sputtered as Jackie pulled from the parking lot onto Elm Street. Alarmed, she shoved in the clutch and gunned the gas, hoping the fuel thingy wasn't about to go bad again. Last year she'd paid almost two hundred dollars to have the whatever-it-was replaced, and she didn't have that kind of money right now. Thankfully, an extra gulp of gas appeased the cranky engine, and the car rumbled toward Alice Farmer's house without further protest.

Jackie shook her head at the memory of Mrs. Farmer's fury over the poor UPS man. People tended to shy away from the woman because of her constant complaining, but Jackie was used to it. Her aunt Betty had been exactly like that in the years before she passed away. No one could do anything to suit her, and everything sent her off into long tirades of bitter whining. Of course, Aunt Betty had an excuse—she lived with the terrible pain of crippling arthritis every moment. Jackie almost thought of her passing as a blessing—relief from an agonizing existence, even though her death left Jackie completely alone in the world.

Alone. No family. No boyfriend. No friends of any kind, for that matter. An uncomfortable feeling twinged in the back of Jackie's mind, but she pushed it away. Feeling sorry for yourself accomplished nothing. She didn't regret her years of caring for Aunt Betty, even though she'd missed every single basketball game her senior year and had to drop out of the band because she couldn't be gone

for a full week of band camp. She didn't care, truly. The
need for friends fell by the wayside when your only relative
needed you so desperately.

The drive to Mrs. Farmer's house was pleasant in the
evening twilight, the temperature just warm enough to
leave the windows rolled down. It wouldn't last. By the end
of the month the high humidity would set in, making travel
without an air conditioner impossible to endure. Jackie
hated driving anywhere in the heat of the summer. Especially when the car's air conditioner didn't deserve the
name. It was a disgrace to air conditioners everywhere.

Alice Farmer lived in a white frame house halfway
down a wooded country road that led to the city dump. Big
trees in the front yard cast a deep and welcome shade but
deprived the soil of sufficient sunshine to produce anything
resembling a lawn. A few hardy weeds provided the only
green in the otherwise bare stretch of land.

Jackie parked in a dirt driveway behind Mrs. Farmer's
red Escort and climbed three cement stairs to the front
porch. The doorbell wasn't lit, and when she pressed it she
heard no sound. Broken. A tap on the wooden frame of the
screen door sent a chip of white paint fluttering to the
porch. No response. She opened the screen and knocked
loudly on the front door.

She thought she heard a sound from inside, like a moan,
or a soft cry. The hair at the base of her skull prickled.
Should she go in? What if nothing was wrong and she
barged into Mrs. Farmer's house uninvited? She worried at
a stray strand of hair and tucked it behind her ear. But what
if something was wrong? With a glance around the empty
yard, she twisted the doorknob. Unlocked. She pushed the
door open a couple of inches and called through the crack.

"Mrs. Farmer, are you home?"

Again she heard a moan from somewhere within the house—this time she was positive. Someone was in pain. Setting her jaw, she opened wide the door.

"Mrs. Farmer, it's Jackie Hoffner from church," she said in a voice loud enough to carry through the house. "I came over to help you get those boxes down from your attic."

Silence.

"I'm coming in, Mrs. Farmer."

She stepped across the threshold and heard a crash. Anxious, she hurried through the empty living room, following the sound.

The strong odor of vomit hit her like a physical slap when she stepped into the short hallway. She took a momentary step backward. Then, bracing herself and breathing through her mouth, she hurried toward the back of the house. The door to a bathroom stood open, displaying evidence that someone had been too violently ill to make it all the way to the toilet. She fought a gag reflex as the stench nearly overpowered her.

In the bedroom just beyond, she found Mrs. Farmer lying lengthwise across the bed, her nightgown saturated with vomit and sweat. An alarm clock lay shattered in pieces on the hardwood floor as though she had been trying to reach it. A telephone also lay on the floor, the receiver under the bed with the base upended. Mrs. Farmer looked at her through glazed eyes and moaned.

Jackie rushed to the bed, swallowing hard. She ignored the soiled nightgown and took the elderly woman's hand.

"It's okay, Mrs. Farmer. I'm here."

A vein in the old woman's throat pulsed with a wild rhythm, and her hand felt clammy. Sweat dampened her forehead and neck, and her skin was chalky-white. Her mouth moved as she tried to speak, but Jackie shushed her.

"Don't try to talk. I'm calling 911. You'll be all right as soon as the paramedics get here."

Jackie grabbed the phone from the floor and held the button in until she got a dial tone, then dialed 911. After giving the address and a description of the emergency, she ran to the bathroom and snatched a washcloth off a towel rack. As cool water ran over the cloth, she whispered a prayer.

"Lord, I don't know what to do here. Please help!"

Back in the bedroom, she sat on the mattress and wiped Mrs. Farmer's face, whispering soothing words to the barely conscious woman the way Aunt Betty used to when young Jackie was hurt or frightened, and the way Jackie herself had during her aunt's later years.

"It's going to be okay. Don't worry now. You're going to be fine."

Minutes later, Jackie heard the ambulance's siren screaming down the road. She ran out to meet them and then was politely but firmly pushed aside as the paramedics went to work. Orders were shouted, a gurney retrieved, and Mrs. Farmer strapped onto it. As they whisked her away, one of the paramedics curtly commanded Jackie to follow them to the hospital so the necessary paperwork could be filled out. Then they were gone.

Jackie stood in the silent bedroom staring at the empty bed. Paperwork? She barely knew Mrs. Farmer and certainly knew none of the information the hospital would want. She needed to call someone.

A desk stood in the corner of the bedroom, and she opened the drawer hoping to find an address book. Bingo. An ancient-looking leather booklet with worn alphabet tabs lay inside. When she picked it up, her gaze fell on the church directory beneath it.

"Of course! I'll call Pastor Palmer."

Relieved, she dialed the Palmer home and quickly explained the situation when Margaret answered the phone.

"Find Mrs. Farmer's purse," Margaret ordered. "She's bound to keep her insurance card in it. Earl is at a deacon meeting at the church, but I'll call and interrupt him. We'll meet you at the hospital in forty-five minutes."

Relief flooded Jackie, leaving her limp. The pastor's wife was a real take-charge woman, just the sort of person you wanted to call in an emergency. Jackie sagged onto the edge of the mattress. "Okay."

She hung up the phone and found Mrs. Farmer's purse on a table by the front door. She stared at it for a moment. Margaret would meet her in forty-five minutes? The drive to the hospital only took ten. Hospitals gave her the creeps. She wandered down the short hallway and stared at the empty bed.

Silence claimed the house. As her glance circled the room, nervousness overtook her; her fingers felt fidgety. Instead of spending half an hour sitting along in the hospital waiting room, she might as well make herself useful. Someone would have to clean up before Mrs. Farmer returned. The poor woman couldn't come home to filthy sheets and a terrible smell.

Glad to have something helpful to do, Jackie went to work.

Forty minutes later, Jackie stepped through the wide automatic doors into the hospital emergency room behind Margaret and Pastor Palmer. In her hands she clutched a small overnight case she had found in the bedroom closet, filled with the essentials she knew Mrs. Farmer would want. Her nostrils tingled as the smell of antiseptic assaulted her. This place smelled just like the hospital where her parents had died. She could almost feel her small hand clutching Aunt Betty's as the doctor delivered his terrible news.

With a conscious effort, she thrust the memory away. This waiting room was smaller, with brightly painted walls and a plastic box full of toys in one corner. A man and woman sat together in a row of cushioned chairs, the woman hunched over a clipboard filling out forms while the man stared intently at a television in the corner. A nurse in pink surgical scrubs behind a desk looked up from her computer monitor as they entered.

Jackie felt filthy after having scrubbed Mrs. Farmer's toilet and bathroom floor. She'd thrown the soiled sheets into the washing machine, and planned to return to the house later to put them in the dryer. Thank goodness, Margaret had taken on the task of searching through the old woman's purse when she met them in the parking lot. Jackie would have felt like an intruder going through another woman's purse, no matter how important the circumstance!

Pastor Palmer approached the nurse. "We're here to see Alice Farmer. She was brought in a little while ago by ambulance."

The nurse gave them a measured look. "Are you relatives?"

"No, I'm her pastor. She doesn't have any relatives that I'm aware of, but I've got her insurance card right here."

Because Pastor Palmer was new to Heritage Community Church, he had called Russell Price, the head of the board of elders, to find out about Mrs. Farmer's relatives. Mr. Price hadn't been much help, though. He promised to make some calls to various church members and contact them later with any information he discovered. In the meantime, Margaret had instructed Jackie to search Mrs. Farmer's purse to find her Medicare card and a set of keys so the house could be locked for the night. Jackie had reluctantly agreed to handle that chore. As far as she was concerned, a woman's purse was even more private than her underwear drawer.

The pink-clad nurse's gaze slid away. "Wait right here, please."

"But could you tell me—"

The nurse ignored Pastor Palmer's question and disappeared through a door behind the desk. Margaret looked questioningly at her husband, who shrugged.

Moments later the nurse returned.

"Could you come this way? The doctor would like to talk to you."

Jackie, Margaret and the pastor followed her into the emergency treatment area, a wide corridor partitioned by floor-to-ceiling curtains that gave a semblance of privacy to half-dozen hospital beds. To Jackie's relief, none were occupied, though several nurses sat talking quietly at the other end of the hallway.

They were led to a cluttered office, and after a moment a doctor joined them. He was a pleasant-looking man, but young. Jackie was glad she wasn't there for treatment. She would have insisted on seeing his credentials before allowing him to so much as take her pulse.

"I'm Dr. Peters." He closed the door behind him.

"Earl Palmer, and this is my wife, Margaret, and a member of our congregation, Jackie Hoffner."

Dr. Peters shook their hands. "You're Mrs. Farmer's minister?"

Pastor Palmer nodded. "But I've actually only been at the church for about seven months, so I'm afraid I don't know her as well as I would like. I do know she doesn't have any relatives in town, so we brought her insurance information with us. Is she being admitted?"

"No, she's not." The doctor paused, and the look on his face warned Jackie of the news before he spoke his next words. "I'm afraid Mrs. Farmer passed away en route to the hospital. The paramedics did everything they could. They administered CPR until she arrived here, but we weren't able to resuscitate her."

Jackie took a step backward and sat abruptly in a hard plastic chair. Mrs. Farmer, dead. She could hardly believe it. Two days ago she had been complaining about the UPS man. An hour ago Jackie had wiped her forehead with a cool cloth. Now she was dead.

"But how?" Margaret's face registered as much shock as Jackie felt.

"The paramedics' report indicates that she was suffering from severe dehydration and was semiconscious when they arrived. She experienced a mild seizure in the ambulance and then she coded—uh, died. Heart failure."

"She had a weak heart," Pastor Palmer told him. "I've heard her say that often enough."

"And she obviously had the flu or something," Jackie added. "When I got there I could tell she'd been sick for a while."

"Actually, the paramedics said the patient's condition and the evidence they found at the house might indicate a rather severe case of food poisoning."

Jackie's eyes widened. Food poisoning? Could the cause have been leftovers from the church potluck? Mrs. Farmer had eaten some of her casserole. Had she taken some home with her?

Ridiculous! *Don't be paranoid!*

"Regardless," the doctor went on, "if she had a history of heart problems, a flu or food poisoning could put her in a weakened condition, and a seizure could send her into cardiac arrest. Of course, an autopsy will be performed, and we'll know more then. In the meantime, the police have been notified and will probably want to talk to you so they can contact her next of kin."

The police?

"I washed her sheets," Jackie said. They all turned to look at her. "I mean, in case the police want to know who did it."

She felt foolish when the doctor's eyebrows rose. It was an experience she'd had many times in her life. Why did she always manage to say something stupid?

THREE

Jackie backed away from the dresser, trying to get a look at her feet. She really should buy a full-length mirror. The image stopped at her knees, leaving her to guess at how her flat pumps looked with the narrow black skirt. She'd bought the skirt and blouse two days ago when an inventory of her closet revealed nothing even remotely appropriate for a funeral. Her coworkers at the State's division for child-support enforcement would probably fall right out of their chairs when she walked into the office in a skirt, but slacks seemed disrespectful somehow.

Yesterday, she'd shuffled all her Friday afternoon clients off onto other caseworkers, so she planned to work through her lunch break and leave at one o'clock. Plenty of time to get from the state office building in Frankfort to the funeral home here in Versailles before the two-o'clock service.

She gave up on seeing her feet in the reflection and turned to examine the side view. Not bad. Maybe she should wear skirts more often.

The doorbell sounded. Linus, who did not like visitors, leaped from his perch on her pillow to rush to his habitual hiding place beneath the bed. Jackie glanced at the clock. Who in the world would come to her apartment at seven-forty in the morning?

She swiped a brush through her curly hair a couple of times and snatched a black scrunchie off the top of the dresser as she left the room. Twisting it around her hair at the base of her neck, she peeked through the peephole in the front door. The telescopic image of two men stared back at her. One wore a uniform.

The police? Jackie's pulse picked up tempo. A visit from the police before eight o'clock in the morning couldn't be good news.

She unlocked the dead bolt and opened the door. Her eyes were immediately drawn to the uniformed officer. He stood slightly behind the other man, his young face freshly shaved beneath short-cropped hair. Strong, well-muscled shoulders filled out his shirt above a trim waist, and when Jackie looked into his face she found herself gazing at the most gorgeous gray eyes she had ever seen. A tickly sensation in her belly made her look away with a shiver. She focused instead on his left hand, which held a canvas messenger bag. No ring on that all-important finger.

Focus, Jackie!

In front of Mr. Good-Looking Cop, the other man held up a black wallet with a shiny badge. He, too, was clean shaven except for a short mustache, in his late forties or early fifties. He wore a neat gray suit, white shirt, and the ugliest tie Jackie had ever seen.

The older man spoke. "Miss Hoffner, I'm Detective Conner with the Kentucky State Police. And this is Trooper Walsh." The handsome officer nodded a silent greeting. "We're here to talk to you about Mrs. Alice Farmer."

Jackie's tension lessened as the detective flashed an easy smile. He didn't look as if he was about to deliver bad news. She opened the door wider. They probably just wanted to follow up on her statement. "Oh, sure. Would you like to come in?"

"If you don't mind."

She stepped back, closing the door behind them as they walked into the apartment to stand in her tiny living room. As Trooper Walsh brushed by her, she caught a faint whiff of his aftershave. The tickle in her stomach returned. If only she had taken the time to fix her hair this morning.

"Please sit down. Uh…" A pile of newspapers littered one end of her couch, and cat hairs clung to the cushion on the other end. She pointed toward the dinette table. "Maybe there?"

Detective Conner smiled. "That will be fine. I hope we aren't interrupting anything important."

"Actually, I was just getting ready to leave for work."

"This shouldn't take too long." Detective Conner's pleasant green eyes looked into hers, the corners crinkling with his smile. "I'd like to ask you some questions about Mrs. Farmer."

Jackie sat across the table from Detective Conner, super-aware of the handsome young state trooper who sat on her left and extracted a notebook and pen from his messenger bag. She hoped she didn't say something stupid, like she usually did. Should she offer them coffee? She couldn't remember if she had any clean mugs.

"Well, okay, but I told the sheriff's department everything I know on Wednesday."

"I've read your statement. If you don't mind, I'd like to

hear it in your own words. Hopefully I won't make you too late for work."

Okay, if she ignored the good-looking one and focused on the old guy, she could almost relax. And honestly, the detective's smile made Jackie feel she was chatting with a friend. What did it matter if she was a little late? Her boss didn't watch the clock.

She launched into a description of the church picnic and Mrs. Farmer complaining about the UPS man not bringing down the boxes from her attic. Then she told him how she had gone to Mrs. Farmer's house to help and found the poor woman violently ill. As she talked about the call for the ambulance and the subsequent trip to the hospital, Trooper Walsh took notes while Detective Conner nodded, his eyes never leaving Jackie's face.

"And then you cleaned up the house."

"That's right."

"Did you wash any dishes, or put anything into the dishwasher?"

Jackie shook her head. "No, I didn't go into the kitchen at all except to find the mop and detergent. I don't remember seeing any dirty dishes."

"I see. Tell me about this church picnic. Who was there?"

"Just about everyone at Heritage Community Church. Close to ninety people, I'd say."

"And can you tell me what was served?"

Jackie's pulse quickened. Leftovers from the potluck *had* given Mrs. Farmer food poisoning! "Uh, it was a potluck so everyone brought something. There was a lot of food. We had fried chicken and sliced ham and a smoked turkey breast. There were at least a dozen casseroles and a bunch of salads, like potato salad and pasta salad and that green Jell-O—"

"What about spaghetti?" he interrupted. "Was there a dish with spaghetti sauce?"

Her mouth went dry. "Actually, I brought a spiral pasta casserole. But there wasn't anything wrong with it."

"Did you eat any of it?"

"Of course I did. Lots of people did." She shifted her attention toward Trooper Walsh, who stopped scribbling on his pad to look at her with those arresting eyes, and added defensively, "It was good."

Detective Conner went on in the same calm tone. "Did anyone else bring a dish with spaghetti sauce?"

Jackie closed her eyes, picturing the food table. Hers was the only dish with tomato sauce. She wiped her damp palms on her skirt under the table and then shook her head.

"Have you heard of anyone else in the church getting sick after the picnic?"

"Of course not." She raised her chin. "And there was nothing wrong with my casserole."

"One more question. Do you recognize this?"

Detective Conner nodded at Trooper Walsh, who reached into his canvas bag and drew out a container sealed in a large plastic bag. He placed it on the table in front of Jackie. It was one of those disposable Ziploc containers with a blue lid, the inside stained orange with what had been, Jackie assumed, tomato sauce.

She swallowed hard against a dry throat and turned to Detective Conner. "If you mean do I recognize what it is, of course I do. If you're asking if I recognize this particular container, that would be nearly impossible."

He gave her a bland look. "I'm aware of that. Can you at least tell me if it might have contained your casserole from the church potluck?"

A flicker of anger sparked in Jackie's mind. No way were they going to pin this on her. There was nothing wrong with her casserole!

She took a deep breath. "The church keeps dozens of those containers in the kitchen so they have something to put leftovers in to send home with people after potlucks. Some people throw them away, but others wash them and return them to the church when they're finished. So yes, it's possible this one might have contained some of my casserole." She leaned forward, looking directly into his eyes. "But there was nothing wrong with it. It couldn't have given anyone food poisoning."

Detective Conner studied her a moment. "The coroner's report said Mrs. Farmer died of heart failure, brought on as a result of monomethylhydrazine poisoning, not food poisoning."

"Monomethyl—what?"

"Monomethylhydrazine. The coroner called it MMH. It's an uncommon poison, but not all that hard to come by. It's found in certain types of mushrooms."

"Mushrooms? You mean wild mushrooms?"

Jackie had heard of mushroom poisonings. Everyone had. That's why anyone with half a brain stayed away from wild mushrooms.

"Specifically a mushroom called *Gyromitra ambigua*. It's common in wooded areas around here."

"Well, the mystery's solved then, isn't it?" Jackie sat back in relief. "There are woods behind Mrs. Farmer's house. She must have decided to go mushroom hunting and got hold of the wrong kind."

There was no humor in Detective Conner's smile. "I

wish it was that simple. But we don't think Mrs. Farmer picked those mushrooms herself."

The hairs at the base of Jackie's neck prickled. "Why not?"

"Because we took the dishes out of her dishwasher, which, thankfully, you had not turned on when you cleaned the house. We sent them all to the lab, and they found something."

"Was it in the tomato sauce?" *Please say no! Please say no!*

"Bingo."

Jackie's heart thudded in her chest. How could poisonous mushrooms get into her tomato sauce? It was impossible. Her mushrooms had come from the grocery store. She ate them herself.

She shook her head. "At least a half-dozen people took leftovers home, and I haven't heard of anyone else getting sick. Maybe Mrs. Farmer thought the sauce needed some spicing up and she added wild mushrooms at home."

"That's what I thought, too," the detective said. "I know sometimes my wife adds something to leftovers to dress them up a bit. So we went through her garbage very carefully. There was no trace of mushroom stems or pieces. She almost certainly would have trimmed the stems before cooking them."

"Maybe they were chopped up in the garbage disposal," she suggested.

"There is no garbage disposal. And we found the remains of the pasta, which she had scraped off her plate before putting it in the dishwasher. It was full of *Gyromitra ambigua*."

"But surely she could have tasted poisonous mushrooms!"

"Actually, this variety has a very mild taste. When mixed with a spicy sauce, they would be virtually undetectable."

Jackie sat back against the hard chair. Mrs. Farmer, poisoned! That poor woman. Who could have disliked her enough to do something so awful?

And why had they chosen *her* potluck casserole? This news would spread like wildfire. The church gossips would have a field day.

Conner cleared his throat. "I know this is most upsetting, Miss Hoffner. But I'm afraid we need to examine your kitchen."

"My kitchen? But surely you can't think—"

"We don't think anything at this point. We're just following procedure. Will you show us the utensils you used to make your casserole?"

"But…but I've washed them!"

Detective Conner sighed. "I expected that. Still, we need to take them for analysis."

"Are you saying you think I killed Mrs. Farmer?" Blood pounded in Jackie's ears. "Do I need a lawyer?"

He sat slowly back in his seat, his eyes never leaving hers. "We're not here to accuse you of anything, Miss Hoffner. We simply want to eliminate the possibility that the mushrooms came from your kitchen. A necessary step in the investigation, nothing more." He folded his arms across his chest. "If you want to call a lawyer, you're entitled. But we still need to examine your kitchen. If we need to get a search warrant, we will."

Her focus dropped to the surface of the table. If she didn't give them permission to look in her kitchen right now, they would think she was hiding something. She would look guilty. And she had nothing to hide.

"Fine."

Trooper Walsh reached into his bag and pulled out several large, plastic, zippered bags. She knew their purpose from watching *CSI* on television. The police used them to bag evidence at a crime scene.

Her face flaming, Jackie rose from the table and led them into the kitchen. She stood silently, fingernails biting into her palms, and watched the young officer search through her cupboards. He confiscated her cutting board, her casserole dish, and every knife she owned. When he opened the refrigerator, her jaw tightened. Did they actually think they'd find poisonous mushrooms in there? She clenched her teeth as Walsh pawed through the contents and removed several plastic containers. Detective Conner's direct stare made heat rise under her collar, but she did not look at him. He'd tricked her into thinking he was a nice man with that pleasant smile. She wasn't going to fall for that again.

When he finished cleaning out her kitchen, Trooper Walsh gave a slight nod to the detective and turned toward Jackie. "I think that's about everything, Miss Hoffner. I'm sorry for the inconvenience."

Inconvenience? Humiliation gave way to fury, which roiled inside her as she followed the pair to the front door, her lower lip caught firmly between her teeth to keep from spouting angry words. As he stepped through the doorway, Detective Conner turned and gave her that false friendly smile. He extracted a business card from his suit pocket and held it toward her.

"If you're planning any out-of-town trips in the near future, it might be a good idea to give me a call and let me know. Just in case we need to get in touch with you."

She really was a suspect? As though in slow motion, her hand reached out and took the card.

"Thank you, Miss Hoffner. Have a nice day."

Trooper Walsh, his arms full of her dishes, gave a sympathetic nod before following the detective down the breezeway to the parking lot.

Jackie closed the door behind them and sagged against it. Her fury drained as she looked down at the card in her hand. She was a suspected murderer. The police thought she had killed Mrs. Farmer with her spiral pasta casserole.

Why hadn't she taken potato chips to that potluck?

Dennis Walsh popped the trunk on his cruiser and stowed the bags while Detective Conner slid into the passenger seat. That interview had been an education in interrogation. The way the detective handled the questioning was nothing short of brilliant. Sitting across the table from him, Dennis hadn't believed how polite, how approachable, how *nice* the normally arrogant man had been, inviting confidences with his demeanor. Of course, at the end his true personality had emerged. That poor girl had really looked rattled. Just like most of the officers around the station looked whenever Detective Conner deigned to walk through with his usual biting commentary.

But he was the best in the state, no doubt about it. That's why Dennis had finagled this assignment. With any luck, Conner would recommend him for detective when they solved this case.

One thing bothered him, though. That girl didn't look like a killer. She looked like a...well, like an attractive young woman with an open book for a face. If Dennis was any judge of character—and he believed he was—Jackie Hoffner was no murderer.

Slamming the car door and strapping his seat belt in one smooth motion, Dennis turned toward his passenger.

"You don't really believe she killed that old lady, do you?"

Conner shrugged.

"But she doesn't fit the profile," Dennis insisted. "Not even close." .

"Walsh, the first rule you learn in police investigation is this—never make assumptions. Everyone is capable of committing a crime, given the right motivation."

Dennis shook his head. "I'm not sure I buy that. I've studied profiling, and—"

"Everyone." Conner snapped his own seat belt and caught Dennis's gaze in his direct one. "You can trust your mother, Walsh. But check her."

Dennis turned the key in the ignition, nodding. Conner was as cynical as they came. Maybe that's why he was considered the best.

But as he backed out of the parking lot, Dennis couldn't help remembering the way Jackie's lower lip had quivered when he had confiscated her cutting board.

FOUR

A rivulet of rain dripped from Esther Hodge's umbrella onto the top of Margaret's head. When it slid down her forehead, Margaret stopped the trickle with a fingertip and took a sideways step to the green canopy covering the grave site. Lucky Earl. He stood dry beyond the casket, holding an open Bible and waiting for the last of the brave to make the muddy trek to the dubious shelter of the canopy.

The canvas ceiling showed an ominous sag of pooling rain directly above Margaret's head. She took another two steps toward the center.

More people than Margaret expected had turned out for Alice's service. Several elderly gentlemen identified themselves at the funeral home as friends or coworkers of the late Mr. Farmer, and a taxicab had deposited an ancient woman who said she'd retired from the paper factory a few years before Alice.

Heritage Community Church was well represented, too. Six elderly members of the Prime Timer Sunday school class, come to bid farewell to one of their own, perched on wobbly folding chairs in front of the casket.

A backward glance showed Richard and Laura Watson, huddled beneath a black umbrella, bringing up the rear of the wet funeral goers. Interesting. The Watsons and Alice had never seemed close—certainly not close enough for Richard to take time off from his job as a bank vice president to attend her funeral. Margaret wondered if the reason had anything to do with Richard's rumored interest in becoming the church treasurer when Ernie stepped down at the end of the year. Attending an old lady's funeral would earn him brownie points with the elderly members of the congregation.

A flash of guilt washed over her at the uncharitable thought. Maybe he was simply being respectful to a long-time member of his church.

The conspicuous absence of one person disturbed Margaret. Jackie should be here. After all, she'd found Alice ill and called the ambulance. She shifted her gaze to the two policemen watching the proceedings from the back corner. When they came to the parsonage this morning they mentioned they'd just come from Jackie's apartment, and their questions centered rather intently on her pasta casserole. They seemed quite eager to know who, besides Alice, might have taken leftover portions home. Surely the girl wasn't so upset by their questions she'd decided not to attend the funeral.

Earl cleared his throat as the Watsons joined the dripping group beneath the canopy. Margaret directed her attention toward her husband, who looked through the bottom half of his bifocals and read from the scriptures. His vibrant baritone carried beyond the tent and rolled down the softly curving hillside, flooding the quiet cemetery with words of comfort.

"'Love never fails. But where there are prophecies, they will cease; where there are tongues, they will be stilled; where there is knowledge, it will pass away.'"

The funeral goers squirmed, surprised at Earl's selection of a passage of Scripture normally read at weddings. Margaret hid a smile. None of that ashes-to-ashes stuff for Earl; he leaped at any opportunity to talk about God's love.

Unfortunately, he had discussed the subject at length back at the funeral home. Having heard her husband perform this particular funeral service several times, Margaret found herself struggling to pay attention. At least he had the sense to keep the grave-side service short. Some of the elderly mourners had no business being out in this weather.

Earl must have thought the same. Before anyone even had time to start fidgeting, she heard his closing words: "The greatest thing we can do to make this earth more like heaven is to show His love to one another. I'm sure if Alice had the opportunity to make one last request, she would ask us to love one another. Let us pray."

Margaret bowed her head along with everyone else. A beautiful thought, but she wondered if that's what Alice would really have asked. The surly old woman certainly hadn't displayed love for her fellow man, at least not as far as Margaret ever saw.

Flushing, Margaret mentally chastised herself. What was wrong with her today? Her thoughts had certainly taken a harsh turn. She seemed to suspect the worst from everyone.

"Amen."

She looked up to see Earl bestowing a benevolent smile upon the mourners, looking extremely pastoral in his raincoat with his dark suit and tie peeking out at the collar.

"May God bless you as you go."

People filed out of the tent, umbrellas popping open here and there. The police officers watched until almost everyone was gone then slipped quietly away after a polite nod in her direction. Margaret made her way toward Earl, who stood talking quietly to the funeral director. Most funerals ended with a gathering at the home of the surviving family so the attendees could share their condolences personally while they ate a meal provided by neighbors and church members. Since Alice's only relative, a niece, hadn't made the trip from California, Earl and Margaret canvassed the Prime Timer class and made the decision to forgo the usual post-funeral meal. After the policeman's questions this morning, skipping another potluck seemed like a very good decision.

Lyle Howard, a church member and Alice's attorney, approached to shake Earl's hand at the same time Margaret arrived at the front of the tent.

"Second-best funeral I ever attended, Pastor," Lyle said.

Margaret raised one eyebrow. "Second best?"

"When I was a sophomore in college, my friend Kevin O'Connor's grandfather died. They had a genuine Irish wake for the old guy. Of course—" he winked in her direction "—that was in my wilder days."

Margaret grinned. "Of course!"

"Thank you for arranging the service," Lyle told Earl. "Everything was very nice."

"Margaret did most of it." Earl shrugged a shoulder. "I just showed up and did what she told me to do."

"It was no problem," Margaret assured Lyle. "If there's anything else I can do to help settle the estate, just let me know."

"Actually, there is. Not with the estate—it's going to be fairly straightforward. Mrs. Farmer left everything to her niece, who wants me to set up an estate auction. But Ms. Baker did say if the church could use anything from the house, particularly her clothes and personal items, they're welcome. Otherwise, I've been instructed to take them to the Salvation Army. If you want to help, you can find someone to go through the house and see if there's anything you'd like to take for the poor box or the ladies' rummage sale and then donate the rest."

Margaret could think of nothing less appealing than going to Alice's house and pawing through her clothes. But she pasted a rueful grin on her lips. "I'll see to it."

"There's no hurry. We won't get an auction arranged for at least a month or two."

He nodded a farewell and, clutching his collar tightly against the steady downpour, dashed out of the tent and down the gently sloping hill toward his car. Soon the only people left were two men in work clothes who hovered beneath a nearby tree, obviously anxious for them to leave so they could finish the burial and get out of the wet.

Margaret looped arms with Earl and drew close beneath the cover of his umbrella as they sloshed through the wet grass toward their car.

"You did a good job," she told him, squeezing his arm.

He chuckled. "Mrs. Watkins told me she was glad she got to hear me preach a funeral before she died. Now she won't worry that I'll botch hers too badly."

"Who's that, Earl?" Margaret nodded toward a gray car with fogged windows parked behind their Buick.

"Looks like Jackie's car," he said, squinting to see inside.

The driver's window opened a few inches. A pair of lips appeared.

"Psst, Pastor Palmer. Margaret. Over here."

Margaret arched her eyebrows at Earl, who shrugged. They veered toward the car. At their approach, the window opened a few more inches to reveal dark sunglasses beneath a Cincinnati Reds baseball cap.

"Jackie, is that you?"

"Shh! Someone will hear you."

Margaret looked around the empty cemetery. "There's no one here."

"Oh." A brief pause, and then Jackie's lips twisted with suppressed sobs. "Do you have a minute? I...I need to talk to someone."

"Would you like to come back to the parsonage?" Earl gave her a soothing smile. "I'm free for the rest of the day."

Sniffling, Jackie nodded. Margaret and Earl exchanged a glance.

"Earl, you run along and we'll be there directly. I'm going to ride with Jackie."

Earl walked her around to the passenger side and opened the door for her. Jackie picked up a pile of papers and threw them unceremoniously into the backseat, where they were immediately lost in the clutter. Margaret had no sooner seated herself and closed the door than the car leaped forward, speeding down the narrow driveway and taking the curves much faster than she liked. She hastily snapped her seat belt, her heart rate picking up speed along with the car. At the cemetery's entrance, she was thrown sideways as Jackie turned left onto the main road without even slowing down.

"You missed the funeral," Margaret said as she clutched the door handle.

"I couldn't go." A sob broke the last word in two. "I can't show my face around those people ever again."

Jackie turned a corner at forty-five miles per hour. Margaret gasped. Could the young woman see through the fogged windshield and those dark glasses?

"Slow down, dear," Margaret managed. "You're making me nervous."

"Oh. Sorry."

Jackie tapped the brakes until they were down to thirty, and Margaret let out a sigh of relief. "Now what's this about not being able to show your face? It's the casserole, isn't it?"

"Oh, Margaret!"

Jackie sobbed and slammed on the brakes. Margaret grasped the seat belt that stopped her from plastering her face on the windshield. Jackie covered her face with her hands, crying, as Margaret glanced through the rear window. The steady downpour made visibility difficult. Not a good time to stop in the middle of the street.

"Why don't you pull over to the side of the road so we can talk?"

Jackie proceeded to do as she asked, then collapsed across the steering wheel, knocking her cap to the floor. Relieved to be out of the way of traffic, Margaret said, "Now listen, Jackie. No one will blame you. Alice's death was not your fault."

"The police don't agree." Fear showed through the tears in her eyes. "Do you think I'll be arrested?"

"Of course not! I'm sure there's a logical explanation for Alice's death, and that detective will find it."

For a moment, the confidence Margaret poured into her voice seemed to soothe the girl. At least her crying slowed and she gave a slight nod. But then her face crumpled with another wail.

"The police have probably visited half the congregation this morning. I just know everyone is talking about my spiral pasta casserole being what killed Mrs. Farmer. How will I ever be able to walk into church again? How will I ever be able to bring food to another potluck? Everyone will be afraid of me. I knew I shouldn't have cooked anything. I'm going to be known as Typhoid Jackie!"

She jerked the glasses off and threw them into the back seat with force.

"Nonsense. There is not a person in the church who wouldn't eat what you cook, me included. You're making too big a deal over this."

"B-but the church gossips—"

"—are having a great time speculating on who really killed Alice. At the funeral home I heard it blamed on a neighbor who was upset about a tree Mrs. Farmer cut down. I also heard speculation about the manager of the grocery store because she complained about the high prices of his produce. And someone mentioned her niece in California needing money to support her drug habit. My favorite was the prankster teenagers who thought the mushrooms were hallucinogenic and wanted to watch Mrs. Farmer 'tripping.' But no one—not one person—said anything about you."

Jackie sat up and sniffed. "Really?"

"Really. But you can bet they're going to start talking about you soon."

"What do you mean?"

Margaret leaned toward the younger woman. "If you suddenly stop coming to church, they're going to wonder what you have to hide."

Margaret reached into her purse and pulled out a tissue, which Jackie took. "I guess you're right."

"Of course I am. Now the best thing you can do is come to church on Sunday, just like always. Hold your head up high and tell anyone who asks that you hope they catch the creep who had the nerve to use your casserole to commit such a terrible crime."

Jackie gave her a weak smile, eyes reddened but dry. "Thank you, Margaret. I feel a lot better."

"I'm glad. Now take me home and we'll have a nice, hot cup of tea. This rain has me shivering like a wet dog."

Rain pelted against Jackie's bedroom window. No fair! Saturdays should be sunny. Why couldn't rain come during the week, when everybody was at work?

She pulled the blanket up around her shoulders and Linus, curled against her side, gave an irritable grumble at being suddenly buried. She shoved him gently.

"Go sleep in the windowsill like a normal cat."

Displaying his typical disregard for her requests, he crept out from between the sheets and curled into a comfortable ball on the far corner of the mattress to resume his slumber.

Jackie stared at the window, watching tiny waterfalls slide down the glass against the backdrop of a gloomy gray sky. She should have gone to the funeral yesterday. Margaret was right in saying everyone would be talking about her absence and wondering why Jackie Hoffner was too embarrassed to show up. She'd just given them something else to talk about, another reason to link her name to Mrs. Farmer's death. As usual, she had done the wrong thing.

Who cares what they think, anyway?

She rolled over, turning her back to the window. Did it matter if people like Beverly Sanders whispered about her behind her back? Not in the least. She'd waltz into that church tomorrow with her head high and ignore them all. She'd done that plenty of times.

Like back in school, when she came into the lunchroom and the girls at the table by the door fell quiet. Or worse, giggled as they looked at her discount-store jeans and T-shirt. Aunt Betty couldn't afford to spend good money on fancy clothes like the other girls wore. And Jackie wouldn't have wanted her to, anyway. Clothes didn't matter.

Of course, clothes weren't the only thing the other girls in high school had talked about behind her back. No matter how hard she tried to fit in, Jackie always managed to say something stupid. Once she'd joined a cluster of class-mates standing in the hallway outside Mrs. Kavanaugh's room her sophomore year, talking about some hot guy named Justin Timberlake. Jackie had asked innocently, "Who's that, a new kid?" Even now, the memory of the looks they turned her way, the rolled eyes, the snickers, made her cringe.

"He's a lousy singer anyway."

She sniffled into her pillow. Friendships back then had been too hard to figure out. She got along better with Aunt Betty's friends. Older people didn't care if you wore clothes that had gone out of style five years ago.

But Jackie wasn't a teenager anymore. You'd think at twenty-four she'd be able to make friends with women her own age. There were several at church she could spend time with, if she wanted to. Maybe go to a movie or shopping. Instead, what was she doing? Running over to an eighty-year-old's house to do a good deed that only got her into trouble.

Irritated at the turn her thoughts had taken, Jackie sat up in bed. She pulled Linus into her lap and stroked his fur until he began to purr.

No matter what Margaret said, her name would be

linked to Mrs. Farmer's death until the police caught the killer. Who would want to hang out with Typhoid Jackie?

"And I know that detective thinks I had something to do with it."

The memory of his arrogant smile, his direct stare as Trooper Walsh searched her refrigerator made her jaw tighten. Would they even bother looking for other suspects while they wasted time trying to find traces of poisonous mushrooms on her kitchen utensils? Probably not. Even an idiot could see that the poisonous mushrooms had been added after Mrs. Farmer got home with the leftover portion of her casserole. Otherwise they'd have people dropping dead—or at least getting sick—all over the church. But it looked as though the police were going to drag this thing out for months by running tests and chasing false hunches that led to dead ends.

If she was in charge, she'd handle things differently. She'd go visit all the old ladies in the church. They'd talk to her, she was sure of that. Old people liked to talk to young women. In fact, she'd talk to *all* the women in the church, even the younger ones. They'd open up to her like they never would to that conceited detective.

Jackie's hand stopped midstroke and rested on Linus's arched back. That wasn't a bad idea, actually. Women *would* talk to her, would tell her things Detective Conner and Trooper Walsh could never find out. She could probably have this case solved in a matter of days.

But she couldn't just show up at people's houses and say, *Excuse me, but do you know who poisoned Mrs. Farmer?* She'd have to lead into it casually. Since she was new to the church, she really didn't have the kind of relationship with anyone that would allow for a social visit.

But *Margaret* didn't need an excuse. The pastor's wife could show up on anyone's doorstep for a casual chat, and no one would think a thing about it. And if Jackie just happened to tag along...

She jerked the blanket aside and Linus leaped out of her lap as she turned to put her feet on the floor. She'd do it! Somehow she would convince Margaret to help her, and she would track down the killer.

Then, when she had cleared her name, maybe she could even start gossiping about one of those stupid reality shows on television.

"Please, Margaret. You've got to help me. I can't do it without you."

Jackie stood in the cookie-scented front room of the parsonage later that afternoon, staring into the stunned faces of Pastor Palmer and his wife.

The pastor's gaze connected with Margaret's for a second before he spoke to Jackie. "Don't you think the police are better suited to handle the job?"

Jackie shook her head. "You saw the two who've been assigned to the case. That detective obviously doesn't know what he's doing, and Trooper Walsh is only on the case to do the detective's grunt work."

"Detective Conner seemed capable to me," Margaret said.

"You didn't see the way he acted at my apartment. He's convinced I had something to do with poisoning Mrs. Farmer, and he's going to spend his time chasing empty leads while the real murderer walks free."

"But Jackie, you're not a detective." Margaret shook her head. "You don't know anything about solving crimes."

"True, but I'm a woman and I'm a member of the

church. Someone is bound to know who has a grudge against Mrs. Farmer, and I think they'll tell me." She gave Margaret what she hoped was an imploring look. "Especially if you're with me."

"But what about your job? Visiting people is quite time-consuming."

"I've got some vacation time coming. My boss will let me take a week off, no problem." She spoke with more confidence than she felt. Her boss was an easygoing guy, and the rules about time off at the state government office were fairly lax, but she would have to do some fast-talking to get permission to take a week off with no notice.

Jackie clasped her hands together and held them up to her chin. "Please, Margaret."

Margaret threw a helpless look toward Pastor Palmer, whose eyebrows had embedded themselves in his hairline. Jackie watched the silent husband-and-wife communication going on between them. Then Margaret sighed.

"I visit the church shut-ins on Mondays. If you'd like to tag along, I guess that'll be okay."

Jackie bounced on her toes, grinning at them both. "Great! Maybe we'll have this case solved by the end of the week."

FIVE

Jackie slumped behind the steering wheel and watched people file into the church. Yesterday's confidence had slipped a little. Man, she dreaded going into that place. What if Beverly Sanders stood waiting inside the door? What would she say? Or worse, what if she didn't say anything at all, but only stared from across the sanctuary, whispering with the other women about Typhoid Jackie?

I've got to get a grip. Margaret says they're not talking about me at all.

But she didn't believe it, not really. Without a doubt, Mrs. Farmer dying from potluck leftovers was the juiciest piece of gossip this church had heard in years. Of course they would discuss every aspect of the incident, and much as she hated to admit it, Jackie was an aspect.

Still, she wouldn't accomplish anything by sitting in her car. She had her response ready. She'd practiced all morning. With a sigh, she gathered her purse and umbrella and stepped out, glancing toward the dark cloud cover overhead. Threatening but, for the moment, dry. She picked her way carefully over the gravel parking lot. The glass door opened as her foot touched the concrete sidewalk.

"Good morning," said a cheery male voice.

Jackie looked into Bob Murphy's smiling face. He was wearing a name tag identifying him as the day's greeter. "Hi, Mr. Murphy."

He leaned through the door to examine the sky. "Think it'll hold off until we get home?"

"I doubt it."

"Yeah, me, too. But it's good for the garden, I suppose."

Jackie squeezed by him into the church. She almost breathed a sigh of relief when she saw no sign of Beverly Sanders. Instead, Jean Murphy, wearing a name tag identical to her husband's, stood beside the table with the guest book. If a visitor happened to make their way to HCC this morning, Mrs. Murphy seemed determined to ensure that their presence would be duly recorded.

At the moment, no visitors were in sight. Mrs. Murphy crossed the floor in two steps, her hands held toward Jackie.

"My dear, how awful for you." She grabbed each of Jackie's shoulders in a firm grip. "I just can't imagine how you must feel."

Inwardly, Jackie winced. But she forced herself to bestow a calm smile on Mrs. Murphy before delivering her rehearsed response.

"It's terrible," she agreed. "I've hardly slept a wink since the police told me how poor Mrs. Farmer died. I can't imagine why anyone would want to hurt an old lady like her."

Mrs. Murphy leaned forward to speak in a low voice. "Well, you know, she wasn't very well liked in this town." She cast a quick glance around the empty narthex. "Or even in this church, truth be told."

Aha! My very first conversation about the case, and I've already hit pay dirt!

"Really? But why not? I thought she'd been a member here her whole life."

"That's the thing. She knew practically everything about everybody. And she didn't mind making use of any tidbit of information that came her way, either."

Mr. Murphy stepped up beside them and laid a hand on his wife's arm. A look passed between them before he turned a friendly smile on Jackie.

"You'd better get on in there and find a seat. The service will start in a minute or two."

"Oh, yes, of course."

As Jackie turned toward the open sanctuary doors, she congratulated herself. She hadn't been here two minutes and already she had discovered a valuable source of information. Before the day was over, she intended to get Mrs. Murphy in a corner and question her further.

From the front of the sanctuary, Pastor Palmer said, "Let's bow together in prayer."

Startled, Jackie glanced at her watch. He had, indeed, preached for his usual forty minutes, but she couldn't remember a thing he'd said. Her mind had been too busy planning her questions for Mrs. Murphy and any other lady who seemed willing to chat about Mrs. Farmer. She bowed her head and whispered an apology to the Lord for ignoring the sermon, ending as Pastor Palmer said, "Amen."

After four verses of "Beneath the Cross of Jesus," the congregation slapped their hymnals shut. Jackie gave her full attention to her pastor, who stood holding his Bible and letting his gaze sweep the congregation.

"If you're on the men's softball team, Phil has copies of the game schedule and will be in the narthex handing them out, so be sure to see him. Also, don't forget that we're starting a new Bible study this Wednesday night, so please come out and join us."

He paused, and the smile melted from his face. Jackie clenched her fists. Was he going to mention Mrs. Farmer?

"As you all know, a long-time member of our congregation, Alice Farmer, passed away on Tuesday."

Blood rose slowly to heat her face. Was it her imagination, or had the heads of half the congregation swivelled toward her? She kept her eyes forward, focused on Pastor Palmer.

"Her passing is especially disturbing because it appears as though someone tampered with some food she took home from our church picnic last Sunday. Because of that, I've been asked to request that anyone who took leftovers and experienced any sort of stomach upset this week contact Detective Conner of the Kentucky State Police. Detective Conner is here this morning and will be in the back of the sanctuary if you'd like to talk to him."

Jackie twisted to look behind her. Here? Detective Conner was here, in her own church? He must have come in after the service started, because she would have seen him if he'd been there when she arrived. Sure enough, her eyes were drawn immediately to the unfamiliar sight of a uniformed figure on the back pew. Trooper Walsh. Perhaps drawn by her movement, he looked straight at her and, with a slight shrug, smiled. Her stomach experienced that same tingling sensation it had the day she met him. Flushing, she looked away, to his left. Beside him sat Detective Conner, wearing the same ugly tie he had worn when he came to her apartment. Her face went cold at the hard stare he leveled on her.

She turned her back on him, swallowing hard. The nerve of that man, coming to *her* church! How dare he follow her around like this! Stalking, that's what it was. Police weren't allowed to stalk people, were they?

Jackie filled her lungs with a calming breath. On second thought, maybe his presence was good. She needed to tell him of her plans to clear her name by finding the murderer. Maybe they'd even share clues with her, though she doubted it. She'd seen enough television to know that was unlikely.

Pastor Palmer's voice reclaimed her attention. "…hip surgery, and also Mr. Lewis as he recovers from a broken wrist. And now…" He raised his hand toward the congregation and gave the benediction.

The first person out of her pew, Jackie beelined across the sanctuary toward the place where Jean Murphy stood chatting with Ellen Clarke. As the center aisle filled, Jackie slipped into the pew behind the pair and waited quietly for their conversation to end. When Mrs. Clarke turned away, Mrs. Murphy, wearing an expression of polite inquiry, shifted her focus to Jackie.

Jackie cleared her throat. "Um, Mrs. Murphy, I've been thinking about what you said this morning. You know, about people not liking Mrs. Farmer."

Mrs. Murphy glanced quickly toward the end of the pew, where her husband stood talking to two men. "I really shouldn't have said that. Bob says I talk too much, and I'm sure he's right. I don't want to gossip, you know."

"Of course not." Jackie gave her a reassuring smile. "But in this case, with Mrs. Farmer dead and all, any information might be helpful in finding the person responsible. Or," Jackie went on quickly when Mrs. Murphy's brow creased with alarm, "in clearing the members of our church of suspicion. I'm sure the police being here this morning means they think someone here knows something."

"Oh!" Mrs. Murphy paled as her eyes flew toward the back of the sanctuary. "I don't want to be questioned by the police!"

"Trust me," Jackie assured her drily, "you don't. But if you know anything, perhaps you could tell me and if I think it's important, I'll pass it along as an anonymous tip."

"Well…" The woman's face took on a cautious expression, and she lowered her voice. "I don't want to cast suspicion on anyone. But it's no secret that Alice was known for having a…well, a rather judgmental attitude. She was quick to find fault, and she held a grudge."

"Against who?"

"Practically everyone. With my own ears I've heard her criticize everything from the placement of the flowers on the altar to the selection of hymns for the order of service. She even found fault with Pastor Palmer's audition sermon because he preached on the subject of God's love instead of calling people to repentance." Warming to her topic, the woman leaned close, giving Jackie a whiff of stale coffee breath. "She was the single dissenting vote in offering him the job. I've even heard her talking about getting up a petition to have him removed. Of course, everyone loves Pastor Palmer, so that would have failed. But that wasn't always the case."

Her mouth snapped shut abruptly. Jackie looked into her rounded eyes and prompted, "She was successful sometimes?"

Mrs. Murphy's gaze dropped. "You really should talk to Esther Hodges if you want to know about that. Anything else I can tell you would just be gossip, since I don't know firsthand."

This was exactly the kind of information Jackie had

hoped to discover. If she could keep Mrs. Murphy talking she was sure to uncover some more interesting tidbits. But at that moment Mr. Murphy turned away from the cluster of men at the end of the pew and glanced toward his wife, who threw a guilty look in his direction. Jackie flashed him her best smile and spoke in a low voice.

"Thanks, Mrs. Murphy. And don't worry. I won't say a word to anyone about our conversation."

Mrs. Murphy gave her a grateful smile before stooping to collect her raincoat and purse. Jackie slipped out of the pew and headed toward the rear of the sanctuary.

Detective Conner and Trooper Walsh stood alone like lepers, the members of Heritage Community Church making a wide path around them. One glance into Officer Walsh's face told Jackie he felt conspicuous standing there in his uniform beside the smiling detective. The younger man managed to avoid looking directly into anyone's face. But as Jackie approached, he locked eyes with her for an instant. Those high cheekbones and long, curling lashes drew attention to hidden depths in his eyes. She noticed a tiny fresh cut along his right jaw where he had nicked himself shaving.

She had to stop feeling like a schoolgirl every time she looked at him. In church, no less! She turned to Detective Conner, her chin high.

"Miss Hoffner." His head dipped forward in a polite greeting while his eyes remained fixed on her face.

"Detective Conner. Trooper Walsh." Jackie nodded to each of them. "I'm glad you're here."

"And why is that, Miss Hoffner?"

"Because it saves me the trouble of calling you tomorrow. Have you gotten any leads on the case?"

Trooper Walsh opened his mouth to answer, but Detective Conner shook his head. "No one has spoken to us besides Pastor and Mrs. Palmer. Were you going to give me a lead tomorrow?"

"Not a lead. Just some information." She squared her shoulders. "I wanted to let you know that I'm on the case."

"On the case?" The detective's eyebrows arched. Next to him, Trooper Walsh hid a quick smile.

Jackie nodded. "I'm taking the week off work to search for clues, and I wanted to tell you I'll pass along any helpful information I find. I'm hoping you'll do the same for me."

"Miss Hoffner, please don't do that. I assure you, we are trained in investigations of this kind, and we don't need help from civilians."

"But I can get information you can't," Jackie argued. "I'm a member of this church. I'm a woman. I'm—"

"Don't," he repeated with force. "We're dealing with someone who has committed murder. We don't know his or her mental state, but the situation could be dangerous. Just leave things to us."

"But—"

He held up a hand, and Jackie fell silent. Frustrated, she turned to Trooper Walsh, who shrugged. Couldn't they see how important it was to her to clear her name? It would be so much easier if she could work with the police. They had experts, crime labs, all sorts of things she couldn't access. Of course, she knew the police hated having civilians involved in their cases, but she couldn't stand by and do nothing. She would follow her plan, with or without their help.

Watching her face, Detective Conner's eyes narrowed. "You're going to ignore me, aren't you?"

In answer, Jackie gave him the sweetest smile she could manage.

* * *

As their feet crunched across the gravel parking lot, Dennis cast a sidelong glance at Conner. The detective's jaw bulged from the force of his clenched teeth. Dennis knew the reason without being told.

"She has a point, you know."

"And what might that be?"

"Women talk to other women." Dennis lifted a shoulder. "They sure didn't talk to us today."

It was true. The entire congregation had ignored them, except for Jackie and the Palmers. If Dennis hadn't seen the members greeting one another, he would have assumed Heritage Community Church was the most unfriendly church in town. But a uniform and a badge had apparently frozen some of their tongues to the roofs of their mouths. He might have gotten a different reception as a real visitor instead of an investigating police officer.

Actually, for a while he had almost forgot he was on duty. Pastor Palmer preached a good message in a compelling style. This place reminded him of his own church in Lexington, where he still attended with his mom and dad every Sunday he didn't have to work. He'd never really considered finding a place to worship here in Versailles, because the fifteen-minute drive to Lexington was an easy one. But Heritage Community Church might just change his mind.

Except, he reminded himself, someone there was probably a murderer.

"We can't afford to have that girl messing around in our case, Walsh." Conner shook his head. "I've seen it before. She's NBT."

Dennis cocked his head. "NBT?"

Conner's lips twisted. "Nothing But Trouble."

SIX

"Look what I got." Standing in the doorway of the parsonage on Monday morning, Jackie reached into her purse and extracted a silver box the size of her palm. She held it out for Margaret's inspection.

"What is it?"

"It's a digital voice recorder. I went to the mall in Lexington yesterday and bought it. Look how small it is. It'll fit into my purse and no one will even know it's there."

Margaret shook her head. "Don't you think it's impolite to record conversations? Is it even legal?"

Jackie had spent a long time considering those questions yesterday as she stood in the aisle of the department store, examining the display of recorders. She didn't want to do anything wrong, but she was afraid people would clam up the minute she started to scribble on a pad of paper, the way Walsh had done in her apartment. It would inhibit their conversations. And if she tried to make notes after she left, she was sure to miss some important clues.

"They do it all the time on TV. And don't worry, I'll be discreet," she assured Margaret.

Heaving a resigned sigh, Margaret stepped back and

gestured for her to come inside the house. "Go on into the kitchen. Earl's just finishing his breakfast."

Jackie walked through the living room, fiddling with the device. "I got this one because it has an external microphone. The recorder can be hidden in my purse, but the mic clips onto the strap. See?"

She plugged a thin cord into the recorder and demonstrated. The microphone at the end was practically unnoticeable, if you didn't look too closely.

"I can't imagine what you think you're going to discover talking to old people in a nursing home."

They arrived in the kitchen to find Pastor Palmer sitting at a round breakfast table, sipping coffee. He looked up from his newspaper, eyeing Jackie's recorder with interest as she slipped into an empty chair.

"Actually," he said, the corners of his mouth twitching, "you never know what Mr. Sheppard might come out with. He's a colorful old guy at times."

Margaret held the coffeepot toward Jackie, a question on her face. Jackie shook her head. She didn't want to be rude, but she hoped Margaret didn't intend to hang around the house too much longer. The sooner they got started, the sooner they would discover something to help her identify the killer.

To her relief, Pastor Palmer refused a refill and began folding his newspaper. Margaret turned the coffee warmer off and leaned against the kitchen counter. She eyed Jackie with obvious hesitation. "Just remember one thing, please. We're visiting church members, not interrogating criminals."

Jackie bit back a sharp response. Did Margaret think her completely incapable of finesse? Did she expect her to go in there with a bright spotlight and a rubber hose to bully a bunch of old people into a confession?

She was trying to come up with an appropriate response when Pastor Palmer said, "You never know. They might be one and the same."

"Oh, Earl!" Margaret's hand rose to her throat. "Do you really think someone in our church is a murderer?"

"I don't know." He shrugged. "I suppose it's possible. We've known these people less than a year."

"Well, I don't believe it."

Jackie leaned forward, her elbows planted on the table. "Maybe it isn't anyone in our church. I hope not. But Mrs. Farmer has been a member for a long time. Those people know her better than anyone, and someone is bound to know something that will help us identify her killer."

Uncertainty tinged Margaret's features, but she gave a single nod. "I suppose you're right. Let me get my things and we'll leave."

Pastor Palmer stood and took his coffee mug to the sink. Jackie left the table and trailed after Margaret down a short hallway and into an office.

"Your boss was okay with you taking off work?" Margaret asked.

Jackie grimaced. "Well, he wasn't thrilled, but I convinced him. I had to promise to come in if they run into problems later in the week."

Actually, her boss had told her she was crazy for wanting to mess around in a murder investigation and she should get a life. But she didn't see any reason to tell that to Margaret.

"How many people will we see today?"

"Four." Margaret slid open a desk drawer. "I usually

only have three, but since Mrs. Sawyer's still recovering from surgery I've been stopping by her house, too."

She retrieved a handful of church bulletins, then opened another drawer and removed a stack of cassette tapes. A pink tote came out of a third drawer, and she stuffed everything into it. She handed the tote to Jackie and motioned for her to follow as she left the room. Back in the kitchen, she added two Baggies full of cookies.

"I like to take a little something to Mrs. Harrod and Mr. Sheppard," she said. "The dining room there at the nursing home is nice enough, but I think they appreciate having a little snack in their own rooms."

Jackie peeked into the tote. The cookies looked like oatmeal, or maybe peanut butter. Two of her favorites.

Margaret picked up a worn Bible from the counter. "I'm ready."

Finally! Tote bag in one hand, Jackie slung her purse across her shoulder as Pastor Palmer bestowed a kiss on Margaret's cheek. "Tell them all I said hello and I'll be along later in the week."

During the trip across town, Jackie fiddled with her recorder. Margaret had announced that they would visit Mrs. Sawyer's house first, since it was the farthest away, and work their way back to the parsonage. A couple of times Jackie noticed her opening her mouth to say something, her forehead creased with lines, but then closing it again. She was probably concerned that too many questions might upset the old people, but she had nothing to be concerned about. Talking to old people was one of the things Jackie did best.

They paused on Mrs. Sawyer's front porch while Jackie

turned on her little device. When everything was ready, she nodded toward Margaret, who rang the bell.

Mrs. Sawyer greeted them, moving slowly with the aid of a walker. Margaret hugged the older woman gently. She looked so frail Jackie worried a breeze might overbalance her. She had to be at least eighty, but until her hip surgery a few weeks ago, Jackie had seen her often at church, both on Sunday mornings and Wednesday nights. She was a member of the Prime Timer Sunday school class, the one Mrs. Farmer had attended.

"It's nice to see you up and around," Margaret exclaimed as they followed her into the tiny living room. "You look stronger than last week."

"I hate this thing," Mrs. Sawyer confided, "but at least I'm able to walk on my own." She lowered her voice. "My daughter was glad to go back to work. I think I was getting on her nerves."

"Oh, I'm sure that's not true."

"Well, she was getting on my nerves sure enough." The old lady smiled. "It's good to be able to go to the restroom by myself."

Margaret laughed. "I'm sure it is. You know Jackie Hoffner, don't you?"

The older lady turned her wrinkled smile on Jackie. "Of course I do. How nice to see you. Young people don't visit us old folks much these days."

Jackie returned the smile with a wide one of her own and took the extended hand gently. "We've missed you at church, Mrs. Sawyer."

The older woman gestured for them to sit on the couch and then dropped into a Queen Anne wing chair with obvious relief. "I would offer you coffee, but you'd have to make it yourself. Marsha leaves my lunch on a plate in the refrigerator, and getting it to the table is the extent of my ability with this thing. But I'm learning!"

"That isn't necessary," Margaret assured her.

The old lady looked at Jackie with a shrewd stare. "I hear you've been having some excitement lately."

Settled on the couch, Jackie tried not to grimace. "What do you mean?"

"I heard somebody murdered Alice," Mrs. Sawyer said. "Someone dumped poison in her drinking water, they say, and you found her dead body."

Obviously the grapevine reaching into Mrs. Sawyer's home operated on a several-day delay, and without much accuracy. She hadn't heard about Pastor Palmer's announcement yesterday morning.

"Actually," said Margaret, "her water wasn't poisoned, her food was."

"Really?" Mrs. Sawyer's eyes widened, and Jackie detected a twinkle of excitement. Yes, just like Aunt Betty's friends.

"And when I got to her house she was still alive," Jackie added. If the gossip was going to get spread around, at least it should be correct.

"My goodness, how frightening. One of our own, poisoned."

The old lady shifted in her chair and glanced toward the telephone. She'd be on the phone the moment they left, spreading the news. If there was anyone who hadn't yet heard, that is.

Jackie leaned forward on the couch. "Did you know Mrs. Farmer long?"

"Oh, yes, dear. For nigh on thirty years, ever since my

husband and I moved to Versailles when he retired, God rest his soul."

"Do you know anyone who might want to harm her?"

Margaret shot her a look. What? Mrs. Sawyer didn't seem offended by the direct question. In fact, she seemed eager to talk. She leaned against the upholstered back of her chair, her lips pursed for a moment as she thought.

"I expect so. Alice wasn't exactly a friendly person. We all loved her, of course, because she was one of our own, but she had sharp eyes. She knew things about a lot of people in that church. The stories she used to tell!"

"Such as?"

This was just the sort of thing Jackie had hoped to hear. She picked up her purse and set it in her lap, the little black microphone pointed toward Mrs. Sawyer.

The old lady tapped her finger against the molded leg of her walker. "Why, I can't think of a single one at the moment!"

Jackie hated to ask leading questions, but maybe she could discover a little more information about the incident Mrs. Murphy had alluded to yesterday at church. "Did you happen to hear anything about, uh, difficulties between Mrs. Hodges and Mrs. Farmer?"

Beside her on the couch, Margaret's back stiffened. Jackie glanced her way, surprised to see a spot of color high on each cheek. Her expression was unreadable. Mrs. Sawyer didn't seem to notice.

"Of course!" The old lady brightened. "That's a perfect example. Esther's son Joshua was a wild one. Drugs, you know. Trouble with the police, too. Oh, the trials Esther had with that boy! But he straightened himself up, and when he got out of high school he went to Bible college somewhere up north. Then he got a job as a youth pastor at a big church in Ohio." Her attention shifted toward Margaret and then back to Jackie. "Alice didn't believe someone with a past like his should be leading youth, so she wrote a letter to the board of elders at his new church. They fired him."

Jackie gasped. What a terrible thing to do to someone. Malicious, even. Had Mrs. Farmer never heard of forgiveness? Didn't she think people could change?

"Why would she do that?" Margaret asked.

Mrs. Sawyer gave a delicate shrug. "Alice had high standards. And that's one reason Nick Carlson is probably resting easy about his promotion out at the factory since she's gone."

A new name! Jackie shifted the purse to the edge of her knees, as close to Mrs. Sawyer as she could get it without shoving it under the older lady's nose. "What do you mean?"

Mrs. Sawyer included both of them in her smile. "Well, it's no secret Alice disapproved of his speedy marriage to Sharon, and especially when the baby was born just a few months later."

Another person with a motive. This was exactly the sort of information the police would take weeks to discover. And she had gotten it her first day on the case!

Jackie opened her mouth to ask for more details, but Margaret stood abruptly. "Look at the time! I'm afraid we need to leave."

"So soon?" Mrs. Sawyer asked, surprised. "You've barely arrived."

"Yes, Margaret," Jackie agreed, looking sideways up at her. "We've barely arrived."

Margaret had evidently had enough. "We have three more visits this morning, and I'm afraid I have plans for the afternoon."

A lame excuse, if Jackie had ever heard one. But the look on Margaret's face kept her from asking anymore questions. She sat quietly as Margaret gave Mrs. Sawyer a cassette tape of last week's sermon and a bulletin and then led them in a quick prayer.

They saw themselves to the door, leaving Mrs. Sawyer sitting comfortably in her Queen Anne chair. As Jackie pulled it closed behind them, she saw Mrs. Sawyer reach for the telephone.

"What was that all about?" she demanded, trailing after Margaret toward the car. "Why did we leave in such a hurry?"

Margaret whirled on her. "What on earth made you ask about Esther Hodges?"

"Something I overheard at church yesterday. And my question paid off."

Margaret's lips pressed into a hard line. She stalked to the car and jerked the door open. Jackie slid into the passenger seat as Margaret slammed her door shut. Harder than necessary. Jackie shut her own door as quietly as possible. What had she done to make Margaret so angry?

Margaret turned in the seat. "What do you mean by that—that your question paid off?"

Jackie shifted in the seat and looked out the window. Anywhere but at the outrage on Margaret's face. "I'm assembling a list of possible suspects, people with a motive for killing Mrs. Farmer. Obviously, I've just found the first two."

Margaret gasped. "Esther Hodges is a good, Christian woman! She wouldn't hurt a flea!"

Jackie shrugged and kept her tone apologetic. "Maybe she is. But Mrs. Farmer hurt her child. Revenge is a pretty strong motive."

"That is ridiculous." Margaret twisted the key in the ignition and the engine roared to life.

Jackie held her tongue as the car backed out of the driveway and pulled onto the street. Margaret's hands gripped the steering wheel, her knuckles white.

"Is that the kind of conversation you intend to have every time? Because if so, I don't think I want to go with you anymore. That wasn't simply a matter of asking questions. That was nothing but gossip."

Jackie looked toward her, surprised at the accusing tone. "I wasn't gossiping. We have to ask about people who have a grudge against Mrs. Farmer. How else will we find the murderer?"

Margaret took a few deep breaths, an obvious attempt to calm down. "Jackie, you might not have intended to gossip, but Mrs. Sawyer did. Esther is my friend, and though I don't know Nick and Sharon Carlson, Nick's father, Vince, is our choir director and a friend of Earl's. That conversation left me feeling sullied and low."

The look Jackie had seen on Mrs. Sawyer's face as she related the story of Mrs. Hodges's son certainly proved Margaret's point. No doubt the old woman was on the phone right now, passing along the information she'd gotten from their visit.

Still, without a doubt Mrs. Sawyer had already been gossiping before their arrival. If anything, Jackie and Margaret had just set the record straight. At least now the gossip would be true. A look at Margaret's tight lips told Jackie now was not a good time to argue that point.

"Listen, Margaret, I don't want to gossip, I really don't. But you can't get upset every time I question someone. I have to talk to people if I want to get to the bottom of this."

Margaret took her eyes off the road to give her a quick look. "Why, Jackie? Why is it so important to you to find the murderer?"

"I don't want my name coming up every time Mrs. Farmer is mentioned. And it will, Margaret. You know it will."

That was true. But it wasn't the whole truth. Jackie turned away, staring at the line of trees they passed and admitted the truth to herself. *Because I want to prove I can do something right. I want people to like me.* It was the answer she couldn't give to Margaret. To anyone. Except maybe Linus.

Margaret remained quiet a long time. Finally she sighed. "You're making way too much out of this, Jackie. I'd prefer to leave this interrogation business to the police. But if you're determined to continue, I guess you need me along to temper the conversations."

Normally, Jackie would have flared with indignation at a statement like that. She could certainly handle a conversation all by herself, for cryin' out loud! No one needed to "temper" anything for her. But she didn't want Margaret mad at her.

So she simply said, "Thanks, Margaret. I appreciate your help."

"Besides," Margaret went on, "the Bible says older women should teach younger women. Maybe this is an opportunity the Lord is giving me to teach you something. Here." She picked up the Bible that lay on the seat between them and thrust it into Jackie's hands. "Before we get to the nursing home, I want you to read Proverbs chapter eleven."

Jackie obeyed. And tried not to fume when she got to verses twelve and thirteen.

* * *

On the den sofa, Margaret snuggled into the curve of Earl's shoulder. She loved this time every evening, when the supper dishes were put away and the nightly news programs had ended. Strands of Tchaikovsky washed over her, clearing her mind and easing away the day's tension.

"How did the visitations go?" Earl asked.

"Terrible."

She told him about the visit to Mrs. Sawyer and about Jackie's list of "suspects."

Earl shook his head. "She's quite a character, isn't she? I'll bet she causes quite a stir at lunch tomorrow."

Margaret avoided Earl's eyes. "After today, I didn't have the nerve to invite her to lunch. These lunch dates are one of the highlights of my week, and I don't want tomorrow's ruined by uncomfortable questions." She flushed with guilt at her selfish desire to exclude Jackie from a perfect opportunity to talk with several of the church ladies.

Earl stretched his legs out in front of him and pulled her closer. Margaret closed her eyes, listening to the music and breathing in the faint scent of his aftershave. She supposed she should invite Jackie to her weekly ladies' luncheon. The girl would jump at the chance, because Esther would be there. But could she be trusted to handle the situation tactfully?

"Did she add anyone else to her list after the other visits?" Earl asked, interrupting her thoughts.

"No. Mrs. Snedegar was entertaining her neighbor, so we didn't stay long. And Mrs. Harrod was more interested in my cookies than in Jackie's questions."

"And Mr. Sheppard?" He grinned. "Did he have any interesting stories for his pretty young visitor?"

"He behaved like a gentleman." Margaret sighed and plucked at a loose thread on the sofa cushion. "Do you think I should invite Jackie to lunch with the ladies?"

Earl shrugged. "Whatever you think. I'm sure you'll make the right decision."

She already knew what that decision would be. She wouldn't enjoy herself if she didn't extend the invitation. She'd be thinking the whole time of Jackie sitting home alone, and how hurt her feelings would be when she found out she had been excluded.

But not tonight. She'd call her young friend in the morning. Tonight she just wanted to relax and forget all about gossip and murder investigations.

She pressed her face into Earl's shoulder and grumbled, "I *hate* making the right decision."

SEVEN

Yawning, Jackie poured coffee into a mug while Linus twined around her legs, verbalizing his impatience for breakfast. Day two of her vacation. Yesterday had not been as productive as she'd hoped after the informative talk with Mrs. Sawyer. The old people in the nursing home hadn't delivered any new leads on the murder case. Still, she knew they'd enjoyed her visit. Mrs. Harrod kept patting her arm while she munched on Margaret's cookies, and Mr. Snedegar showed her a bunch of pictures from his war days.

Hopefully today would prove more profitable. She planned to talk with her two main suspects, Sharon Carlson and Esther Hodges. Sharon was easy. She had been out when Jackie called the Carlson residence last night, but a few subtle questions asked of her teenage daughter, Samantha, had revealed Sharon's place of employment. Jackie planned to drop by her office this morning. With the experience of a few visits under her belt, she didn't think she'd have any problems leading into a conversation about Mrs. Farmer.

Talking to Mrs. Hodges would be a little more difficult to arrange. Margaret was so protective of her.

The shrill ring of the telephone blared into the apartment's silence. Jackie grabbed the receiver and propped it on her shoulder, leaving her hands free to open a can of cat food.

"Hello?"

"Jackie? It's Margaret."

"Hey, I was going to call you in a bit. Do you want to go by Sharon Carlson's office with me this morning?"

A pause on the other end. "Uh, no, I don't think so. I've only met Sharon once, so I doubt my presence will help you, and if we're both there it might look like we're ganging up on her."

"Well, I've only met her once, too." Linus's yowling grew louder as she plopped the smelly mass of congealed whitefish into his bowl. "That time Samantha had a solo in the Easter pageant is the only time I've seen her at church. And I've never seen Samantha's dad."

"He works third shift, so he sleeps during the day. That's why Samantha comes to church with her grandfather." Another pause. "Listen, Jackie, I called to invite you to lunch."

"Linus, back off!" The little fiend made walking impossible. She deposited his breakfast onto the floor mat beside his water bowl. "Sorry to yell in your ear, Margaret. Lunch sounds great. What time?"

"Actually, it's not at my house. Some of the ladies at church have gotten into the habit of meeting for lunch every Tuesday. We started back when Earl and I first came to HCC, and Esther decided it would be a good way for those of us who don't work outside the home to get to know each other."

Jackie's grip on the receiver tightened. "Esther Hodges?"

"That's right. And Laura Watson and Sylvia Graham

and Julie McCoy. Sometimes others join us, but that's who'll be there today."

A perfect chance to question her number-one suspect! "Where and what time?"

"We're meeting at Shaker Village at eleven-thirty, but I'll stop by and pick you up at eleven. Will that be okay?"

"Perfect. I'll have my recorder ready."

Margaret's sigh sounded loud through the receiver. "Jackie, please don't make this an uncomfortable lunch. These women have been nothing but kind to me since I arrived. They're my friends."

And one of them might be a killer! But Jackie kept her thought to herself. Margaret probably wouldn't appreciate hearing it.

"I'll be good," she promised. "See you at eleven."

She disconnected the call and turned to Linus. "I've got two interrogations today. With luck, I'll have this case solved by suppertime."

Unimpressed, Linus ignored her.

Dennis pulled his cruiser into the parking lot of police headquarters promptly at seven forty-five. Yesterday, he'd arrived a few minutes past eight and received a lecture from Conner on the necessity of developing good investigative habits. The detective considered punctuality right up near the top of the list. "Being late implies laziness, and there's no room in the force for a lazy investigator."

Dennis endured the dressing-down silently, aware that a half-dozen pairs of eyes watched covertly from behind cluttered desks around the room. He had to remind himself he was lucky to be working with Conner, who reportedly changed partners more often than a teenage girl changed clothes. He was beginning to see why. Not many would willingly perform all the grunt work while the arrogant detective refused to dirty his hands.

But Dennis would suffer that and worse to learn from the best investigator in the state. One day he hoped to lay claim to that title himself.

He picked up the folder containing the notes he'd printed off at home last night. For the most part, his job so far in this case had been great. He'd faithfully recorded notes of every conversation, every interrogation Conner conducted. Their case file was growing. True, they didn't have much to go on yet, but the detective's techniques were inspiring. He was certain to weasel out relevant information sooner or later.

Dennis made his way down the hallway toward the crowded room where Conner's desk was located. The lab report they'd received yesterday had indicated no evidence of *Gyromitra ambigua* on any of the utensils they had confiscated from Jackie Hoffner's kitchen. True, they had been washed, but the wooden surface of her cutting board bore trace amounts of onions, peppers and ordinary mushrooms. Jackie hadn't chopped *Gyromitra ambigua* on that surface. While she might not be a great dishwasher, Conner seemed ready to concede she wasn't a viable murder suspect. Far more likely that the poisonous mushrooms were planted in a leftover portion of her pasta after it arrived at the victim's home.

Dennis grinned, remembering her expression on Sunday as she faced down Conner. That was one determined girl. While he was in complete agreement with Conner that she needed to stay out of their investigation, he couldn't help but admire her spunk. If she carried out her plan to talk to the women in that church, she might just dig out a clue or two.

Conner was already at his desk, reading through a typed report. He looked up when Dennis approached, his eyes fixing on the folder. "Those yesterday's interrogation notes?"

"Yes, sir."

"Good. I needed them an hour ago."

He snatched the folder. Dennis bit back a sharp retort as Conner pulled out the neatly printed pages and scanned them. Yeah, he was learning a lot working with Conner. How to act like a good investigator. And how not to act like a total jerk.

Tomorrow he'd be here at seven.

He stood while Conner scanned the notes. The detective chewed a corner of his mustache while he read. When he finished the last page, he gave a nod. "Looks like it's all there."

That was as close to a compliment as Dennis was likely to get. "Thanks."

Conner shuffled the papers and pulled a two-hole punch from a drawer. "I've got a team meeting us at the victim's house at noon. I want to go through there one last time."

"But we already—" Dennis cut off his argument mid-sentence at a glance from Conner.

"I want the surrounding property combed, too." The detective punched holes in Dennis's notes and slid them onto two metal prongs inside the folder he'd been reading when Dennis arrived. "Then we can cut the tape and release the house to the estate."

Dennis's cell phone rang. With an apologetic grimace at Conner, he unclipped it from his belt and glanced at the display. His parents' number. Before eight o'clock in the morning? Something must be wrong.

He flipped open the cover. "Hello?"

"Dennis." Relief saturated his mother's voice. "I'm so glad I got you."

The speed of his pulse kicked up a notch. "What's wrong, Mom? Is Dad okay?"

"Why wouldn't he be? He's out in the garage, as usual, fiddling with the lawn mower."

Dennis felt the weight of Conner's stare. He turned his back. "Mom, is this important? I'm working."

"Of course it's important. I wouldn't be calling otherwise. I need you to come to the house for dinner tonight."

"Dinner?" Dennis lowered his voice and took a couple of steps away from the detective's desk. "Why is that important?"

"Because I've invited someone I want you to meet, and this is the only evening she can make it."

He closed his eyes. Lately his mother's efforts to see him married off to a nice girl had crossed the line of mere nagging and become downright frustrating. "Mother, I am not coming to dinner tonight to let you parade another girl in front of me."

An outraged puff sounded in his ear. "Are you taking a tone with me, young man?"

He took pains to reply calmly. "I'm in the middle of an important case. I don't have time for this right now."

"But will you come tonight? I promised Kelly Jean you'd be here."

"Then you'll have to call her back and unpromise her."

"I can't do that!" A hint of desperation crept into his mother's voice. "The poor girl will be so disappointed. She's already made plans to be here."

"I hope you have a nice time with her," Dennis said, leaving no room for argument. "I'll be working late."

"Honestly, who would have thought that such a sweet, compliant little boy would become such an irritating man?" She humphed. "An irritating *unmarried* man."

Dennis raised his eyes to the ceiling. "Goodbye, Mom. Tell Dad I said hello."

He closed the cover and clipped the phone onto his belt. When he turned, he found Detective Conner watching him, arms folded across his chest.

"Whenever you're ready to get to work," the surly detective said, "we have something a little more important than your love life to attend to. Like a murder to solve."

Jackie parked her car in front of a single-story brick house that had been converted into an office building. A sign on the door read Hockensmith Transcription Services. Sure that her recorder was turned on and the microphone clipped unobtrusively to her purse, she pushed her way through the front door. The jangle of bells announced her presence. She stopped just inside, faced with a maze of chest-high cubicle walls.

A head appeared over the top of the nearest one, and a young woman peered at her from behind dark-rimmed glasses. "Can I help you?"

"Uh, yeah, I'm looking for Sharon Carlson."

Another head popped up a few cubicles beyond the first, this one blond, wearing a headset. "I'm Sharon."

"Hi. I'm Jackie Hoffner, from church. Uh, Samantha's church."

Sharon looked at her, waiting for her to go on. Jackie shifted her weight to the other foot. Now that she was here, she wasn't sure how to begin. But she certainly couldn't shout her questions across the room. "I wanted to ask you about something. Do you have a minute?"

Sharon exchanged a look with the brunette, then shrugged. "Sure, I can take a break."

She removed the headset and stepped out from behind the partition, and gestured for Jackie to follow. "Come back here where we can talk privately."

Following her past a row of cubicles, Jackie ignored the inquisitive looks the occupants cast her way. They rounded the last wall and stepped into a small break room where Sharon took a bottle of water from an ancient refrigerator and held it toward her.

"Or there's coffee, if you'd rather."

"This is great, thanks."

Jackie took the proffered bottle and sat in one of three chairs at a round table that dominated the room. She set her purse on the table, off to one side. Hopefully Sharon wouldn't look closely enough to notice the microphone.

Sharon joined her and twisted the top off her own bottle, watching Jackie in silence with piercing blue eyes. She looked amazingly like her daughter. Blond hair swung in wispy locks around an oval face that was completely free from any sign of age. If she wore makeup, Jackie couldn't detect it, but her skin shone with health. Her lithe frame belied the fact that she had ever given birth to a child.

"Thanks for taking the time to talk to me," Jackie said, stalling. Sitting across the table from Sharon's expectant expression, her confidence from yesterday's visits flagged. How did one casually bring up the subject of murder? This had been a lot easier with eager old Mrs. Sawyer.

"I've got to admit, I'm curious. No one from the church has ever come to my office before. Is Samantha in some sort of trouble?"

"Oh, no." As Jackie shook her head, an idea for an

opening sprang to mind. "In fact, I wanted to make sure she's okay. I'm sure you've heard about the death of Mrs. Alice Farmer."

Sharon's expression did not change. "My father-in-law told us last week."

"It has been really upsetting to a lot of us at church," Jackie continued. "And for a young, impressionable teenager like Samantha, it must be frightening."

"Not really." Sharon shrugged. "I'm sure she knew the old woman, but they weren't especially close."

"You've never heard Samantha mention Mrs. Farmer at all?"

Sharon cocked her head. "Why would you ask that? Do you think Samantha is somehow involved in her death?"

"No, of course not."

"Then why are you here?" Her eyes narrowed. "And don't give me any garbage about being concerned for Samantha, because she's never mentioned your name, either."

Swallowing a mouthful of water to relieve a throat gone suddenly dry, Jackie's mind played tag with itself. Maybe she should have written out her questions before she arrived. Too late now.

"I know what this is about." Sharon sat back in her chair and folded her arms across her chest. "You aren't here to check up on Samantha. You're here to check up on me."

Busted!

Jackie forced herself to remain calm as she screwed the lid back on her water bottle. "Actually, I did come across some information that might indicate you and your husband didn't exactly get along with Mrs. Farmer."

Slamming a fist on the table, Sharon groaned. "Those gossiping old biddies at that church just can't let anything go, can they? It was fifteen years ago! And they'd still like to paint a scarlet A on my forehead." She leaned forward suddenly, looking directly into Jackie's eyes. "And your Mrs. Farmer was the worst. That old bat had the nerve to call my house when she found out Nick was up for promotion and tell me she didn't think he was *suited* for a job supervising people."

Jackie drew a breath. "Why would she do that? Why would she think her opinion mattered to you?"

"Because she worked a million years at the Schilling Paper factory, and she still has friends there. She wanted to let Nick know if he moved forward with applying for that supervisor job, she intended to make sure her friends knew why he shouldn't have it."

"That's ridiculous," Jackie said. "Lots of people have children and never even bother to get married. Surely that wouldn't make any difference."

Sharon shook her head, her lips twisted. "You have no idea. This is a small town, and Schilling Paper is a family-owned business. The owners are *Christians*—" she spat the word "—and nobody holds a grudge like a Christian."

Jackie's back stiffened. "Hey, I'm a Christian. I don't hold grudges."

Blue eyes stared at her for a moment. When Sharon spoke, her voice dripped accusation. "You're here, aren't you?"

A flash of shame heated Jackie's face. Though she wasn't here to accuse Sharon of getting pregnant before she married, she *was* here because of an old woman's gossip. Not a very good reflection on the character of a Christian.

She met Sharon's gaze. "Not because I hold any sort of grudge or even make any judgment about you. I'm just following up on a lead, trying to get to the bottom of a murder. If your husband had a reason—"

Sharon placed both palms on the table and stood. She leaned across the surface until her face was inches from Jackie's.

"Leave my husband out of this. Leave my daughter out of this. And leave me out of it, too. That nasty old spider never did anything but spread her poison and cause us heartache. If you keep at it, you'll end up just like her."

She left without another word. Stunned, Jackie sat in the silent room. Had she just been threatened? Reaching into her purse, she pulled out the recorder and saw that it was still running. Good. If she turned up dead, at least the police would have a record of the threat.

Her hand shook as she slipped the device back into her purse. Rarely had she been on the receiving end of such anger. Was that the reaction of a murderer trying to cover her tracks? It might be. But something about the fierce fury on Sharon's face made Jackie wonder. The emotion might also have been that of a wrongly accused woman who had been hurt by malicious actions too often in the past.

She had botched this interview, for sure. Maybe she owed Sharon an apology. But how did one apologize to a furious potential murderer?

She rose from the table and wound her way through the building toward Sharon's desk.

But with guilty relief, she discovered she wouldn't have to figure it out today. Sharon's cubicle was empty.

"And whatever you do," Margaret told her, "don't accuse anyone of anything."

Jackie kept her attention on the road through the windshield of Margaret's Buick. The last thing she needed this morning was a lecture from the pastor's wife.

"And I don't just mean not to accuse anyone of murder," Margaret went on, "but *anything*. Don't accuse anyone of disliking Alice or of having a reason to resent her or anything. This is supposed to be a fun lunch, not a cross-examination."

"Yes, Mother." Jackie didn't bother keeping the sarcasm from her voice. Out of the corner of her eye she saw Margaret's head jerk her way.

Actually, if Jackie's mother had survived the car accident, she would be about Margaret's age. Aunt Betty had been a wonderful parent, but she was really a great-aunt, and much older than Jackie's real mother. What would it have been like, having someone like Margaret around during her teenage years?

Her mind turned to the teenager most often in her thoughts today: Samantha Carlson. Was she close to her mother? When Samantha was younger, had Sharon gone to her piano recitals and school plays? Had she taught her how to turn cartwheels in the grass, and do duck-unders on the swing at the park? A sick, guilty heat churned in the pit of Jackie's stomach as she pictured Sharon's face across the break-room table. The way she'd sneered at the word *Christian* revealed a deep disgust, maybe even hatred, toward anyone associated with the church. No wonder she never attended with her daughter. And Jackie certainly hadn't done anything to change her opinion.

She turned toward Margaret. "Do you think Mrs. Farmer was a Christian?"

Margaret shot her a startled look. "What a question! Why do you ask?"

"Sharon Carlson."

"I wondered how that went."

"Terrible. She really doesn't like Mrs. Farmer, and she apparently thinks all Christians are out to get anyone who makes a mistake." She looked down at her lap. "Me included."

"Ah. That couldn't have been a comfortable conversation, then."

"It wasn't." Jackie looked up again. "But what gets me is the look in her eyes when she realized why I came to see her. She was angry, yes, but I think she was also…" She fell silent.

"Hurt?" Margaret's voice was a soft breeze.

Jackie nodded. "And she blamed me, just because I'm a Christian. Guilt by association, or something. When she talked about Mrs. Farmer and others at the church, I felt… ashamed. I didn't want to be associated with Christians if that's how they acted."

She looked away, embarrassed by her admission. They rode in silence for a moment.

"Christians aren't perfect, Jackie," Margaret said finally. "We all give in to the temptation to sin every now and then. Unfortunately, some sins hurt other people."

She executed a turn from County Road 68 onto the long driveway leading to Shaker Village. Jackie stared out the window at acres of green pastures framed by black plank fences. Horses grazed or stood serenely in pairs, soaking up the spring sunshine. Outside the car, peace reigned in those verdant fields. Inside the car, Jackie's thoughts disturbed any pleasure she might have gotten from the charming scenery as Margaret steered the car down the narrow driveway and rolled to a stop in the shady parking lot.

Margaret turned in her seat. "When Christians sin, we can so injure another person that it keeps them from accepting the Lord. How that must grieve Him! We're supposed to be His representatives, and instead we turn others away by our actions."

Jackie felt pierced by Margaret's regard.

"Gossip and spite are sins, Jackie, and Christians aren't immune to them. Sharon Carlson is a victim. We need to pray for her and do everything in our power to show her what Christian love is all about."

The memory of Sharon's anger and pain were branded in Jackie's mind. Margaret was right. Anyone who had been hurt like that needed prayer.

"But what if she and Nick killed Mrs. Farmer?"

Margaret shrugged. "They need Christ just like everyone else. The sooner the better, preferably before they go to prison."

Jackie gave a slow nod. She should pray for Sharon Carlson…and maybe ask for a little forgiveness herself.

Her spirits lighter, she turned a smile on Margaret. "I'm starved. Let's go eat."

EIGHT

Jackie stepped inside the restaurant, an old Shaker building dating back to the mid 1800s now in use as a bed-and-breakfast. They informed the hostess of the number in their party, and then spent a few minutes admiring the furnishings. On each side of the entry hall, identical spiral staircases rose to the upper levels, their hand-carved wood railings gleaming with years of polish. A small room to the left of the front door held antique furniture and a display of Shaker items.

"Here they come," Margaret announced, gazing through a side window.

Jackie performed a quick check of her recorder. She pressed the record button and clipped the microphone to the shoulder strap. Her conversations with Mrs. Sawyer and Sharon sounded perfect, but the mic's range had been unobstructed. She couldn't very well set her purse on the table at lunch, and she worried that their voices wouldn't pick up well if she shoved it under the table.

The ladies arrived at the entrance in a group, Margaret and Jackie standing inside to welcome them. The first through the door, Laura Watson greeted Margaret with a hug and then caught sight of Jackie and smiled broadly. "Jackie, what a nice surprise."

Laura was the ultimate Southern lady, in Jackie's opinion. Her soft voice, pitched pleasantly low, held just a touch of attractive Southern drawl with none of the harsh hillbilly twang. She wore her dark hair in a short, respectable style that complemented her oval face, and her makeup always looked professionally applied. Her nails were perfectly manicured, as usual, and her purse matched her shoes. Standing beside Laura, Jackie felt like a poorly dressed waif in her khakis and comfortable loafers.

"Jackie has the week off work," Margaret explained to them all, "so I invited her to join us."

Behind Laura, Julie McCoy gave a quick "Hello, Jackie," on her way to admire a sturdy Shaker chair against one wall, leaving a scented trail of lilac in her wake. Jackie had become acquainted with her since they both attended the women's Sunday school class and liked her quiet personality. She was a bit older, though, and married, with two teenagers.

"You picked a great day to come along, Jackie," announced Sylvia Graham. Towering a full head over Jackie, she wore a straight red dress that complemented her slender figure and deep tan. "I haven't been to Shaker Village in years. I'd forgotten how beautiful the drive is."

"We're so glad to have you come along!" exclaimed Esther, pressing forward to take Jackie's hand in her warm one.

Jackie's smile froze as she faced her number-one murder suspect. Esther Hodges wore her habitual open expression and toothy smile. The air around the woman seemed vibrant, constantly churned by hands that never ceased their expressive movements. In her midfifties, her broad face and ruddy complexion were perfectly crowned with a mop of unruly dark hair. She spoke in a loud voice that seemed harsh after Laura's soft, cultured drawl.

"Sorry we're late, and it's all my fault. Locked my keys in the car, so Julie had to come get me."

"Oh, no," said Margaret. "Not again."

"Yep. Third time this month." Esther shook her head in disgust. "And that hide-a-key thing Jim put under the back bumper musta fell off, because I couldn't find it. And he's out of town again and has my spare on his key ring."

"What will you do?" asked Sylvia.

"Oh, not to worry. I'll call Triple A when I get home. They're getting so they know my voice."

"You need to get another spare made immediately," said Laura. "This time, put it someplace where it won't fall off."

"I keep a spare key inside the gasoline door," Jackie volunteered. "The little box fits right in there, and it can't fall off with the door closed."

"Hey, that's a good idea." Esther turned a grateful smile on her. "Never thought of that."

Margaret awarded Jackie a proud smile. Honestly! Did she think Jackie couldn't be civil? Was she worried Jackie would pounce on Esther and shriek *Murderer!* the moment she came through the door?

"Our table's ready," announced Julie from across the room.

A hostess wearing a plain gray dress covered with a white starched apron and shawl led them to a wooden table surrounded by six chairs. Sunlight streamed through wide floor-to-ceiling windows lining one side of the room. They looked out onto an old Shaker building converted to a gift shop and, beyond a plank fence, a big vegetable garden. Jackie selected a place next to the wall and hung her purse over the chair back, the microphone pointed as unobtrusively as she could manage toward the rest of the ladies. Across the table, Margaret caught sight of the purse and sighed. Jackie pretended not to notice.

When everyone had taken a seat, the hostess gave each of them a one-page menu announcing the day's lunch selections of breaded catfish or porcupines, along with a variety of vegetables and relishes.

Jackie stared at the menu. There had to be some mistake. "They don't serve real porcupines, do they?"

Esther laughed. "No. I guess they're a Shaker thing, because I've never seen them anywhere but here. There're made with ground beef." She slapped her menu onto the table. "That's what I'm having."

"Sounds great," agreed Margaret. "And real sweet tea to drink. I'm splurging today."

They placed their orders, and, after the server had disappeared in the direction of the kitchen, exchanged smiles.

"What a great place," Julie said, examining the make of the sturdy wooden table. "I've never been here before. Is the furniture all original?"

"I don't think so," Sylvia answered. "But they've taken pains to make sure they kept everything looking as authentic as possible."

Directly across from Jackie, Esther leaned forward to speak. "After lunch we can take a stroll around the grounds. Everything's so green and beautiful this time of year."

"I'd like that," Julie said. "I think I'm going to bring the girls here one day this summer. They'll love it."

The server arrived with their drinks and placed a big bowl of coleslaw and a basket of cornbread in the center of the table. When she walked away, they bowed their heads. Feeling slightly embarrassed, Jackie did, too. She wasn't accustomed to saying a blessing in restaurants.

"Gracious Father," Margaret prayed quietly, "thank You for this wonderful group of women. I'm so grateful for their friendship. And thank You for this beautiful day and the food we're about to eat. Bless those who work to prepare and serve it for us. In Jesus' Name, Amen."

"Amen," echoed four voices softly.

Jackie opened her eyes. That hadn't been too bad. No one was staring at them or anything.

At the opposite end of the table, Laura raised her napkin and discreetly removed something from her mouth. She slipped the folded napkin into her purse, then noticed Jackie's stare.

"Braces," she explained with a shy smile.

"You're kidding!" Jackie shook her head. "I didn't notice you were wearing braces."

"Good. They're supposed to be invisible." Laura sipped from her tea glass.

"My dentist mentioned them," said Sylvia. "Are they working?"

Laura nodded. "I've only had them three months, and I can tell a difference already. I like them because I can take them out when I want to, like a retainer. The worst part is going to the dentist every month."

"But Laura," said Margaret, "your teeth aren't crooked. Why do you need braces?"

"They are a little uneven." She gave a modest shrug. "I've always been sensitive about them. Richard and I are planning a big anniversary trip next spring, an Australian cruise, and I don't want to feel self-conscious smiling for photos."

"Wow, an Australian cruise." Jackie leaned forward. "I've always wanted to go on a cruise, but I couldn't afford it."

Laura laughed. "Actually, cruises are an economical way to vacation. We've gone on several. But this one is a bit pricey, and the airfare to Sydney is outrageous."

"My daughter-in-law had those invisible braces," commented Esther around a mouth full of coleslaw. "They worked for her. Teeth straight as anything now."

Daughter-in-law? Would that be the wife of Joshua, the one Mrs. Sawyer had told her about? Jackie racked her brain, trying to think of a question that would get Esther talking about her son.

Margaret beat her to it. "How are Joshua and Emily doing up in…is it Cleveland?"

"That's right." Esther beamed, pride suffusing her humble features. "He's the associate pastor of a big church there, and Emily teaches third grade. I expect they'll make me a grandmother one of these days."

"An associate pastor?" Jackie ignored Margaret, who was trying to catch her eye. "That's great. Has he always wanted to go into the ministry?"

She raised her eyebrows at Margaret. *See? I can be discreet.* Margaret settled back in her chair with a relieved smile as Esther answered.

"Law, no! That boy was a pistol growing up. Into trouble all the time. I stayed on my knees, and every chance I got I told him the Lord had a hold on his life and he couldn't run forever." She smirked. "I was right."

"So, he must have had some pretty tough odds to overcome, to go into the ministry with a past like that."

Two spots of red appeared on the woman's ruddy

cheeks. "He surely did. But he was lucky to find a church that understood what it means to be saved and have your past mistakes forgiven." She looked down at her bowl, speared a forkful of slaw with a vicious stab, and added softly, "The second time."

"So," Margaret said in a voice louder than necessary, "Julie, how are the girls? Has Amber decided on a college yet?"

"She's still waffling between EKU and the University of Kentucky."

As Julie expounded on her daughter's college decision, Jackie spread butter on her corn bread. How frustrating! She hadn't asked any embarrassing questions or accused Esther of anything. Why did Margaret have to change the subject so abruptly? But Esther's anger when she mentioned her son's first church assignment had been patently obvious. Now, how to turn the discussion to Mrs. Farmer and see what kind of reaction she got?

Their food arrived, momentarily sidetracking the conversation as the women exclaimed over their lunches. Jackie's porcupines—rounded mounds of hamburger and rice covered in tomato sauce—tasted almost exactly like Aunt Betty's meat loaf. She should have ordered the catfish.

"So," she said as the women chewed, "that's awful news about Mrs. Farmer, isn't it?"

Laura put her fork down on her plate. "Must we talk about that terrible business?"

"And over food, too," put in Julie.

Esther gave a loud snort. "At least it's not potluck food."

Jackie's lips tightened, which Esther must have seen. She reached across the table toward Jackie. "Oh, I'm sorry, honey. I didn't mean anything personal. Everyone knows it wasn't your fault someone picked your casserole to plant the poison in."

"Of course it wasn't," agreed Margaret, and all the heads around the table nodded.

Mollified, Jackie dipped her forehead in acknowledgment. "I still can't imagine who would want to hurt a nice old lady like Mrs. Farmer."

An uncomfortable silence descended upon the table. No one met her eyes. Laura picked up her fork again and became absorbed in her catfish. Sylvia grabbed for her glass and gulped tea. Beside her, Julie bit into a dainty glazed carrot, her eyes fixed on the far wall.

Esther's lips pursed. "Well, she wasn't a nice old lady by any standard I ever heard. I can think of several reasons someone might want to get rid of her."

"Esther," whispered Margaret, her voice heavy with warning.

"It's true," Esther insisted. "Everybody here knows that. I'm just stating a fact."

Sylvia leaned forward to speak around Julie. "She's right, you know. Alice wouldn't have won any popularity contests Since Margaret and Jackie are new, they haven't had the opportunity to be on the receiving end of her tongue. Let me tell you, it wasn't a pleasant experience."

"Her tongue," added Esther, "or her poison pen."

Margaret closed her eyes, and Jackie wondered if she was praying. And if so, what for? For the truth to come out? Or for her friends to shut up?

"What do you mean?" Jackie asked.

"Alice was famous for writing letters, letting people know what she thought. She wrote a letter once to our former pastor, telling him his wife's skirts were too short and that she was purposefully tempting the men in the congregation to have sinful thoughts."

"I remember that," said Laura. "It really hurt Marcia's feelings."

Esther bit her lip, her face flushed with anger. "And she wrote a letter to my Joshua's first church, telling them he was a troublemaker and shouldn't be around young people. That one got him fired."

"That's terrible," exclaimed Julie. "What a cruel thing to do."

Esther nodded. "So you see what I mean. That woman was just nasty, that's what she was."

"Even so," said Margaret, "she was a child of God and didn't deserve to be murdered."

"Of course not," agreed Sylvia.

Esther toyed with her food, pushing it around on her plate without taking a bite. "Yeah. Of course not."

"I wonder if we'll all be questioned by the police," said Julie. Her gaze slid to Jackie. "I dished up those leftovers."

"Oh, surely not," said Laura, looking disturbed at the idea.

"What if we are?" Sylvia shrugged. "We just tell them where we were from Sunday afternoon until Tuesday night, when Alice was found. I'm sure none of us paid Alice a visit during that time. No big deal."

"Not if you have an alibi," said Esther. "Jim was out of town on a business trip, as usual. There's nobody's to vouch for me."

Jackie cast a triumphant look at Margaret. Esther Hodges was still bitterly angry with Mrs. Farmer over that letter. Maybe even angry enough to kill her. And she had no alibi.

NINE

After a dessert of Shaker lemon pie and a leisurely stroll around the lush grounds, the group split up. Jackie rode in the silence of Margaret's car, jotting down thoughts from her two interviews of the day. Margaret, staring pensively ahead, refused to be drawn into conversation.

As the car approached town, they passed the turnoff to the city dump.

"Hey, look at that." Jackie pointed toward a police car in the road, a blinker signaling its intention of turning onto Mrs. Farmer's street. As Margaret's car whizzed by, Jackie caught sight of the man in the passenger seat. "Wasn't that Detective Conner?"

"I think so. I wonder if they're going back to Alice's house for something."

Jackie twisted in her seat to watch the police car execute the turn and disappear down the street. "Why don't we follow them and find out?"

"Sorry, I don't have time. I have an appointment this afternoon."

Jackie studied Margaret's suddenly closed expression. Did she really have an appointment, or was that just an excuse to get rid of her?

"You know, Margaret, I know you don't approve of my investigation—" she tried to keep the hurt out of her voice "—or think I'm capable of handling it."

"It's not that." Margaret gave her a quick smile before returning her eyes to the road. "I'm sure you can find things out, maybe even some things the police wouldn't be able to find. I just worry about all the people who might be hurt in the process."

"I know, I know. Gossip is terrible. But I think I handled myself pretty well at lunch."

"You did, but that's just what I'm talking about. I don't believe for a minute that Esther killed Alice. But your questions dredged up some painful memories for her, just like they did for Sharon this morning. Who else will be hurt before this is over?"

Jackie resolutely ignored the memory of Sharon's furious expression and the twinge of guilt that accompanied it. She would apologize to Sharon the first chance she got, and from now on she would handle things better. Still, she couldn't ask questions about Mrs. Farmer without dredging up unpleasant feelings. The old woman seemed to have that effect on people. "You know what they say. You have to break a few eggs—"

"—to make an omelet. I know." Margaret smiled wryly. "I hate making omelets. They never turn out like I want them to."

When Margaret's Buick pulled out of the parking lot of Jackie's apartment building, Jackie went straight to her own car. She needed to get some cat food anyway, and since she was going out, she might as well drive by Mrs.

Farmer's house. If the police were looking for new clues, she intended to be there when they found them.

A police car and a white van filled the narrow driveway. Jackie left her car parked on the street and walked across the yard. The front door opened while she was still several feet away.

"Miss Hoffner," said Detective Conner, spearing her with a green gaze. "What brings you here on this fine afternoon?"

Jackie ignored the arrogance in his tone. "I was going to ask you the same."

"We're here on official business. And you? Come to do some more housecleaning?"

At that moment, three men came around the side of the house, saving Jackie from trying for an appropriately scathing response. Two wore jeans and button-down shirts, and one of them carried a sophisticated-looking camera. The other held several large plastic zipper bags, the same kind Trooper Walsh had used to cart off the contents of her kitchen. No surprise, the third man was the young state trooper himself.

Eyeing the bags, Jackie tried to make out their contents. One looked like it held a dirty paper plate. Another had a balled-up wad of something she couldn't identify—something translucent. And the third… She gasped. A knife! A small one, like a kitchen knife. They'd found a knife in the backyard! Or maybe in the thick woods behind the yard?

"Got what we need, Detective," one of the men told Conner as they brushed by Jackie. "We'll run these over to Frankfort today. The lab boys should be able to ID the trace material on the knife. The rubber gloves look clean, though."

Rubber gloves!

"I want the photos on my desk in an hour," the detective responded. He gave Jackie one more direct stare, then retreated into the house and closed the door behind him.

As the two plainclothesmen pulled away in the van, Jackie walked toward Trooper Walsh. She gestured with her head toward the closed door.

"Is he always so condescending?"

The young man shrugged a shoulder. "He's the best."

"He'd have to be, to get away with that attitude." Jackie studied him. Maybe without Detective Conner around to commandeer the conversation, she could actually get this guy talking. "So you found a knife, huh?"

His eyes slid toward the house before returning to her. "I don't think the detective would appreciate me talking to you about the case."

Jackie scuffed a toe in the packed dirt. Flirting had never worked out well for her, so she hesitated trying it now. But how could she get him talking?

"He wouldn't have to know," she suggested. "And besides, I already saw the knife. I'm just trying to figure out whether or not the killer intended to use it if the mushrooms didn't work."

No answer except a slight shake of his head.

"Don't tell me there's another victim. You didn't find that knife in a body out back, did you?"

His eyebrows rose. "That's quite an imagination you've got there, Miss Hoffner."

She waved a hand. "Call me Jackie."

"Jackie."

Her name, spoken in his low voice, sent a delicious shiver coursing through her.

Okay, so maybe a *little* flirting wouldn't hurt.

"Tell you what, Trooper—"

"Dennis." His lips twitched into a sideways grin that made her mouth go dry.

"Tell you what, Dennis. If you tell me what you found in the backyard, I'll promise to tell you if I find any hard evidence. Not just rumors, but actual clues."

"You've heard rumors?" He stood straighter. "Anything we should know about?"

"I don't know." Jackie looked pointedly toward the backyard. "Maybe."

"You know I can't talk to you about the case." His grin teased her, almost as if he knew what he was doing to her stomach.

A glance down the driveway, toward the back of the house, showed her the deep wooded area behind Mrs. Farmer's backyard. Thickets of scrub bushes and trees grew freely between the house and the neighbors, providing plenty of cover for someone sneaking into the backyard from those woods. And mushrooms grew in woods, right?

She cocked her head and looked up at him disarmingly. "So that paper plate I saw, was it lying near the knife?"

Watching him carefully, she saw the grin melt a tiny bit.

"Like maybe someone had been using them both," she went on. "Maybe slicing mushrooms, while wearing rubber gloves?"

Aha. Now the grin faded completely and his focus slid toward the house. She was on the right trail.

"You know," she said, trying to hide her growing excitement, "you can lift fingerprints from the inside of the gloves. I saw it on *CSI*."

The crooked grin returned. "We know."

"But this proves that no one at the church could have done it. At least not at the potluck." She thought of Julie

McCoy, who had dished up the leftover portions of the casserole. "The killer chopped the mushrooms in the backyard, or maybe even in the woods, and then slipped into the house to plant them in the leftovers."

No bites on that fishing expedition. Crossing his arms, he pursed his lips and gave her a stern look. "I want to talk about those rumors. If you discover something relevant to the case, you have to tell us. Withholding evidence in a murder case is a crime."

Jackie knew he was right. On the other hand, so far she'd only heard gossip, and she really didn't want to pass on gossip. Especially gossip about Sharon Carlson.

But he *was* the police. Besides, if she cooperated by telling him at least part of what she'd discovered, maybe she could convince him to return the favor. He was certainly a lot more likely to talk to her than Detective Conner.

"Well, it seems Mrs. Farmer has made a few enemies around the church. She apparently liked to write letters pointing out what people were doing wrong. She was well-known for them."

"Any specific letters you've heard about?"

Avoiding his gaze, she answered, "There was one a while back, to the former pastor, complaining about the way his wife dressed. I heard there've been others, too." She stopped. If he didn't ask *which* others, she wasn't going to volunteer the information. "I guess not many people at church liked her."

"What about—"

Behind them, the door was thrown open, and the detective's voice barked, "Walsh!"

They both turned. Jackie swallowed hard, feeling like she had been caught doing something she shouldn't. One glance at Dennis's face told her he felt the same.

"Yes, sir?"

"I need you in here." Conner glared at Jackie. "If you can spare the time, that is."

As he turned to walk toward the house, Dennis lifted his shoulders and gave her a brief smile. "See you later."

Watching him close the door, Jackie hoped so.

At three-fifteen, Margaret pulled onto the street that ran beside the high school. She drove slowly, scanning the teenagers crowding the sidewalk until she caught sight of an arm waving her down.

"Hi, Mrs. Palmer," said Samantha as she slid into the passenger seat. She put a bulging backpack on the floor at her feet. "Thanks for giving me a ride."

"I'm glad to do it." Margaret drove to the end of the street and then turned right. "Is there anyplace you need to go, or do you just want me to take you straight home?"

When Samantha called the parsonage this morning and asked if she could bum a ride home from school, Margaret suspected the teen had more on her mind than just a ride. Looking at the troubled expression on her face now, she was sure of it. The girl avoided eye contact as she absently twirled a blond lock of hair in front of her ear. It had been almost ten years since Margaret's boys lived at home, and she had never been blessed with girls, so she didn't have much experience reading the nonverbals.

"Or do you want to go somewhere and get a Coke?" Margaret asked.

Samantha nodded.

Margaret drove through town, the silence between them growing awkward. She racked her brain, trying to come up with something to say, something to draw the girl out, but nothing came to mind.

Lord, I can tell she needs help. Can You give me a hand, here?

On the other side of town, Margaret turned right onto U.S. 60 and then into the parking lot of the first fast-food restaurant she saw, a Wendy's. She parked the car in the space nearest the road and turned to look at her passenger.

"Maybe I'm out in left field somewhere, but you seem worried. Is there anything I can help with?"

Sometimes people just needed an opening. That was certainly true of Samantha, because her eyes filled and her chin started to quiver.

"I have this friend," she said as a tear slipped down first one smooth cheek and then the other.

A friend? Was this going to be one of those "friend with a problem" stories?

"Go on."

Samantha's breath shuddered as she inhaled. "My friend has a drinking problem. I'm pretty sure of it, but she says she doesn't."

Margaret struggled to keep her expression impassive. Not pregnant, which was a big relief, but an alcohol problem? Sweet little Samantha? Her grandfather would be devastated.

"What makes you think your…friend…has a problem?"

Samantha glanced sharply at her. "It really is my friend. Her name is Liz. I don't even drink." She paused, then looked away and added softly, "Anymore."

Margaret didn't detect any sign of dishonesty. She dropped her hands to her lap. "Anymore? So does that mean you have in the past?"

Samantha nodded.

"I see. And maybe you've even been drinking with Liz?"

Samantha closed her eyes and nodded again.

"Do you want to tell me how it started?"

The girl sat for a long moment before speaking. "We used to sneak out of the house on Friday nights. I have to sneak," she said with a quick glance, "'cause I'm never allowed to do anything."

A trace of teenage disgust colored her tone, reminiscent of Margaret's own sons' frustration over household rules stricter than their friends'. Margaret hid a smile and nodded for her to continue.

"At first it was no big deal. It was just fun. We'd walk up to the McDonald's where some of the kids hang out, and everyone would sit around on the hoods of their cars and talk. Sometimes we'd get to go cruising down Main Street with someone who had room in their car.

"That's when we first tried drinking. This guy had a bottle of cherry vodka, and we bought Cokes and made cherry Cokes." She paused. "You won't tell my parents, will you?"

Margaret caught her gaze and held it. "You're not drinking anymore, are you?" Samantha shook her head. "Then no, I won't. We'll consider this a counseling session, so what you say stays between us."

"I thought only preachers had counseling sessions."

Margaret grinned. "Preachers' wives have them, too, on occasion."

The girl's shoulders relaxed. "Thanks. Anyway, that first night I drank way too much. After I got home I barfed out my bedroom window all night. The next morning I had to take a hose out there and clean it up before anyone saw."

"Lovely," Margaret said drily. "And you enjoyed yourself so much that you went out the next Friday night and did it again?"

"Something like that. Anyway, once we started drinking, it seemed like everyone we met had alcohol. Beer, whiskey, vodka, wine. Every week it was something different."

"Where do they get it?"

"Oh, it's not hard. There are people who'll get it for you. Anyway, one day I went to school—it was a Monday—and Liz called me over to her locker. She had a bottle of vodka in there."

"And that's when you knew she had a problem."

Samantha nodded. "I told her it was a bad idea, we might get caught. But she didn't care and she said if I didn't want any that just left more for her. That was about a month ago. She drinks every day now, and sneaks out almost every night. And sometimes she gets so trashed she's…getting into other stuff."

"Drugs?"

"No." Samantha gulped. "Sex. She gets so wiped out she tells me the next day that she can't remember who she was with. That's happened more than once."

Tears spilled down her cheeks. Margaret reached into the backseat for a box of tissue and handed her one.

"Have you tried talking to her?"

Samantha nodded. "I even looked up some stuff on alcoholism so I could tell her what could happen to her. That was scary. I went to the library downtown in case my mom and dad checked the Internet history at home and somebody from church came in. I was afraid I might get caught looking up Web sites about alcoholism, but I don't think they saw me."

"What does Liz say when you try to talk to her?"

"She doesn't want to hear it. She tells me she's just

having some fun, and there's nothing wrong with it. She says I've turned into a goody-goody."

Margaret heard the pain in Samantha's voice and watched her blot at a fresh batch of tears.

"It's my fault, Mrs. Palmer. I'm the one who wanted to take the first drink with the cherry vodka. Liz really didn't want to, and I talked her into it. She doesn't go to church, and I do. I know better. And look what I've done!"

The tears fell freely now, and Margaret slid across the seat to put her arms around the sobbing girl. She ached for this poor child who was learning a painful lesson in integrity—one some people never managed to understand.

When the sobs subsided, Margaret handed her a fresh tissue.

"Are you a Christian, Samantha?" Blotting at her eyes, the girl nodded. "Then the first thing you need to do is ask God to forgive you for anything you've done wrong. And then start praying for Liz. I will, too."

"Okay." A huge sniff, and reddened eyes turned Margaret's way. "But what else can I do?"

"Well, I think you need to continue to be honest with Liz and tell her why you're worried about her. And maybe you could invite her to church."

"She'll never come. I can't even get my mom to come to church with me."

Margaret wanted to ask a few questions about that, too, but bit her tongue. Now was not the time.

"Then we'll pray about that, too. I'm sure God will show you what to do."

Jackie turned from Main Street onto U.S. 60, heading toward the grocery store for cat food. The first traffic light turned red as she approached, and her car glided to a halt. She glanced through the passenger window.

Wasn't that Margaret's Buick in the Wendy's parking lot? Yes, it sure was. Margaret herself sat in the car, along with someone else. Who?

The light changed, and Jackie inched forward. A blonde sat in the passenger seat. It looked like… Was it Sharon Carlson? Jackie nearly wrenched her neck staring as she drove slowly past. As she came parallel to the window, Margaret leaned back and the other woman leaned forward, giving Jackie a clear view of her face. No, it wasn't Sharon. That was Samantha Carlson in Margaret's car.

What in the world was Margaret talking so intently about with the daughter of one of Jackie's murder suspects?

Another pair of eyes, peering through the window of a bigger car, glimpsed the blonde in the passenger seat of the tan Buick.

This development was most disturbing. Something had to be done about it.

Quickly.

TEN

Linus leaped onto the dinette table, directly in the center of Jackie's notebook.

"Get out of the way, you goof." She picked up the cat and stroked his soft fur a couple of times before returning him to the floor.

Not to be deterred, Linus sauntered around to the other side of the table and leaped again. He sat primly at the far end of the table, his tail curled around his body and his amber eyes fixed on Jackie.

"As long as you stay over there, you're okay."

Jackie picked up her pen and punched play on the recorder. She was thrilled with the quality of the recording from lunch. Esther's voice sounded as clear as if Jackie had held the microphone right under her nose.

"Well, she wasn't a nice old lady by any standard I ever heard. I can think of several reasons someone might want to get rid of her."

"Esther." That was Margaret.

"It's true. Everybody here knows that. I'm just stating a fact."

Jackie pushed Stop and scribbled in her notebook below a heading in neat block letters that read ESTHER

HODGES. She pressed Play again, listened all the way to the end, and double-checked her notes to make sure she had all her thoughts written down. Then she turned off the recorder and looked at the page.

"I don't know, Linus. I mean, she's certainly still angry over the letter that got her son fired. But the guy's okay now. He has a good job and a nice wife with straight teeth. Mrs. Farmer wasn't a threat to him anymore."

She tapped the pen against her lips.

"So that means her motive is revenge, plain and simple. But she just doesn't seem like the vengeful sort. Especially when she's looking forward to having a grandchild someday soon. Why would she jeopardize that?"

Immobile, Linus watched the tapping pen with rapt fascination.

Jackie flipped the page and stared at the notes beneath the heading SHARON CARLSON. Sharon had a motive— trying to protect her husband's chance for a promotion at the paper factory. There was no doubt she disliked Mrs. Farmer, but enough to kill her?

"If only we could get a look in her kitchen and see if she has a set of knives matching the paring knife the police found."

Jackie flipped to another page, this one labeled CLUES. She had spent the afternoon surfing the Internet to research poisonous mushrooms. Her computer, a clunky thing about a million years old with a dial-up modem, was more frustrating than helpful. She hated it. The old thing ran so slowly it almost wasn't worth using, and the connection dropped frequently without warning. But she suffered through several hours of surfing to make sure she had her facts straight before she wrote anything on her list of clues.

She read the short list to Linus.

"*Poisonous mushrooms in the woods behind Mrs. Farmer's house.* That's the only possible explanation for the plate and knife the police found back there. But the mushroom site on the Internet said that's nothing unusual—they grow just about everywhere this time of year."

"*Mushrooms planted in leftovers.* Well, yeah. But since that kind of poisonous mushroom usually only makes you sick, the killer would have to know that Mrs. Farmer had heart problems." She shrugged. "That's just about everybody at church, and probably everybody who knew her outside of church, too.

"*Knife.* The one I saw was small, like a paring knife. We don't know for sure if that's what the killer used, but it's likely. Unfortunately you can get a paring knife anywhere, even the dollar store. So unless they can find fingerprints, it probably won't help much. I don't think they'll find anything on the knife, because of these."

She drummed the tip of the pen on the next item on her list.

"*Rubber gloves.* Not the yellow kitchen glove variety, but the thin, translucent doctor's-office kind. Those could be the break we need, if the police can get fingerprints off the insides. Of course, you can probably buy rubber gloves in a drugstore, but I'm guessing a killer wouldn't want to have a box of gloves with only two missing laying around his house for the police to find. It would be a lot safer to pick up a couple from someone else's box. So we need to know who has access to rubber examination gloves. Doctors, of course, along with anyone who works for them. And who do we know who works for doctors?"

Linus remained silent, his eyes following the pen in Jackie's hand.

"I'll tell you who. Sharon Carlson." Jackie flipped the page in her notebook. "See, I wrote right here after talking to Samantha on the phone the other night that Sharon would be at work *as long as she wasn't out doing deliveries.* A medical transcriber delivers the documents she types to the doctor's offices. So that means Sharon has access to the rubber gloves there."

Jackie pictured her own doctor's office. On the counter in each examination room, next to containers of cotton swabs and alcohol rubs, sat an open box of examination gloves. It would be so easy to take a few and stash them in a purse or shove them in a pocket. No one would ever know.

Then she remembered. She had seen a box of examination gloves recently, and not in a doctor's office. Where? She closed her eyes and scrunched her nose, trying to picture the open box of gloves. It had been in a wire rack hanging on the wall at…

"The nursing home!"

Linus started at Jackie's shout.

"There were rubber gloves on the wall right inside the door in both the rooms we visited at the nursing home yesterday, Linus. Anybody can walk into a nursing home on the pretext of visiting someone there."

Her mind hovered around a thought, but she refused to go there. Instead she got up abruptly from the table and went into the kitchen. Snatching the telephone from the wall, she paused a moment before dialing. Then her fingers flew over the numbers.

"Hello?"

"Hi, Margaret. It's Jackie."

"I was just talking about you. Sylvia called to tell me what a good time she had at lunch today, and how glad she was that you were able to join us."

"Yeah, I had a good time, too. Thanks for inviting me." She clutched the receiver. "Uh, Margaret, I happened to drive past you and Samantha Carlson this afternoon at Wendy's."

A pause. "Oh, that was nothing. She needed a ride home from school, and we decided to stop for a Coke."

"You seemed to be talking pretty intently. And since I just talked to Sharon earlier in the day, I couldn't help but wonder what you guys were talking about."

A longer pause. "I really can't say, Jackie."

"Why not? It might be important."

"I can tell you it didn't have anything to do with Alice or Sharon. Trust me, it's something completely unrelated and private."

Jackie heard the resolve in Margaret's voice. She wouldn't budge. Getting anything out of her tonight seemed unlikely.

"Well, okay. If you say so. You might be interested to know that Esther is no longer my number-one suspect."

"She's not?" Margaret sounded relieved.

"No, Sharon is."

A pause. "You know, Jackie, you really should be careful."

Goose bumps rose across the back of Jackie's neck. "Why do you say that?"

"Earl said something the other day that has me worried. If someone in our church really did kill Alice, they won't be too happy when they hear you're running around asking all these questions. It could be dangerous."

Of course Margaret wouldn't threaten her; she was too

nice for that sort of thing. And how sweet that she and Pastor Palmer actually worried about Jackie's safety.

"Don't worry about me, Margaret. I'll be careful. I promise."

"Well…okay. Will I see you tomorrow?"

"Sure. Maybe I could come over in the morning and we could pick a few more people to visit."

"I'll have coffee ready at nine."

"Sounds good. Bye, Margaret."

Jackie replaced the receiver and rubbed her neck. Why did Margaret sound so evasive about her conversation with Samantha? What secret could a teenager possibly have that would make her confide in the pastor's wife?

Well, teenagers kept lots of secrets. And of course Margaret would have to keep whatever she said in confidence. But maybe Samantha had seen something that connected her mother with the murder. Whatever the secret, Jackie was sure it was important, and Margaret hiding the information was getting in the way of her investigation.

Mrs. Murphy's words at church on Sunday morning came back to her. Mrs. Farmer had been the single dissenting vote against Pastor Palmer, and had even talked about getting up a petition against him. Margaret might have heard about that.

And she had access to rubber gloves at the nursing home.

"No," she said, her voice harsh in the empty kitchen. "I don't believe it."

But enough doubt niggled her mind that she walked back to the table with a slow step. If she wanted to be thorough in this investigation, she needed to identify *all* the suspects, even the ones she didn't believe for a minute were guilty. She would have to make a new page with the name MARGARET PALMER at the top.

"Hey, where's my pen?"

From beneath the table, Linus looked up with innocent, round eyes. When Jackie confiscated his new toy, he gave her a wounded look and slunk toward the bedroom.

The evening's first lightning bugs hovered a foot above the freshly mowed grass when Dennis turned from Walnut Avenue into his driveway. No light shone in the windows of the main house. He glanced at his watch. Eight forty-two. Twelve minutes past Mr. Montgomery's bedtime. Dennis missed the old guy standing at the front window, watching as he parked his cruiser beside the house. The presence of a police car in his driveway gave Mr. Montgomery a sense of security, especially since all his family lived up in Ohio. And he gave Dennis a discount on his rent because of it.

Dennis let himself into the garage apartment and flipped on the light. The three small rooms were plenty for him. Five long steps took him across the combination living room/kitchen and into the bedroom, where he unhooked his belt and laid it on the chair beside his bed. He unsnapped the holster strap, readying his pistol for a quick retrieval, grinning as always at the useless habit. Nothing ever happened in sleepy little Versailles.

Except something had happened. Someone had murdered an old woman.

His thoughts turned to the afternoon's discovery as he rummaged in the refrigerator for something to eat. The knife and gloves were the first real clues they'd found, though Conner wasn't confident they'd lead to the identity of the killer. They couldn't very well search every kitchen in town, looking for a telltale set of knives with one missing. And fingerprints only identified a perpetrator if they already had a record. If not, they were almost as useless as putting a saddle on a cat. You weren't going anywhere anyway, so why bother?

A dried-out slice of leftover pizza went into the garbage can, and that pretty much cleared out the fridge. He pulled a couple of pieces of bread from the plastic wrapper and inspected them. Was that a spot of mold? Nah, couldn't be. This loaf was only a week old. Or was it two?

Now Jackie showing up had been an interesting development. As he spread peanut butter on the bread, he smiled at the memory of her excitement when she caught sight of the knife. She was really into this investigation.

NBT—Nothing But Trouble, Conner said. Was she, really? Some women could weasel information out of another woman that it would take a guy years to find out. His mother was like that. How many times had he seen her stop to talk to a perfect stranger in a grocery-store aisle, and know the woman's life story by the time they said goodbye?

The problem was Jackie didn't really seem the sort women talked to. She was so…pushy. Not like Mom at all. In fact, Jackie might be one of those police groupies Mom had warned him about. And they really did exist. The minute Dennis put on the uniform, they seemed to come out of nowhere, smiling and batting their eyelashes and letting him know they wouldn't mind if he stopped by after work.

Nah, Jackie didn't seem that type, either. Though she had batted her eyelashes once or twice this afternoon. She was cute when she did it, too. But mostly he figured what she wanted was information.

He dropped onto the couch, bit into his sandwich. Lousy luck she showed up on the scene today in time to see their evidence recovery. And it was patently obvious she had ignored Conner's demand that she stay out of the case, too. At least she'd seemed willing to tell him what she discovered. Like those rumors and the victim's letter-writing habit. A shame Conner had interrupted before she'd told him anything of substance.

Maybe he ought to find out if she knew anything helpful. He chewed thoughtfully.

He should probably let it go. Conner was right when he said civilians had no place in a murder investigation. Especially one who was as closely involved as Jackie. Not a murder suspect, but without a doubt she was on the inside of this mess, even if she didn't mean to be.

On the other hand, Jackie had glanced away this afternoon when he asked for specifics about those letters. A trained investigator watched for evasive behavior like that. It didn't necessarily mean Jackie was a criminal, but it did mean she was hiding something.

He wanted to know what that something was. If it turned out to be important, Conner would praise him for sniffing it out.

He tossed the last of the sandwich into his mouth and dug the white pages out of the pile of books on the kitchen counter. There he found a listing for *Hoffner, J* with no address. He smiled. At least she possessed enough sense to keep her first name and address out of the phone book. Single women should never make it easy for a man to find them.

Channel surfing made Jackie tired. Horizontal on the couch, her head propped on the arm and Linus curled into the curve of her tummy, she struggled to keep her eyes open as she searched for something on television to hold her interest. A medical drama she liked came on at nine, and hopefully it wouldn't be a rerun. If she could just manage to stay awake for another ten minutes—

The telephone sounded like an alarm, its shrill tone piercing through the low hum of the TV. She jerked upright, sending Linus off the couch at a run, and shook off the last of the drowsiness as she jogged into the kitchen and grabbed the cordless.

"Hello?"

"Hey, Jackie, this is Dennis Walsh."

Her jaw and fingers slackened at the same time, and the phone almost slipped out of her grip. Dennis Walsh, the world's most gorgeous cop, was calling her? An image of gray eyes and a crooked grin swam to the front of her mind.

"Are you there?"

"Uh, yeah, I'm here. What's up, Dennis?" His name sounded good on her lips.

"Not much. I just got home from work a few minutes ago. Listen, I was wondering if you'd be willing to meet me for coffee some morning."

"Coffee?" She sank against the doorjamb for support. Was Mr. Good-Looking Cop asking her out on a date? No, she couldn't be so lucky. Her dates—and there hadn't been many of them—tended to be more along the lines of pizza-delivery guys. There had to be another explanation.

"Yeah. We sort of got interrupted today, but I'm really interested in hearing more about those rumors you mentioned. How does Thursday look for you?"

Rumors. Jackie stood upright and bit back a disappointed sigh. She was right. Of course this wasn't a date. She didn't have *that* kind of luck with men. He just wanted to get information from her.

"Thursday's good, I guess." Her voice sounded calm, even casual, she noted with pride. "Will your *boss* be there, too?" A touch of acid slipped into her tone.

"No, he's tied up in Frankfort on Thursday mornings. It'll just be the two of us." He paused. "I hope that's okay."

Was that a hint of uncertainty in his voice? Like maybe he hoped she wanted to spend time with him alone? Jackie shook her head. *Stop grasping!* This was about the murder case, and this guy was all business.

"That's fine. Where and when?"

"How 'bout McDonald's around nine. Is that too early?"

"No, that's fine. I'll see you there."

His voice flowed warmly through the phone. "I'm looking forward to it."

She heard the click indicating he had hung up, but for a moment she couldn't move. Had her imagination taken over, or had his voice gotten softer at the end, like he really *was* looking forward to seeing her?

Stop it! This isn't a date!

Moving slowly, she replaced the phone and returned to the couch. Much as she didn't want to admit it, she was really looking forward to seeing him again, too. Date or not.

ELEVEN

Jackie sat at Margaret's round table, her elbows propped on a daisy-covered tablecloth, sipping from a steaming mug of honey-sweetened coffee. Bright shafts of morning sun shone through the kitchen window, setting the yellow curtains aglow. The light glinted through a crystal prism suspended nearby, sending dancing rainbows all over the gleaming white cabinets. This morning, sitting in Margaret's cheery kitchen, her suspicions of last night seemed ludicrous. Margaret was no more a killer than she was.

"My aunt Betty used to sweeten her coffee with honey," she commented, blowing on the surface of the hot liquid before taking a sip. "Mmm. This is a real treat."

Margaret turned from the counter to smile in her direction. "You don't use honey at home?"

"Splenda. Low-carb, low-cal."

"Ha. As if you need to worry about your weight. Here, have one of these."

A plate of banana muffins, fresh from the oven, tantalized Jackie's nose with a sweet, beckoning aroma. She'd had her morning oatmeal already, but…

"Oh, yum." Eyes closed, she chewed with pleasure. "These are awesome."

"I'm glad you like them. They're Earl's favorites." Coffee mug in hand, Margaret took the seat opposite Jackie's. "So what's on your agenda today, Miss Detective?"

"I want to talk to some more old people. You know, someone who might give me another lead. Don't worry," she added when Margaret drew breath to speak, "I'm not going to gossip."

"I'm sure you'll handle yourself diplomatically."

Jackie washed down a mouthful of muffin with coffee. "What made you change your mind? Yesterday you lectured me about spreading gossip."

"I've prayed about it, and I've said my piece. That's all I can do. I still think the police are better equipped to find the murderer." She shrugged an apology. "But if you're determined to question every person in the church, I'll help however I can. You're my friend. And I do want this murderer brought to justice, you know. The sooner the better."

Nodding, Jackie watched Margaret bite into her own muffin. She did consider Margaret a friend. Not the kind to go shopping or to the movies with, but sort of like a mother-type friend.

But still…why the sudden change of attitude? Was Margaret hoping to keep Jackie focused on someone other than herself?

Stop it. I don't believe Margaret is a killer.

An image of the page she'd added to her notebook last night flashed into her mind. Less writing covered that page than the others. To be honest, she could write nearly as much on a page with her own name at the top.

"So." She smiled across the table. "Who should we visit today? I want to talk to someone who knew Mrs. Farmer pretty well."

"Then I suggest we pick someone in the Prime Timer Sunday school class," Margaret replied. "Let me get the church directory."

While Margaret left to look for the directory, Jackie sipped her coffee and wondered if she should mention Dennis's call last night. For some reason, she wanted to talk about it. Maybe if she did, she could get her mind off his voice and onto something else.

When Margaret returned with the directory, Jackie flipped the cover open and scanned the names. "By the way," she said nonchalantly, "you'll never guess who called me last night."

"Who?"

"Trooper Walsh."

"Really?"

The unconcealed glee in Margaret's voice made Jackie look up. "Why do you say it like that?"

"Because just the other day I was thinking the two of you would make a cute couple."

Heat suffused Jackie's face. "Oh, please."

"Seriously," Margaret insisted. "I talked with him for a few minutes at church on Sunday, and he's very intelligent. He's a Christian, too."

Jackie stared at the directory, though the tornado in her brain made it hard to focus on the names.

"You can't deny he's handsome. And those muscles! He must work out."

Handsome? Jackie wouldn't call him handsome, exactly. Much of the night had been spent thinking of how she *would* describe Dennis Walsh. With those high cheekbones and broad shoulders, he was more like…drop-dead gorgeous.

"I suppose he's cute enough." She flipped a page. "But

I don't think he's interested in me. He just wants to get together to talk about the case."

Across the table, Margaret's eyes gleamed as she straightened. "Get together? When? Where?"

"Tomorrow morning at McDonald's."

Margaret deflated. "McDonald's?"

"It's not a date, Margaret. We're just going to have coffee and talk about the case." She looked up and leaned forward to confide, "I think Detective Conner has a meeting or something on Thursday mornings, which is why we're waiting until then. I got the impression Dennis doesn't want him to know we're talking."

"Dennis? You're calling him Dennis?"

Margaret's grin sent a new wave of heat to Jackie's face. Maybe she wasn't ready to talk about Dennis after all. She tapped on the directory and changed the subject.

"Who should we visit today?"

Margaret continued to grin a moment, cocking her head to stare across the table. Jackie breathed a relieved sigh when she apparently decided to let the subject drop and looked down at the pictures in the directory.

"There's Mrs. Anderson, but she volunteers at the hospital during the day. You could try to catch her at church tonight, though."

"Okay." Jackie flipped a few pages. "Mrs. Stafford, then."

Margaret shook her head. "She works."

"Mrs. Whitehouse?"

"Out of town this week, visiting her daughter in Kansas City."

Jackie turned back to the front. "What about Mrs. Coates?"

"She goes to a different Sunday school class. I don't know how well she knew Alice."

"But she's on the prayer chain, so she has connections in the church. Anyway, it's a place to start."

"True." Margaret's pensive expression cleared. "She and her husband are both retired, so they might be at home."

Jackie slapped the directory closed. "Let's give her a call."

"Sad news about Alice." Audrey Coates shook her head. "You expect to hear about things like that on television, but right in our own church?"

"It's terrible," Jackie agreed.

She and Margaret sat on a tan sofa in Audrey's living room. Her home bore evidence of years of happy living, with every surface covered by a cheerful array of knick-knacks. Dust catchers, Aunt Betty used to call them.

Audrey's husband, Ron, had greeted them and then excused himself to the garage to perform an oil change on a neighbor's car.

"It has been quite a shock for everyone," Margaret said.

"And especially you, my dear." Audrey cast a sympathetic glance toward Jackie. "How terrible to have your casserole used as a weapon."

Jackie swallowed a curt reply and smiled. "Which is why I'm doing everything I can to help the police catch the murderer."

"You are? My goodness."

Audrey's expression became eager. Ah, here was a woman who wanted to talk. No need to tiptoe around the issue.

"That's what brings us here this morning." Jackie leaned forward, arms on her legs. "We hoped you might be able to tell us if you've ever heard of anyone having a grudge against Mrs. Farmer."

"Oh, my dear, that could be just about anyone." One

corner of her lips twitched in a humorless grin. "Alice led a sad life, really. Known by a lot of people, but loved by few. She was her own worst enemy."

"Yes," put in Margaret, "we've certainly discovered that, poor woman."

"I suppose you've heard about Joshua Hodges, then?" Both Jackie and Margaret nodded, and Audrey shook her head slowly. "A sad thing, that was. Something like that could have damaged the boy's career for the rest of his life. And it was just spite on Alice's part."

"We heard there have been other spiteful things Mrs. Farmer did." Jackie shot a quick glance at Margaret. "We don't want to gossip, of course."

"Certainly not." Audrey's forehead creased. "But of course that's what Alice did. She gossiped about everyone. Poor Vince Carlson, when his son first married—"

"Yes," Margaret said quickly. "We know about that, as well."

Audrey sat back, smiling. "My, my. You've already heard a lot. And poor Kathy Dorsey, too, I suppose?"

Jackie straightened. A new name! Kathy Dorsey, a young woman not much older than Jackie, was a divorced single mother and a regular attendee at HCC. Beside her, Margaret drew herself up, as well.

Audrey nodded. "I see you haven't. Well, it really is a perfect example. Kathy is a teller at the bank where Alice did business, you know. A few months ago, it seems the poor girl made a mistake in counting change from a customer's deposit. Bad luck must hover over her, because the customer was none other than Alice."

"Oh, dear." Lines creased Margaret's forehead.

"Alice spoke quite sharply to her every time she saw her,

even at church. I heard that myself. Poor Kathy scurried to
get out of her way, you can believe that. Alice didn't mind
telling me why, when I asked why she was so hard on the
girl. Told me she thought Kathy was unfit to hold any job,
much less one at a respectable bank where Alice held stock.
I'm surprised you two didn't hear about that yourselves."

"People don't really pass gossip along to the pastor's
wife too often," Margaret said.

"And nobody ever tells me anything," Jackie put in.
"I'm still the new girl, I guess."

A concerned expression came over Audrey's features.
"Please don't think I'm accusing poor Kathy Dorsey of
killing Alice. I'm sure she's incapable of doing anything
so terrible. A sweeter girl never walked the earth. I'm just
giving you an example of Alice's behavior. I'll bet every
person you ask could come up with a different one. That's
how she was."

"Yes, that's what we're finding out," said Margaret.

Jackie remained silent. Maybe Kathy Dorsey really was
a sweet girl…or maybe her sweetness was a front for something ugly. Either way, Jackie intended to ask her a few
questions about that bank deposit.

TWELVE

The sweet scent of honeysuckle tickled Jackie's nostrils when she pulled into the church parking lot that evening. Big, overgrown bushes covered with pale yellow blossoms lined one side of the field where they'd held their picnic.

Jackie shuddered. She did *not* want to think about that picnic!

The parking lot held no more than a dozen cars. She was among the first to arrive. Wednesday nights didn't typically draw a big crowd, except for the kids' classes. Some parents liked to use Wednesdays at the church as a free babysitting opportunity. Judging by the amount of whooping and laughter that drifted into the sanctuary from the downstairs activities, Jackie didn't think the kids minded.

A red Chevy glided to a stop on the far side of hers. Jackie halted her progress across the parking lot. Providence was on her side tonight. Kathy Dorsey and her twins had arrived.

Kathy turned to speak to her sons in the backseat, her voice carrying clearly through the open window. "Charlie, if you hit your brother at church tonight, there will be consequences."

Through the back window, Jackie glimpsed the four-year-old's pensive expression as he considered his mother's warning. "What consequences?"

"A big one. No television all day tomorrow."

"*All day?* Aw, Mom."

Jamie raised his chin to smirk at his brother as the trunk popped open. Kathy got out of the car and headed toward the rear. Jackie didn't know much about her beyond the obvious fact that she was a single mother of rambunctious twins and one of the reality-show group. She glanced at Jackie as she rounded the back of the car.

"Oh, hi." She lifted her nose and inhaled. "Mmm, doesn't that honeysuckle smell wonderful?"

"It sure does," Jackie responded. "Do you need any help? Looks like you've got a load."

"That would be great. It's my night to bring snacks."

Jackie took a bulging grocery sack in each hand as the boys tumbled out of the car and headed for the church at a gallop.

"Don't run inside the building," Kathy shouted after them, then grinned at Jackie. "I don't know why I bother. The dog listens better than they do."

Jackie had no experience whatsoever with kids or dogs, so she limited her response to a smile. Kathy took a gallon jug of fruit punch in each hand and closed the trunk. The two women followed the boys toward the church at a more leisurely pace.

Though she had a bit of practice under her belt, Jackie still bumbled around with trying to turn the conversation to Mrs. Farmer. As she sifted through a few possible openings, dismissing each one as too obvious, Kathy took the situation out of her hands.

"I didn't get a chance to speak to you on Sunday, but I wanted to tell you how sorry I am about what happened."

She gave an embarrassed shrug. "You know, with your casserole."

"It wasn't my casserole that killed her," Jackie said, too quickly.

"Oh, I know," Kathy rushed to agree. "The boys and I ate some of it. It was really good."

Her ruffled feelings placated, Jackie nodded. "But I have had a terrible time. Especially being interrogated by the police." She peered sideways into Kathy's face. "Have you been questioned yet?"

The girl started and gave her a quick look. Her light brown hair formed a widow's peak in the center of her forehead, giving her round face a heart-shaped look that was more interesting than flattering. Especially with her eyes rounded like that.

"No, of course not. Why would I be?"

"Well, I figured someone would eventually mention that little problem you had with Mrs. Farmer."

Kathy's face went pale. "I don't know what you're talking about."

"Oh." Jackie shrugged. "But I heard about it so it's probably just a matter of time before the police hear it, too. I'm sure they'll want to talk to you."

They arrived at the door, and Kathy stopped. She turned her back to the building and stood staring toward the empty field. Jackie watched, seeing her throat move convulsively as she swallowed. Was that fear on her face?

She spoke without looking at Jackie. "We had a disagreement, that's all. No big deal."

"I heard she went around telling people you shouldn't be allowed to keep your job."

Kathy didn't answer. Jackie's conscience twinged. The

girl really did look frightened. But did she look guilty? Jackie couldn't decipher that stare and convulsive gulping. Whatever the reason, Kathy certainly knew something.

"Hey, look, I'm not accusing you of anything. I'm just saying if I heard that rumor, the police are going to hear it. And you know, I'm working with the police on this case." Jackie paused. Not a lie, exactly. After all, Dennis wanted to hear any information she discovered, didn't he? "So if you have anything to say, you might want to tell me. That way I can report that I've talked with you and it's no big deal."

Another car pulled into the parking lot, and they both looked toward it. Margaret's Buick. Kathy's attention remained fixed on Margaret and Pastor Palmer as they got out and headed toward the church.

"I made a mistake on her transaction. I corrected it before she even walked away from my window, but she harped on it for weeks."

"That's all? She didn't threaten to get you fired?"

Kathy shook her head but continued to watch the approaching couple, her shoulders so tense they shook. Jackie felt a flash of sympathy. The girl looked really scared. But about what? If she was innocent, why wouldn't she tell Jackie what had her so frightened?

"Hey," called Pastor Palmer as he and Margaret reached the concrete walkway, "you two look like you could use a hand."

He ran up the sidewalk to open the door, reaching for one of Jackie's sacks. Margaret looked questioningly toward her, and Jackie shook her head. She'd talk to Margaret later.

And Kathy Dorsey, too. That girl still had some explaining to do.

* * *

"So what are you wearing tomorrow?"

Someone tugged her shirt, and Jackie turned to find Margaret following closely as she exited the sanctuary. Pastor Palmer still stood up by the altar, talking with a group of lag-behinds.

"I don't know." She shrugged. "Probably jeans and a T-shirt."

Margaret's horrified expression spoke volumes.

"It's not a date," Jackie reminded her. "We're meeting to talk about official business."

"There's no reason it can't be both official business *and* a date."

"If the guy wanted to ask me out on a date, surely he'd pick someplace besides McDonald's."

Margaret dismissed that with a wave of her hand. "His intentions don't matter at this point. What matters is that you make the most of the opportunity." She gave Jackie a stern look. "You may not wear jeans. Don't you have a nice spring skirt and blouse?"

A mental review of her closet revealed nothing of the sort. She did have that black skirt she'd bought for the funeral. That looked good on her. But she'd worn it the morning Dennis and Detective Conner came to her apartment.

She shook her head.

"I know!" Margaret's face brightened. "The outfit you wore to the picnic was very flattering. That pink blouse really set off your dark hair. And, Jackie…" Her focus swept upward. "Wear your hair down tomorrow. In front of your ears."

Jackie's hand went self-consciously to the side of her head. "What's the matter with my ears?"

"Not a thing, dear. But your hair is lovely, and it frames your face beautifully."

At that moment, Emilee Howard approached and claimed Margaret's attention to discuss some matter related to Vacation Bible School. Still stinging from the ear comment, Jackie walked to her car.

Inside, she swiveled the rearview mirror so she could examine her reflection. The scrunchie came out, and a toss of her head set her hair free. She did have nice hair, if you were into uncontrollable curls. How many times had Aunt Betty told her that lots of women paid big money to get curls like Jackie's? Turning her head from side to side, she decided wearing it down did make her jaw and chin look softer, a little more feminine.

She smoothed the hair behind her ears with a quick gesture and looked again. That looked…controlled. Neater. But her nose did seem to take up more of her face this way, and her ears did stand out a bit…

Forget Margaret, anyway! There was nothing wrong with her ears. She jerked the thick mane through the scrunchee, scowling at the mirror. She would wear her hair however she liked!

A movement outside drew her attention. The Dorsey twins soared past her front bumper, racing to their car. Kathy followed at a slower pace carrying a grocery sack in one hand. Now might be a good time to continue their interrupted conversation.

But when the young mom looked toward Jackie, her expression froze. She looked quickly away and picked up her pace, as though she hoped Jackie had not seen her, though they both knew she had.

Jackie remained in her car while an uncomfortable

feeling settled in her stomach. It was like high school all over again. Kathy was only a few years older than Jackie. Under different circumstances, they might have been friends. But Jackie had to go and act like a big-time interrogator, so of course Kathy wanted to avoid talking to her.

But the questions were necessary! How else could she get to the bottom of Mrs. Farmer's death? And without a doubt, Kathy knew something she wasn't telling.

Jackie watched the other woman snap the boys' seat belts before getting behind the wheel, all the while keeping her back to Jackie's car. Jackie chewed on a fingernail as the Chevy pulled out of the parking lot.

What did that girl know that made her so afraid? If they'd had a few more minutes before Margaret and Pastor Palmer arrived earlier, Jackie would have gotten it out of her. Another question or two would have done the trick.

She turned the ignition key and the Toyota roared to life. Whatever Kathy knew, Jackie intended to find out tonight. Nicely, of course. Diplomatically. They'd just have a little girl talk, and Kathy would share her secret and clear up the issue.

If Kathy's secret turned out to be something important, Jackie could alert Dennis in the morning.

While going through the church directory, Jackie had noted the Dorsey address because it wasn't far from her apartment. She drove there now, catching a glimpse of Kathy's red Chevy ahead of her every so often. She turned onto Taylor Avenue in time to see Kathy pull into a driveway halfway down the street.

The houses here were modest-sized, single-story buildings, each with a pair of trees in the front yard. No garages, so Jackie pulled over to the side of the road several houses away from Kathy's and watched as the boys ran from the car to the front door of a rectangular brick home. Kathy, carrying her grocery sack, followed with her keys and let them inside.

Should she go in right now? Jackie's stomach fluttered at the thought. Maybe she should wait a few minutes. It was almost nine o'clock, surely close to the boys' bedtime. Maybe after they were in bed, Kathy would talk more openly.

One fingernail reduced to a nub, Jackie switched to another.

A vehicle passed. A white Grand Cherokee, new by the looks of it. She noted it in passing, her attention focused on deciding the right time to continue her interrogation. The vehicle passed Kathy's driveway and parked on the street two houses beyond. A man got out. He slammed the door, walked a few steps away, and turned to point a remote-controlled power lock at the Cherokee.

When he walked quickly toward the Dorsey residence, Jackie sat up in her seat. Average height, dark hair, gray suit. Hard to make out details in the rapidly diminishing twilight, but this was a professional man, by the looks of him. He took long strides, carrying himself with confidence. He—

Wait a minute! When he stepped into the ring of light shed by the porch lamp, Jackie got a good look at him. She recognized this guy. That was Richard Watson, Laura's husband. What was he doing at Kathy Dorsey's house at almost nine o'clock at night?

The front door opened. From her vantage point, Jackie couldn't see who stood inside the house, but she saw Richard say something, and then he stepped across the threshold. The door closed behind him.

Jackie threw herself against the backrest. This felt big.

Richard Watson was a vice president at Versailles Bank and Trust, the same bank where Kathy worked as a teller. What possible reason would a vice president have for visiting the home of a teller, unless…

She shook her head. No. No way. Richard was married to a beautiful, gracious woman. He had a great job and was respected in the church and the community.

They were both *church* members, for cryin' out loud! They couldn't be having an affair.

On the other hand, if they were having an affair, and if Mrs. Farmer had somehow found out about it, her poison pen would certainly not have dawdled over this one. Imagine the scandal that sort of news would cause! Richard would probably lose his job at the bank.

The fear on Kathy's face loomed large in Jackie's mind. Her job would probably be in jeopardy, too. Was this the secret Jackie saw lurking in her eyes, the one she refused to tell?

Something else occurred to her. That day at the picnic, when Mrs. Farmer was going on about the UPS man, what had she said? Something about people wallowing in sin. Jackie scrunched her eyes shut, trying to reconstruct the scene. They'd been sitting at the picnic table, Mrs. Farmer on Jackie's left, Margaret and Pastor Palmer across from them. Pastor Palmer said Christians should pray for people who struggled with sin, and Mrs. Farmer said struggling was one thing, but wallowing in sin was another. The old woman had been glaring at someone. Jackie remembered looking in the same direction.

What if Mrs. Farmer had been referring to someone there?

Jackie pounded her palm on the steering wheel. She couldn't remember. Who had been standing there?

She couldn't be 100 percent sure, but she thought Richard and Kathy had both been in the general vicinity of Mrs. Farmer's glare. She did remember Kathy washing spaghetti sauce from the twins' faces, because she'd felt a surge of pride that they'd eaten her casserole. She was almost sure Richard stood nearby.

So Mrs. Farmer's "wallowing in sin" comment might have been directed at Kathy or Richard or both of them.

Jackie's scalp prickled. She might have found the murderer, and there might be more than one.

TWELVE

At precisely nine o'clock Thursday morning, Jackie pulled into the McDonald's parking lot. A police car sat near the door, the driver's seat empty. A quiver began in her stomach as she retrieved her notebook from the passenger seat. She debated whether or not to bring it, because her scratchings would surely seem amateurish to an experienced investigator like Dennis. She didn't want him to think her a dope.

On the other hand, she wanted him to know how much work she had done on this case.

Standing, she smoothed the wrinkles out of her white slacks and brushed the cat hair off her pink blouse. She caught her hand as it tried to perform its habitual gesture. Drat Margaret. She'd never be able to push her hair behind her ears again without thinking about it.

The restaurant was practically empty, with only a few tables taken. At a booth in the corner, near the restrooms, sat Dennis. He stood when she entered and raised a hand to catch her attention.

Jackie stopped dead in her tracks at the sight of him. She'd expected him to be wearing his uniform, not jeans and a T-shirt. A formfitting T-shirt.

She clutched her notebook to her chest and swallowed against a suddenly dry throat.

"Hey, Jackie," he said. "I didn't order yet, because I didn't know what you wanted."

He walked up to her, forcing her to raise her chin to look him in the eye. The quiver in her stomach transformed itself into a full-fledged flutter.

"Uh, coffee," she managed to stammer. "Just coffee."

"Not a morning person, huh?" His lopsided grin took her breath. "I hope you don't mind if I eat. I went to the gym at seven, and I'm starved."

She tore her eyes away from his face. "Sure. Go ahead."

"Grab a seat, and I'll be right there."

Jackie slid into the booth and gave herself a stern talking to while she waited for him to return from the counter. She would *not* act like a moonstruck teenager. They were here to discuss a serious matter. She would keep her mind on business and *not* allow herself to become distracted.

By the time he returned, Jackie had herself under control. She even managed a friendly thank-you when he placed a cup of coffee and a handful of packets in front of her.

"I wasn't sure how you take it."

She picked up a blue package of sweetener. "This is fine. I try to stick with the low-cal stuff."

His eyes swept over her. "I can't imagine why."

I will not blush! I will not! By sheer force of will, Jackie managed to return his grin with a polite smile.

He unwrapped the first of his two biscuit sandwiches, and the scent of bacon enveloped them. Two bites later, the sandwich was gone.

Okay, so he could use a little work on the table manners.

"What do you have there?" He nodded toward the spiral

notebook, then took a sip from his steaming cup and un-wrapped the second sandwich.

"My notes." Jackie flipped open the cover, revealing the first page of her neat script. "At night I write down every-thing I've discovered during the day. It helps me get my thoughts organized."

He gave an approving nod. "That's smart. It's a good idea to make notes while a conversation is still fresh in your mind, so you don't forget anything."

"Oh, I don't have to worry about that." She picked up her purse and plopped it down on the table between them. "I'm recording all my conversations."

His eyebrows arched as he studied the black micro-phone clipped to her shoulder strap and Jackie's stomach sank. What if she had been breaking the law?

She leaned forward and spoke in a low voice. "Is that all right? I mean, is it legal?"

His forehead cleared. "Oh, yeah, don't worry about that. Kentucky is a one-party consent state." She must have looked blank because he explained, "In some states, both parties must be aware that a conversation is being re-corded in order for the recording to be considered legal evidence. In others, like here, only one person has to be aware."

Jackie sat back. That was actually kind of scary. She thought about some of the conversations she'd had over the years. Though she'd never done anything illegal, having a conversation she considered private suddenly show up in court as public evidence creeped her out.

"So are you going to give me those recordings?"

Startled, she looked up at him. "No! I didn't make them to turn over to the police. I just did it because I have a terrible memory and I wanted to make sure I got the details right if I happened to learn something important."

"And have you? Learned anything important, that is."

"Maybe." She awarded him with a brief smile before assuming a businesslike tone. "I'm prepared to share my findings with you, Trooper Walsh, if you're prepared to tell me what you've discovered."

"You've already obtained inside information. The knife and gloves."

"True. But I saw those myself, so that really doesn't count."

He shrugged a shoulder, not conceding the point but apparently not prepared to argue about it. "You know I can't give you any information about this case. But here's something new that's a matter of public record. Yesterday we got the toxicology report, and it confirmed the coroner's preliminary findings of monomethylhydrazine poisoning."

"That's not new." Jackie dismissed his news with a wave.

"No, but it does allow us to more accurately pinpoint the time of the crime." He glanced at her purse. "Are you recording this conversation?"

Actually, she'd intended to, but when she'd seen Dennis looking like a regular guy instead of a police officer, she'd forgotten to push the button. Relieved, she shook her head.

He placed both forearms on the table, his coffee cup held loosely between his hands. "Since the lab found no trace of toxic mushroom on your kitchen utensils, and since we've been unable to find anyone else who was ill after eating your casserole—" He grinned at Jackie's sudden exhalation of relief "—we can be fairly confident that the mushrooms were added at Mrs. Farmer's house."

"You knew that already," Jackie reminded him. "From the knife and gloves."

He spoke as one delivering a particularly sage piece of wisdom. "The first rule of detective work is *Never make assumptions*. Until we get the lab results, we only *assume* the knife and gloves are related to this case."

Jackie picked up her coffee stirrer and folded it in the middle. "Okay, that's fair. So did the toxicology report tell you anything else?"

He nodded. "It told us the approximate time Mrs. Farmer started digesting those mushrooms. Around five-thirty on Monday, the day after the picnic."

"But she didn't die until Tuesday night." Remembering the smell in Mrs. Farmer's house and the state of her bathroom, Jackie shuddered.

"That's right. Symptoms for that type of mushroom poisoning generally set in seven to ten hours after ingestion. Deaths are rare, and usually caused by liver damage, but in Mrs. Farmer's case—"

"She had a weak heart."

Dennis nodded. "The strain of severe abdominal cramps, vomiting and diarrhea proved too much for her. Just like a bad case of the flu would have done. In fact, she probably thought she had a touch of the flu at first."

"Which explains why she didn't try to call for help until later. The telephone had been knocked off the table and was under the bed when I got there."

"By then she was too weak to pick it up."

They sat silent for a moment, Jackie thinking how terrible the last day of Mrs. Farmer's life must have been. "So *assuming* the knife and gloves were used to chop those mushrooms—" she flashed a grin at her disregard for the first rule of detective work "—that means someone planted them in my casserole between one-thirty on

Sunday afternoon, which is about when she got home from the picnic, and five-thirty Monday evening. That's a long time."

"Yeah, but it's what we have to work with." Dennis took a sip, then set his cup on the table. "Your turn. What have you found out?"

Jackie squirmed on the hard seat. She really didn't consider this gossip. She was talking to the police, after all. In the name of justice, she needed to turn over any real evidence she had.

Only problem was she didn't have much *real* evidence. Not like knives or gloves. She had a lot of "he said, she said" stuff and a couple of really good assumptions. She knew what he'd say about her assumptions.

"I haven't found a lot," she admitted.

His shoulders lifted a fraction. "Let me decide for myself."

"You remember what I told you the other day about the letters?" He nodded. "Well, turns out Mrs. Farmer has written several that could provide a motive."

She turned in her notebook to the page labeled ESTHER HODGES. Dennis read the heading upside down and nodded.

"Yeah, we know about that one."

"You do?"

"We talked to her yesterday. We've been questioning people since Friday, and her name came up several times. Apparently, that nasty letter caused quite a stir in your church." He finally picked up his second biscuit and devoured it as quickly as the first.

Well, that certainly let a bit of air out of her balloon. She hadn't considered that the police might find out the same information she had. In fact, she had been fairly confident she could weasel out rumors they would never hear.

Wouldn't Margaret be shocked to find out Jackie wasn't the only one who considered Esther a suspect?

She looked at Dennis. "Do you think she did it?"

"Do you?" he shot back.

"She's still pretty mad at Mrs. Farmer over that letter."

He shrugged again. "Wouldn't you be?"

Yeah, she probably would. It was a nasty thing to do.

"What else have you got?" He read her upside-down handwriting.

"Sharon Carlson." Jackie flipped the page. "She and her husband—"

"Nicholas. Yeah, we got them, too."

Jackie sat back in disgust. Did Dennis know *everything* she knew? "So what do you think of them as suspects?"

He took a quick sip from his coffee. "I can't discuss that."

But Jackie saw an odd expression cross his features before they closed down. She hid a smile. He'd just told her what she wanted to know. His attitude was casual when discussing Mrs. Hodges, but guarded when she mentioned the Carlsons. A thrill of excitement zipped through her. He'd given her insider information, whether he'd intended to or not.

"Of course," she assured him, "just a word of advice— I think you should check out Sharon. She has access to rubber gloves, you know."

Dennis shrugged. "Everybody does. You can buy them at any drugstore."

"Maybe, but you should have seen how angry Sharon got when I mentioned Mrs. Farmer's name."

"That's good to know."

Jackie drank her coffee, which had gone lukewarm. She wasn't even going to bother mentioning Margaret. Besides the fact that the idea of Margaret being a killer was ludicrous, Jackie would feel like a complete fink admitting she'd considered her friend even for a moment.

In fact, Dennis probably already knew about the petition to oust Pastor Palmer. He seemed to know everything else, which left her feeling a bit disconcerted.

There was one thing she'd wager he didn't know.

"So have you come across any mention of Richard Watson in your investigation?"

Dennis eyed her speculatively. She hid a smile. Yep, just as she'd thought. She had something new to offer after all.

"I've heard of him. He's a big shot down at the bank, isn't he? Does he go to your church?"

"Oh, yes. He and his wife have been members there for years."

"Don't tell me Mrs. Farmer wrote a letter about him, too?"

Jackie pushed aside the discarded sugar wrappers and napkins and leaned forward. "No, but I think maybe she was getting ready to."

She told him what she'd seen last night, satisfied when his eyes widened appreciatively.

"And this Kathy Dorsey. What do you know about her?"

"I know Mrs. Farmer went around telling everyone she was incompetent and shouldn't be allowed to work at the bank. At first I thought that might be her motive. But after last night…" She shook her head.

Dennis reached across the table suddenly, resting his hand on hers. The warmth of his touch made her mouth go dry.

"Jackie, this is a great lead. Thank you."

Rational thought evaporated. *Say something, you idiot!*

A cheery voice cut through Jackie's fog. "What a pleasant surprise!"

Jackie's hand seemed to jerk away of its own volition, and she felt a flash of regret at its treachery. But only a flash, because in the next instant all the blood in her body rushed to her head, flooding her face with fire.

What in the world was Margaret doing here?

"Hello, Mrs. Palmer." Dennis pulled his hand slowly back across the table, hiding a grin at Jackie's red face. He rose politely and smiled at the new arrival. "Won't you join us?"

"Oh, no." She shook her head. "I'm in such a rush. I've got about a million things to do today."

Still seated, Jackie turned a look on the preacher's wife that could almost be described as angry. Dennis pocketed his hands. Was she embarrassed to be seen with him?

"McDonald's is on your list of errands for the day?" Jackie asked, studying Mrs. Palmer intently.

The older woman's smile deepened. "I was on my way to the grocery store and realized I felt a little snackish. You should never do your grocery shopping hungry, you know."

Disbelief colored Jackie's expression. Dennis didn't believe Mrs. Palmer, either, but he would never be so impolite as to show it. He was opening his mouth to say something to ease the tension when he noticed the expression on the woman's face. He had seen that look before. In fact, his own mother wore it every time she introduced him to a girl.

He felt a sudden and intense desire to escape. Quickly.

"We were just about to leave," he said, drawing surprised stares from both women. "I need to get dressed and over to the station before Detective Conner arrives."

As he spoke, he piled the trash from his breakfast onto a tray, ignoring the look of dismay Jackie turned on him.

"When will we talk again? About the case, I mean."

"Call me if you hear anything important." He pulled his wallet from a back pocket and fished out his card. "My home number is on the back."

Jackie glanced down, and then back up. "And you'll do the same, right?"

"Yeah, sure. Thanks for talking with me."

With a farewell nod at Mrs. Palmer, he made a hasty retreat, the weight of their stares boring into his back as he dumped the contents of the tray into the trash can. As he opened the door, he thought he heard Jackie hiss, "Way to go, Margaret!"

In the safety of his cruiser, he sat back and heaved a sigh. Why did he feel he'd just narrowly escaped the hangman's noose? After all, the past half hour hadn't been bad. He'd thoroughly enjoyed talking with Jackie, watching that quick smile of hers flash unexpectedly and then disappear. It made him want to say something to make her smile again. And he'd liked the intense way she looked at him when he talked about the toxicology report, as if she had never heard anything so fascinating in her whole life.

You egotistical jerk. You're just soaking it up because you think she's attracted to you.

He shifted into Reverse and backed out of the parking lot. Unease warred with the biscuits in his stomach. Conner would be furious if he found out Dennis had discussed the coroner's report with Jackie. Yeah, it was public record, but would she have known where to find it on her own? Probably not. And he knew he'd inadvertently verified that the Carlsons were being investigated. What kind of cop was he, to let his defenses drop just because a pretty girl flirted with him? He needed to toughen up.

Honestly, he could be attracted to Jackie. She was cute, and obviously she had a brain in that pretty head. And he'd always been a sucker for curly hair.

He shook his head. No, he wasn't going there. Jackie might be pretty and smart, but he wanted more in a woman. He wanted someone to look at him the way Mom looked at Dad, even after thirty years of marriage. Some of his college pals had tried marriage after graduation, and more than a few of them were already divorced. Not him, buddy. No way. He'd grown up basking in a living example of love that lasted and had determined a long time ago to settle for nothing less.

Cute as she was, he just didn't think Jackie was a likely candidate.

THIRTEEN

"I still can't believe you showed up at McDonald's."

Jackie glared across the daisy-covered kitchen table-cloth, and Margaret had the grace to look away. Esther Hodges would arrive any minute, and then the three of them planned to go to Mrs. Farmer's house and sort her clothing for Goodwill.

Two spots of pink appeared high on Margaret's cheeks. "I'm sorry. I couldn't help myself. Earl says my matchmaking will get me in trouble one day, but I wanted to see the two of you together. You can tell all sorts of things by the way a man looks at a woman across a table."

Somewhat appeased by the apology, Jackie sipped iced tea from the tall glass Margaret had placed in front of her. She toyed with a napkin, her mind wandering back to the gray depths of Dennis's eyes.

"And?"

Margaret looked up. "And what?"

Jackie gave a frustrated grunt. "And did you see anything?"

"Are you kidding?" A grin spread across Margaret's face. "That was no casual coffee meeting, Jackie."

Jackie couldn't help her response. "Do you think so?"

"Absolutely. He was so into you he didn't even see me until I was standing over him. And he was holding your hand."

A thrill of warmth shot through Jackie at the memory. "He wasn't holding my hand," she corrected. "He happened to touch my hand right before you walked up."

"Uh-huh. Whatever he was doing, he couldn't take his eyes off you. And I don't blame him, dear. You do look lovely today. You should wear spring colors more often."

Jackie rolled her eyes. "You're not going to lecture me again about my clothes or my hair, are you?"

"Of course not. I just thought—"

Jackie was left to guess at Margaret's thought, for at that moment the doorbell rang.

"That's Esther," Margaret said, sliding her chair back from the table. She paused on her way to the front door. "You will be nice, won't you?"

Jackie threw both hands in the air. "I'm always nice."

Margaret left, and a moment later the air in the cozy kitchen erupted with activity as Esther Hodges burst through the doorway.

"Gracious sakes alive, I just can't handle Jim traveling all the time. He's gonna have to get a new job, that's all there is to it." She jerked a chair away from the table and collapsed into it, her forehead damp above ruddy cheeks. "The AC on that piece of junk I drive is blowing hot air again. I told him to have it checked before he left, but did he listen?" She leveled a direct gaze on Jackie. "Of course not. Never does. Men!"

She grabbed a napkin from the holder in the center of the table and fanned herself furiously. Unruly dark curls around her forehead waved in the breeze. With her conversation with Dennis fresh in her mind, Mrs. Hodges seemed far less sinister than before. Jackie found herself enjoying the older woman's blustery manner.

"Hello, Mrs. Hodges."

She waved the napkin in Jackie's direction. "Call me Esther. How are you doing, honey?"

"I'm okay." Jackie rested her chin in her hand. "I heard the police talked to you about Mrs. Farmer yesterday. How did that go?"

Margaret placed a glass of ice water on the table, and Esther threw her a grateful glance. She downed half of it in a single gulp before answering.

"They wanted to drag up that business about the letter and talk it to death. Said they'd heard about it from people in the church." She took another gulp, and then sat back. "Bunch of nosey old tongue-waggers. But I just told 'em what happened, and they seemed okay with that. Detective Conner is the nicest man, isn't he?"

"Yes, he is," Margaret agreed with a look in Jackie's direction.

Jackie didn't answer. Nice? *Yeah, right.* He might look like a friendly Labrador retriever at first, before he turned on you. Like a pit bull. Then again, if Esther hadn't seen the pit bull emerge, that verified what Dennis had said earlier: Detective Conner must not consider her a murder suspect.

"So is it just us today, or is anyone else coming along?" Esther asked.

"Several others said they would meet us there," Margaret answered. "Laura and Emilee and maybe Lois."

Esther turned her head to smile at Jackie. "It's good of you to join us, honey. Not a pleasant thing to do on your vacation, pawing through a dead woman's underwear."

"Oh, I'm looking forward to it," Jackie said.

The women appeared dubious, but Jackie really was looking forward to the afternoon. Not that she expected to find any clues in Mrs. Farmer's house after Detective Conner and his crew had combed through it. But Laura Watson would be there. Maybe she could learn something about Laura's relationship with her husband.

Unfortunately, if problems existed in her marriage, Laura Watson was too much a lady to discuss it. After an hour and a half of working side by side, Jackie had been unable to detect even a hint of evidence that Laura was grieving over her husband's affair. On the contrary, as they sorted, folded and stored clothing in boxes to be delivered to the Goodwill donation center, she spoke with unmasked pride about Richard's important job at the bank and how he had such compassion for the underprivileged and impoverished.

In no mood to listen to the praises of a cheating scoundrel, Jackie bit her tongue and folded a blue dress with a matching jacket. Was it possible Laura didn't know about her husband's affair? Surely every wife knew at some level. There were always signs, weren't there? Too many nights working late at the office, matchbooks from hotels left in a jacket pocket, unexplained expenditures on the credit card statement… You heard about that sort of thing all the time.

She also knew some women chose to ignore the telltale signs. Maybe Laura was one of those.

She placed the folded dress and jacket into an almost-full box. That was the last article of clothing in the bedroom. She arched her back, stretching tired muscles. The others had moved to the kitchen, and Jackie could hear the low murmur of their chatter as they packed up Mrs. Farmer's dishes.

Her eyes fell on the small desk in the corner. A lamp sat on one edge of the otherwise clear surface. Had the police taken all of Mrs. Farmer's papers? With a glance through the door to ensure no one was coming down the hallway, Jackie crossed the room in three quick steps and jerked open the center drawer. Order seemed to be one of Mrs. Farmer's strong points. A compartmentalized plastic organizer held pens, pencils, paper clips and a roll of stamps. Beside it rested the worn personal address book Jackie had seen the night Mrs. Farmer died. She flipped the cover and fanned through the yellowed pages. The spidery script was faded in some places. This address book was probably older than Jackie.

Beneath the booklet lay a volume she recognized, the Heritage Community Church directory. Heart pounding, she checked out Kathy Dorsey's entry. The page was clean. Too bad! She'd thought she might find the address circled or something. The C and W pages were clean, as well—no circles, no checkmarks, no writing at all. With a sigh, she put everything back and then opened the top drawer on the right.

There she found Mrs. Farmer's stationery resting neatly in another plastic sorter, notepaper in a variety of pastels with matching envelopes. She fingered a piece. Was this the paper on which the old woman had written her vicious letters? Seemed sort of ironic, sending a poison-pen letter on lavender-colored paper.

The remaining drawer held file folders. Jackie's hopes rose. Maybe she would get lucky here.

The same spidery script she'd found in the address book scrawled across the tabs on a row of manila folders. Annual Reports—SP, Annual Reports—VB&T, Bank Statements, Medical Receipts, Tax Deductible Receipts. Suddenly uncomfortable, Jackie flipped through the tabs but did not open the folders. Mrs. Farmer's personal financial documents were none of her business. Looking at them would be even worse than going through her purse.

Sliding the drawer closed, Jackie heaved a sigh. If there had been anything here to find, the police had already taken it.

She folded the flaps of the clothing box to seal it and carried it down the hallway to pile in the living room beside the two boxes she'd filled earlier. Then she joined the others in the kitchen.

"Would you look at this?" Seated on the floor in front of an open cabinet, Esther held up a heavy black skillet with both hands. "Here's an old one. You can't find these anymore, not with a smooth surface like that. This will fetch a pretty penny at our rummage sale next month."

Margaret, standing at the counter, turned from a stack of newspaper and an assortment of coffee mugs. "I thought those old iron skillets were unhealthy."

"That's bunk," said Esther. "I've used one for years. The only way one of these'll hurt is if you bash someone over the head with it."

"Actually," said Laura as she tore off a piece of newspaper, "it is true that they add iron to your food. But I think that's supposed to be good for you."

"Really?" Esther inspected the skillet with consternation. "Maybe that's what's making Jim feel off his feed. Too much iron."

Jackie opened an empty cabinet, and then a second one. "Looks like you've just about finished in here."

"There." Margaret nodded toward a cabinet beside the refrigerator. "That one's still full. Grab a newspaper and start wrapping."

Jackie did as she was told. Rolling a green juice glass in a piece of paper, she wondered how she could turn the conversation toward Richard again without having to listen to a list of his accomplishments.

On the other hand, maybe she was taking the wrong approach. Maybe she shouldn't be asking about Richard at all.

Quickly, she emptied the contents of the cabinet onto on the kitchen table. That way she could sit opposite Laura while she worked.

"Guess who I ran into in the grocery store the other day?" Jackie asked the room in general.

"Who?" asked Margaret.

"Kathy Dorsey. She looked great, really pretty. I think she's a little thinner lately. Do you think she's on a diet?"

From the floor Esther said, "I don't know about a diet, but running after those twins of hers would melt the pounds off anyone. They're cute, but they're a handful."

"They sure are," Margaret agreed, giving Jackie a measured stare.

Jackie ignored Margaret, her attention fixed elsewhere. Across the table, Laura smiled and nodded absently as she rolled another coffee mug in paper. Jackie studied her expression, searching for the slightest indication that Laura was less than happy with the young mother.

Nothing. Absolutely nothing.

FOURTEEN

"I can't believe it's Friday already."

Jackie sat once again at Margaret's kitchen table, staring sullenly at the steam rising from a plate of blueberry muffins. Friday. The last day of her vacation, and she was no closer to solving the murder case than the first day.

Margaret reached across the table to pat her hand. "Don't look so down, dear. You've made a lot of progress."

"Yeah?" Jackie reached into her bag and pulled out her notebook. "I've taken a lot of notes and recorded a bunch of conversations, but I don't know about progress."

She slapped the notebook down on the table and glared at it.

"You've also met a nice man and made a good impression on him," Margaret reminded her. "And you've gotten to know several people in our church much better. You've made some new friends."

And a few enemies besides, but Jackie kept that thought to herself. The memory of Sharon's angry face haunted her as she reached for a muffin. She chased the image away with the sweet scent of hot blueberries.

The doorbell rang.

Margaret stood, her brow creased. "I wonder who that is. I'm not expecting anyone."

A moment later, Jackie heard the sound of a woman's sobs and Margaret's soothing voice telling the person to come inside. She put the muffin down and half stood. Obviously someone had come to the pastor's wife in need of comfort. Should she go see who was crying? Or should she leave and give them their privacy?

She sat back down. To leave she had to go through the living room, and that would disturb them. She'd better just wait here instead. Only she felt like an eavesdropper, because she could hear every sound.

"What's wrong, dear?" Margaret asked. "Has something happened to one of the boys?"

"N-no," sobbed the woman. "They're fine. It's…"

Jackie sat straight up. She knew that voice. It belonged to one of her primary suspects.

Kathy Dorsey's tearful hiccup echoed in the quiet house. "It's nothing like that. The…the police just left my house. Oh, Margaret, they said terrible things. They think I killed Mrs. Farmer!"

The pain in Kathy's voice made Jackie cringe. She knew the feeling. When the police had questioned her a week ago, she'd shed a few tears of her own. Compassion stirred in her. She knew what it was like to be questioned by pit bull Conner.

"That is ridiculous. I'm sure they don't think any such thing." Margaret's voice sounded louder, as though she had turned toward the kitchen doorway. "Why don't you come into the kitchen and have some coffee while you tell me about it."

"O-okay."

Panic gripped Jackie's insides. Would Kathy blame her? The police had never even heard of Kathy Dorsey until she told Dennis about her affair with Richard.

She was not prepared to face Kathy right now. She needed time to compose herself, to get her thoughts in order so she could ask the right questions and lead the conversation the way she wanted it to go. But she had no time. At that moment, Margaret stepped through the doorway, her arm around the shoulders of the sobbing young brunette.

Kathy took one look at Jackie and the tears evaporated. "You!"

Jackie's insides sank as Kathy stared daggers across the room. Apparently, Jackie's name had come up during the questioning.

Kathy took a step toward the table, and Jackie leaned as far back as the chair would allow. The young mom looked angry enough to slap her. Margaret stood with her arms hanging at her sides, her attention volleying between the two of them.

Kathy pointed a finger in Jackie's face. "You sent the police to my house. You told them terrible lies about me."

"I did not," Jackie shot back. "I only told them what I know."

Margaret took a step forward. "Jackie? What does she mean? What did you tell the police?"

Kathy whirled. "She told them I'm having an affair with Richard Watson."

Margaret gasped, her eyes going round as melons. "Jackie, you didn't!"

Feeling blood flood her face, Jackie drew herself up. "I did not say that. Not exactly."

"Not exactly?" Margaret repeated. "Then what *exactly* did you say?"

Jackie found it difficult to look at the accusation in Kathy's face, so she kept her gaze fixed on Margaret. "I told Dennis about the mistake on Mrs. Farmer's account, and how Mrs. Farmer threatened Kathy's job." She cleared her throat. "And I told him I saw Richard go into Kathy's house Wednesday night after church."

Kathy sobbed, and Margaret stepped forward to put an arm around her shoulders. She guided the young woman to a chair and seated her, then glared at Jackie from above her light brown hair.

"Well, it was the truth," Jackie said, allowing a touch of anger to creep into her voice.

"I'm sure there's an explanation." Margaret's hand rested protectively on Kathy's shoulder.

After a few moments of quiet crying, Kathy shook her head and made a visible effort to choke them back. This didn't look like a woman caught in adultery. The righteous anger, the devastated sobs, the dejected slope of Kathy's shoulders all had the unmistakable feel of a woman unjustly accused. Jackie shifted her weight in the chair. What if she was wrong? What if there really was an innocent explanation for Richard's visit?

She pulled a napkin out of the holder and offered it to the sobbing woman. Kathy stared at it á moment, as though afraid it might be poisoned, and then took it without looking up. She blew her nose and took a shuddering breath.

"He did come to my house Wednesday night. It's the second time he's been there. The first time was two weeks ago, before Mrs. Farmer died."

Margaret squeezed her shoulder once, and then went to

the counter to pour a mug of coffee. She set it on the table, and Kathy took a grateful sip before continuing.

"Mrs. Farmer thought Richard was stealing money from the bank. She wanted me to use my position to find evidence to prove it." She balled the napkin in one fist, the other hand clutching the handle of her mug. "She told me if I didn't, she would file an official complaint against me and have me fired."

"But surely she couldn't have you fired for one little mistake." Jackie tried to sound as though she didn't believe the tale, but her resolve wavered. Either Kathy was telling the truth, or she was a really good liar.

"She could." Her face a mask of misery, Kathy sniffed. "That wasn't my first mistake. I'm…I'm not a very good teller, I'm afraid. One more complaint and I'll lose my job for sure." She looked up, first at Margaret and then at Jackie. "I can't afford to get fired. I'm barely paying the bills now."

Convicted by the honesty she saw in Kathy's eyes, the last of Jackie's doubt melted away. This woman wasn't a killer, and she wasn't having an affair. She was a hardworking single mother struggling to feed her kids.

Jackie wanted to crawl under the table. What kind of worm would accuse an innocent woman of adultery and murder?

One who was trying to show off by passing along gossip as though it was truth. One who wanted to impress a handsome police officer with her investigative ability.

Heart in her shoes, Jackie reached across the table and took Kathy's hand. "I'm so sorry, Kathy. I was way out of line. I should have come to you first before telling the police what I saw."

Kathy's chin quivered. Her stare was so direct Jackie felt

as though she was being examined from the inside out. She kept her gaze steady, hoping Kathy would see her sincerity.

Finally, Kathy gave a hesitant nod. "I guess you only did what you thought was right. And I guess it did look really suspicious, seeing Richard come to my house."

Margaret, however, didn't seem ready to forgive. "What were you doing at Kathy's house in the first place?" she asked, her voice hard.

Jackie bit back a sharp retort. Instead, she bowed her head and said truthfully, "Snooping."

She looked at Kathy again. "Actually, I wanted to talk to you some more, because I thought you acted like you were holding something back at the church. I guess now I know what."

Kathy nodded. "And the worst part is Richard found out that I was asking questions. I'm just a teller, and I don't have access to any records like Mrs. Farmer wanted. So I talked to a friend in the internal audit department. At least—" her lips twisted into a bitter grimace "—I thought he was a friend. But he told someone about my questions, and it got back to Richard."

"So Richard came to your house to find out why you were snooping around about him at work." Jackie used the word *snooping* deliberately, with a quick glance toward Margaret.

"That's right. I was so upset I didn't handle things very well. I blurted out the truth, and that's when he told me he could have me fired far more easily than Mrs. Farmer." She sniffed again, and reached for another napkin. "And he's right. He's a bigwig at the bank."

Margaret leaned forward. "Do you think there's any truth to Alice's accusations?"

Kathy shrugged. "I don't know. He said there wasn't,

that Mrs. Farmer was just a malicious old busybody who loved to dig up dirt to hold over people's heads. I never found anything suspicious."

Jackie chewed on another nail. If Mrs. Farmer's suspicions were right, then Richard had a strong motive for killing her. Not only would he lose his job, but he would go to prison.

"So why did he come to your house on Wednesday?" she asked.

"He said he wanted to make sure I wasn't spending any more time on Mrs. Farmer's claim." She looked suddenly fearful. "His exact words were, 'Now that Alice Farmer is dead, I hope her accusations died with her.'"

A chill shot down Jackie's spine. By the look on Margaret's face, she felt the same.

"Did you tell this to the police, dear?" Margaret's voice held a hint of urgency.

A flood of tears returned to Kathy's eyes. "I was afraid to. Richard really can have me fired."

Jackie grabbed the young woman's hand and gave it a shake. "If he murdered Mrs. Farmer, getting fired is the least of your worries."

Kathy sniffed and sat up. "I've got to get to work."

"I think you should take the day off," Margaret said.

Kathy shook her head. "I called to let them know I'd be late, but we're short-handed this week so I have to go in. I'll be all right."

Jackie remained at the table as Margaret led Kathy to the bathroom to wash her face. Richard Watson, a murderer. She could hardly believe it. He looked so…so sophisticated. So smooth and gentlemanly.

Correction. No gentleman would threaten a single mother's job. Nor would a gentleman murder an old woman.

Poor Laura. She was so proud of her husband, so obviously in love with him. Did she know about this? Jackie remembered her face yesterday, glowing with pride as she talked about Richard's work for poor families in Appalachia. No, Laura didn't know. And it would break her heart when she found out.

"Thank you, Margaret," Kathy said as she and Margaret came back into the room. "I feel better now."

"I do think you should contact the police and tell them everything," Margaret urged.

Kathy's jaw trembled as she shook her head. "I just can't."

Jackie stood. "I'll walk Kathy to her car," she said with a meaningful glance at Margaret.

The older woman hesitated, clearly struggling over leaving Kathy alone with her accuser. As if Jackie would hurt a flea. But then Margaret gave a quick nod.

Jackie followed Kathy out the front door. The weather had turned hot the past few days, and though it was not yet ten o'clock, the sun had already burned through the morning chill to warm the air. A few hardy pink blooms clung stubbornly to Margaret's dogwood tree, and a bright assortment of dandelions littered her yard. Hidden somewhere in the top branches of a sugar maple, a bird chirped with enthusiasm. If the morning hadn't been so upsetting, Jackie would have been tempted to take a walk in the park just to enjoy the gorgeous spring day.

At the door of her car, Kathy paused. She didn't look at Jackie's face, but stared through the open window. Jackie halted beside her, grasping for words. Apologies never came easily.

"Listen," she said, staring at the ground between them, "I really am sorry. Sometimes I act before I think."

Kathy's gaze slid to capture Jackie's. "What bothers me the most is that you actually thought I would have an affair with a married man. I wouldn't, you know."

Miserable, Jackie said, "I do now."

"Well…" Kathy managed a smile, but her eyes held a hint of sadness that made Jackie feel like the biggest jerk in the world. "What's done is done."

Jackie knew it wasn't done.

"Listen, Kathy, you've got to tell the police everything. They need to know."

The young woman bit her lower lip in hesitation, then shook her head. "I just can't face them right now. I've got to get to work, and that detective…"

She didn't need to finish her thought. Jackie knew all about "that detective."

"What would you think about me telling him?"

She hesitated to even suggest it, because she'd caused enough trouble for Kathy already. But Richard's comment was more than suspicious; it was downright incriminating. Dennis and Detective Conner needed to know about it.

Hope flared into Kathy's eyes. "Would you?"

"Of course, but you know they're going to want to talk to you again."

"Do you think they'll come to the bank?" She looked horrified at the thought.

Jackie didn't blame her. Having the police show up at your job would be humiliating.

"I won't say a word until they promise not to. But," she added, "they'll probably be waiting at your house when you get home tonight."

Kathy swallowed hard, then nodded. This time her smile was genuine. "Thank you, Jackie."

She stepped back as Kathy slid inside the car. When the Chevy pulled away from the curb, Jackie lifted a hand in farewell, watching until Kathy turned off Margaret's street.

She mounted the porch steps at a slow pace, not sure if she was looking forward to calling Dennis or not. He was sure to think her a big dope for jumping to the wrong conclusion about Kathy. But maybe he'd be happy with her for finding out the truth behind Richard's visit.

Jackie closed the front door and crossed the living room to the kitchen. Margaret turned a frown her way.

"Look," Jackie said, "I'm sorry. I was wrong. But you have to admit Richard Watson showing up at her house at almost nine o'clock looked suspicious."

Margaret snorted. "Maybe so, but you shouldn't have said anything until you asked Kathy about it first. That would have been the right thing to do."

"Yeah, you're right. Next time I'll know." She was glad to see Margaret looking mollified. "I'm going to run to the bathroom, and then let's talk about who we're going to visit today. It's my last day, so I need to talk to somebody who knows something. Here." She picked up her notebook and slid it across the table. "Make a list."

She spent a minute in the bathroom, taking in her reflection while she washed her hands. Kathy's expression as she pulled away, her relief that Jackie would talk to the police for her, made Jackie feel like a heel. Would she have been so quick to forgive if she had been in Kathy's place?

When she stepped into the kitchen, she stopped in surprise. In the next instant, guilt settled over her like a blanket. Her mouth went completely dry at the sight of Margaret reading her notebook.

Margaret looked up. The hurt in her eyes impaled Jackie from all the way across the room.

"You think *I* killed Alice?"

FIFTEEN

"But...but..."

Jackie wanted to wither into a pool of misery right there on the kitchen floor. Margaret closed the notebook with a deliberate gesture, deep lines of distress marking her forehead. She sat for a moment with her hand resting on the cover and then left the chair to walk to the sink, where she stood with her back to Jackie.

"Margaret, please let me explain. Of course I don't think you killed Mrs. Farmer. You aren't capable of doing something like that."

"No, I'm not." Margaret spoke quietly, without turning.

The pain in her voice brought a lump of tears to Jackie's throat. She'd never meant to hurt anybody. Especially Margaret. All she wanted to do was discover the truth.

"I was only trying to record every possible—" she caught the word *suspect* before it escaped her lips "—piece of information related to the case. I wanted to be thorough."

"I see. And did you share your *information* with Trooper Walsh, like the information about Kathy? Are they going to come knocking on my door next?"

Jackie wished Margaret would turn around and look at

her. "Of course not. There was no reason to. I know you wouldn't do anything like that."

Margaret did turn then. Jackie wanted cringed before her look of betrayal.

"Kathy wouldn't do what you accused her of, either, Jackie. Nor would Esther."

Wretched, Jackie nodded.

"You are a lovely girl," Margaret said in the manner of one about to deliver a blow. Jackie braced herself. "But you are a little too self-centered. It's not an attractive trait. This murder investigation is a perfect example."

That stung. Jackie knew she had many faults, but no one had ever accused her of being self-centered.

"I only want to get to the bottom of a terrible crime," she said, failing to keep a note of defensiveness from creeping into her tone. "I don't see how that's self-centered."

"Is that all you want? You're interested in nothing more than bringing a murderer to justice? Or is there something else?"

Margaret's question shot straight through her. Was justice the only reason she had taken a week off work to investigate this case? Of course not. What if Detective Conner caught the murderer instead of her? Her name would be cleared either way. It wouldn't matter who found the killer, right?

Inwardly, she cringed. She knew it would matter. She was trying to prove something by solving this murder. From the beginning she'd wanted to show off for the church, for the people at work, for Dennis. She'd wanted everyone to think she was clever, to admire her. She'd wanted to find the killer so she could make friends.

Did a more self-centered motive exist?

Jackie hung her head, unable to look at Margaret as the older woman continued in a gentle but determined voice.

"You are a Christian, Jackie. The Lord asks only two things of you—that you love God and that you love others."

"But someone killed Mrs. Farmer," Jackie insisted. "Am I supposed to love a killer?"

"Actually, yes, you're to love without condoning sin. But that's not what I'm talking about here. Your approach from the beginning has been to suspect everyone of wrong-doing, and that's how you've treated them. You've spread gossip and accusations without meaning to, all because you've been so focused on finding a killer that you have forgotten to love. I'm not asking you to ignore the truth. All I'm saying is that your search for truth should be carried out with love."

Jackie looked up. "How can I act with love without asking questions? I don't understand."

Margaret shook her head, sadness heavy in her eyes. "Alice didn't understand, either, and look what it did to her."

Back at home, Jackie slammed the front door and threw her bag on the table. The traitorous notebook peeked out, but she ignored it. Instead she scooped up a sleeping Linus and threw herself onto the couch. Since Aunt Betty's death, Linus was her only confidant.

"I am such a jerk," she told the startled cat. "Who am I kidding with this murder investigation stuff? I don't know what I'm doing, and I've just hurt two people who didn't deserve it."

A few tears tried to force their way to her eyes, but she refused to give in to self-pity. Pain lodged in her throat as she tried to ignore the memory of betrayal on Margaret's face, the devastation on Kathy's. The worst part was that she liked both of them. A lot. Under different circumstances they might have become good friends. She'd blown that, for sure.

"Margaret's right," she moaned to Linus. "I don't know a thing about love. How can I expect to ever find a husband if I can't even manage to keep a friend?"

Unbidden, an image of Dennis came to mind. Not Trooper Walsh, but Dennis, smiling at her over his coffee cup and downing his breakfast biscuit in two bites. The memory sobered her. Sure, he was a nice-looking guy, and no doubt she was attracted to him, but did she think of him as husband material?

Gulping back a fresh onslaught of tears, she admitted to herself that she did. But it didn't matter. He would think her a complete idiot when she confessed her mistake about Kathy and Richard. Her snooping had managed to spoil not only two friendships, but a potential romance, as well.

Well, her snooping days were over. She was hanging up her recorder. From now on, she would do as God wanted and love people instead of looking for suspicious motives in everyone she met.

First she had to do as she promised Kathy. She had to call Dennis.

Linus leaped away when she released him, running to his hiding place under the bed and therefore removing himself from further use as a confidant and Kleenex. Jackie fished Dennis's card out of her purse.

He answered on the second ring. "Walsh."

"Uh, hi. This is Jackie Hoffner."

"Hey, Jackie. I was just thinking about you."

A delicious warmth lightened her spirits when she

heard the note of pleasure in his voice. He was thinking about her. But he wouldn't be happy when she told him why she'd called.

"Uh, listen, I need to tell you something, but you have to make a promise first."

"What's the promise?" He sounded curious.

"You have to promise you won't act on this information until tonight at least. This person is terrified you'll come to her work, and it will get her in major trouble."

"Well, as an officer, I can't promise that, but we do have a pretty busy afternoon scheduled already."

"Then, first of all, I have to tell you that I was wrong about something yesterday."

"Oh?"

"Yeah. Kathy Dorsey is not having an affair with Richard Watson."

"I don't know about that," he said, sounding unconvinced. "We talked to her this morning, and she was definitely hiding—"

"I know what she was hiding," Jackie interrupted. "That's the information I'm going to tell you."

She relayed her conversation with Kathy, ending with Richard's comment about Mrs. Farmer's accusations dying with her.

Dennis gave a low whistle. "That's a pretty incriminating statement. Are you sure about this?"

Jackie thought of Kathy's face. "Yeah, I am."

"So why didn't she tell us about Richard this morning?"

"Because your buddy—" Jackie nearly spit the word "—scared her to death. And besides, she's a single mother and can't afford to lose her job, but if Richard finds out she talked to the police, that's exactly what will happen."

"If Conner scared her to death," Dennis said, "it's because I told him she was having an affair and had a motive for killing Mrs. Farmer."

Jackie flushed with guilt. So she had made both of them look stupid in front of Detective Conner. "Yeah, all right. I already said I was wrong about that."

"Well, listen, I need to go. I've got to pick up Conner for our next interview. Thanks for the information. And I won't say a word about it until this evening."

Curiosity burned, and Jackie wanted to ask who they were questioning. But she stopped herself. Her investigating days were over.

"Good luck," she said. "Talk to you later."

"Bye."

After she replaced the phone in its cradle, she stared at it, feeling suddenly lighter. He hadn't sounded all that upset. Maybe she hadn't ruined her chances with him after all.

Dennis parked the cruiser in a visitor slot close to the bank's entrance. The building, an older two-story stone structure, faced Main Street, but the back entrance was more frequently used since it opened onto the parking lot.

Conner got out of the car, and Dennis fell into step beside him as they walked up the sidewalk. The egotistical detective exuded confidence, Dennis had to give him that. He walked with a steady step, his head held high, eyes constantly sweeping his surroundings. Nothing got past the guy.

Dennis followed Conner into the bank. Directly in front of them stood a high counter with stacks of blank deposit slips. To their right, four teller windows separated the lobby from the drive-up window. Only two of the windows were occupied. Dennis saw Kathy Dorsey's face go snow-white when she caught sight of them. He tried to reassure her with his smile, but she turned quickly away. Conner ignored her.

Without a moment's hesitation, the detective crossed the lobby to the first of three desks along the left wall. He smiled down at the woman sitting there.

"We're here to see Richard Watson."

The woman's eyes slid to Dennis and back to Conner. "Is he expecting you?"

"No, he isn't. We took a chance that he would have some time to talk with us."

"Just a minute and I'll see if he's free."

She made a call, hung up the phone and smiled at the detective. "Go right up. He's on the second floor."

They took the elevator, and when the doors opened, a smiling woman in a white blouse and blue skirt stood waiting. "Hello, I'm Mr. Watson's assistant. Come this way, please."

She led them down a hallway and past a set of cubicles, ending at a row of offices that lined the front of the building. The nameplate on the second office said *Richard Watson, Vice President of Investments*.

Inside, Richard sat in a high-backed chair, his desk empty except for a neat stack of papers on one corner and a month-at-a-glance calendar in the center. A matching credenza against the back wall held a computer and several pictures of an attractive woman, presumably Mrs. Watson. In front of the desk were two comfortable-looking visitor chairs.

Richard Watson looked every bit the part of a bank vice president. A silk tie complemented his expensive suit. When he came around the desk to shake their hands, the shine on his black shoes spoke of one who appreciated good clothing and took care of it. He might have just stepped off the cover of *GQ*.

"Good afternoon, gentlemen," Richard said. "We haven't officially met, but I recognize you from church last Sunday. Have a seat. Louise, would you close the door, please?"

Conner sat in one of the chairs facing the desk, and Dennis took the other. He pulled a small notebook and pen out of his pocket, ready to record any pertinent information the interview revealed.

"Now, what can I do for you?"

Conner sat with his elbows resting on the arms of the chair, his fingers steepled before him. "We're investigating the murder of Mrs. Alice Farmer."

Richard shook his head, his lips drawn into a sad frown. "The news has rocked our church, I can tell you. It's hard to believe anyone would harm her."

The sympathetic smile—the one that said *I'm your friend, you can tell me everything*—appeared on Conner's face. "We actually received a tip that we need to check out with you."

"Me?" Richard's eyebrows rose.

"Yes. You see, we've been made aware of a possible, shall we say, extramarital relationship that could have a bearing on this case."

Dennis watched closely. The surprise that leaped into the man's face could not be faked. Jackie must be right about the affair.

"You must be joking. Me? Having an affair?" He sat back in his chair and gave a low laugh. "That is ridiculous."

Conner spread his hands. "Nevertheless, we do need to follow up on every lead. I'm sure you understand."

"Of course. But tell me, who am I supposed to be having an affair with?"

Conner's expression did not change, but Dennis felt his intensity increase as he focused on Richard's face. "A member of your church and an employee here at the bank. Mrs. Kathy Dorsey."

Richard threw his head back against the high backrest and laughed out loud. "You've got to be kidding! Where in the world did you hear that?"

Conner's smile tightened. "From someone who saw you going into her house Wednesday night."

At that, Richard sobered. He leaned forward and looked Conner directly in the eye. Dennis watched for any sign of dishonesty, any hint of guilt. Maybe he wasn't having an affair, but if he was stealing from the bank, surely something would show in his face.

"Kathy is having some trouble here at the office. She's been put on probation for mistakes at her window. I know she is upset about it. As the sole supporter of her two boys, she can't afford to lose her job." He took a breath, and then continued. "I did go by her house, to let her know I am willing to help any way I can. I intended to talk to her at church that night, but was tied up here at the bank and didn't make the Wednesday night Bible study. I was there not more than fifteen minutes." His lips twitched. "Hardly time for an extramarital fling, especially with her boys running around."

Richard swiveled his chair and picked up a picture from the credenza. He held it toward Conner and Dennis. "Do you see this woman? She is the sweetest, most loving wife a man could ever have. I would never do anything to hurt her."

Dennis shifted in the comfortable chair. Now would have been the perfect time to bring up Richard's comment about Mrs. Farmer's accusations dying with her. Conner would be irritated when Dennis told him later. They'd have to pay Richard another visit.

Conner's fingers tapped against one another. "Did you like the victim, Mr. Watson?"

"Mrs. Farmer?" Richard shrugged and placed the picture on the edge of his desk. "Not particularly. She was a sour woman, always finding fault with people. I didn't dislike her, either. Certainly not enough to murder her, if that's what you're asking."

Dennis detected nothing in Richard's manner to make him doubt the truth of the man's statement. He did not flinch, nor did he flush. He held his gaze steady, and that wasn't easy to do while being examined by the best detective in the state.

"Do you have a computer at home, Mr. Watson?"

An abrupt switch to a new topic. Dennis recognized this tactic, used to throw the subject off balance. Richard's expression did not change.

"No, I don't." He nodded toward the one on his credenza. "I use this one for business, and the occasional personal e-mail. It's a notebook, so I can take it home if I need to."

"Would you mind if we take a look?"

Richard shook his head. "I'm sorry. I have access to confidential bank records. I can't let you use my computer without a search warrant."

"We'll get one if we need it. Of course that means we'll return with a sheriff to serve it." Conner smiled. "Sheriff's deputies aren't exactly quiet when it comes to delivering warrants, you know."

For the first time Richard's expression changed. An angry red flooded his cheeks. "What do you want to see on my computer?"

Conner's shoulders twitched upward. "Just your Internet history."

"If you're looking for porn sites, I'm not into that. Anyway, we have a filter here that prevents us from accessing sites like that."

"Does it block you from Web sites on poisonous mushrooms?"

His lips a tight line, Richard glared across the desk. "Fine. Check it right now, with me watching."

At Conner's nod, Dennis set down his notebook and rounded the desk. Richard swiveled his chair around to watch as Dennis opened Internet Explorer and displayed the history list. The guy obviously didn't do a lot of surfing. The list only showed about two dozen sites, mostly financial Web sites and news, like *USA Today*. Nothing that looked like a site on mushrooms. Dennis clicked over to the Options window, then turned to look at the detective.

"It's set to keep history for seven days."

Conner gave a humorless smile. "Inconclusive, then."

Richard's face remained impassive. Dennis closed the window and returned to his seat as Conner resumed his questioning.

"Do you mind telling me where you were from noon on May sixth until five-thirty in the afternoon on May seventh?"

If the detective hoped to rattle Richard's composure by bouncing from topic to topic, it didn't seem to be working. "As you well know, that was the day of the church picnic. We left there around, oh, I'd say one or one-thirty. I took my wife home, changed clothes and came to the office."

Conner's eyebrows rose. "On Sunday?"

"I am a vice president," Richard reminded him. "I don't always have the privilege of keeping banker's hours. I had an extremely important investor's meeting the next day and needed to prepare for it. I didn't leave here until after ten o'clock Sunday night."

"Was anyone else here with you?"

Richard shook his head. "But if you need proof, I'm sure the bank's security cameras recorded my arrival and departure. In fact, when I got home, Laura had already turned on our home alarm for the night. You can probably get the records from our security service and see when I turned the alarm off to get in the door, and then back on just a few minutes later from the bedroom. I didn't turn it off until I left for work the next morning."

Dennis didn't need Conner's glance to tell him to write down that piece of information in his notebook.

"Who is your security service, sir?" Dennis asked.

"Sugarcreek. I'll call and tell them to give you whatever you need." He looked at the detective again. "I came straight to work, and arrived here around eight-thirty, as I always do. Any number of people saw me. I worked until well after five thirty that night." He leaned forward. "All I ask is that you be discreet as you verify my statement. I'm an officer in this bank, and any hint of a scandal will be picked up by the media. I don't want my wife upset by this ridiculous accusation."

"Of course," Conner assured him, and then rose.

Dennis got to his feet, as well, pocketing his notebook and pen.

Richard stood but remained behind the desk. "I have an early committee meeting with the Kentucky Bankers Association in Paducah tomorrow, and I planned to drive down this evening to spend the night. Leaving town is acceptable, I assume?"

Tight lines around the edges of his lips were the only signs of the man's anger at having to ask permission to leave town.

Conner shrugged and then gave a single nod. "We'll be in touch," he said as he opened the door.

Even to Dennis, it sounded like a threat.

SIXTEEN

Jackie woke to the tickle of a deeply contented purr vibrating her left ear. Without opening her eyes, she reached up to stroke Linus's soft fur.

"Good morning, fur ball," she mumbled.

The purr increased, and Jackie let a sleepy smile steal across her face. If a more pleasant way to wake up in the morning existed, she didn't know about it.

Then she opened an eye and glanced at the clock. Five forty-seven.

"Ugh!"

She snatched up the extra pillow and pulled it over her face, which sent Linus scurrying away. No fair. Saturdays were supposed to be for sleeping in! Her last morning to sleep late before returning to work on Monday, and that pest had woken her up before six o'clock in the morning?

For a moment she thought she might drift back to sleep, but then she remembered yesterday. Kathy's sobs. Margaret's injured stare. With a sigh she sat up.

"Might as well get moving. Thanks, you rat."

She tossed the pillow at Linus, who leaped out of its way and gave her a reproachful look before sashaying out of the room, his tail held high.

Jackie stumbled into the kitchen to turn the coffeepot on before heading for the bathroom. By the time she emerged from her shower, feeling much more alert, the rich smell of freshly brewed coffee permeated the apartment. She slipped on a pair of jeans and a T-shirt, then poured a mugful and took it into the living room, her hair still wrapped in a towel. Sinking onto a corner of the couch, she turned on the television.

"…where a late-night accident has left a teenager in critical condition. Mike?"

The picture switched to a shot of a television reporter standing in front of Central Baptist Hospital in Lexington, a microphone clutched in his hand.

"That's right, Carl. Late last night, a Versailles teenager was struck by a hit-and-run driver a little past midnight. Fifteen-year-old Samantha Leigh Carlson was airlifted—"

"What?" Jackie sat straight up, slopping coffee into her lap. She barely noticed the hot liquid. A growing horror spread through her as the reporter continued.

"—intensive care with multiple internal injuries. A spokesman for the Woodford County Sheriff's Department said a few moments ago that the driver of the car that struck the teenager has not yet been apprehended. Samantha's condition remains critical. We'll keep you informed as updates are given, Carl."

The television picture returned to the newsroom. Her fingers nearly numb with shock, Jackie pressed the mute button. Samantha Carlson in critical condition? Her mother must be frantic. Jackie shook her head to dispel the memory of Sharon's face peeking at her over the cubicle wall. And what about Samantha's grandfather, the choir director?

Jackie scrambled off the couch and dashed to the

phone. The clock read a little before six-thirty, but so what? Pastor Palmer and Margaret needed to know what was going on.

There was no answer. Jackie hung up without leaving a message. They were probably at the hospital already. And Jackie wanted to go, too. Maybe she could help with... well, something.

Midway down the hallway to finish dressing, she stopped. Sharon would probably not appreciate her showing up at the hospital.

Seized by indecision, she returned to the living room and dropped onto the couch. What should she do? She still owed Sharon an apology, but now probably wouldn't be the best time to deliver it. Plus, the Carlsons were high on the police list of murder suspects, according to Dennis.

But would this development change that? Could this be related to the murder case?

A knock at the door interrupted her troubled thoughts. For a moment, Jackie sat frozen on the couch. No one would show up at her apartment so early in the morning, unless...

She dashed across the room to the peephole. Sure enough, Detective Conner's smug smile filled the lens.

This could not be good. What in the world did that nasty man want this time? Was it something to do with Samantha's accident?

With a deep breath to clear her mind, Jackie opened the door. Two uniformed police officers stood in the breezeway behind Detective Conner. One, a stranger, wore a brown uniform. His badge labeled him as L. Byers. The other hung back, avoiding her eyes. Dennis.

"Good morning, Miss Hoffner," the detective said. "May we come in?"

Suddenly conscious of her towel-wrapped hair, Jackie hesitated.

"That depends. What are you doing here at six-thirty in the morning?"

The detective's smile deepened. "We have some questions related to an accident that occurred last night."

She gripped the edge of the door. "I saw it on television. Do you know what happened? Is Samantha going to be all right?"

Byers stepped forward. "May we come in, ma'am? I need to ask you some questions."

Detective Conner's face went blank, giving Jackie the impression he wasn't happy to have someone else speak in his presence. A quick inspection of Byers's uniform told her he was with the Woodford County Sheriff's Department. Not the state police, then, like Dennis and Conner.

Jackie stepped back and gestured for the men to enter her apartment. Without being invited, Conner led his entourage to the dinette table and stood behind the same chair he'd occupied his last time here. Dennis and Byers also selected chairs, but did not sit until she closed the front door and gestured for them to be seated.

Dennis busied himself with his little notebook. Was he avoiding her eyes? Of course, she probably looked awful in her grubby T-shirt and no makeup. Margaret would be horrified. Should she excuse herself to at least take the towel off her head? A look at the serious expression on the men's faces gave her the answer. She sat in the fourth chair, towel and all. At least she had put on clothes instead of a bathrobe.

Byers spoke first, his eyes holding Jackie's across the table. "Miss Hoffner, where were you last night?"

Conner's lips tightened. Clearly, he was unaccustomed to someone else asking the questions. But why were they questioning her? Jackie glanced at Dennis, whose eyes remained on his notebook, his expression grim.

"I was here," she answered. "All night."

"Can anyone verify that?" Conner asked.

Jackie cast an irritated glance his way. "Just my cat. I live alone, Detective."

Byers spoke up. "Neighbors? Friends? Did you talk to anyone on the phone?"

She did not look at Dennis. "Around noon, but not after that. I did walk down to the park at two o'clock, but I was back by three. I doubt if any of my neighbors saw me, though. Most of them work during the day."

"You didn't take your car?"

"No." Jackie turned her head to look at Detective Conner. "What's this about? You don't think I had anything to do with Samantha's accident, do you?"

"Miss Hoffner." Byers forced her to look back at him. "We believe we have found the car that struck Miss Carlson sometime after midnight last night. It is a gray Toyota, and it is registered to you."

Jackie reeled. "But…but…that's impossible!"

She leaped from the table and ran across the living room to jerk the curtains away from the sliding-glass patio doors. Her numbered space in the parking lot was right outside her balcony.

The Toyota was not there. Instead, it was parked two slots away. And it was surrounded by police officers.

"Someone moved it," she said, whirling back to face the men. "Honest. That's not my parking place."

Jackie would have given anything to see a smile from

any of the three. Even Conner's fake friendly smile would be welcome. But no one smiled.

"When did you last see your car in your parking space, Miss Hoffner?" Conner asked.

"Uh, let me think."

Fog clouded her mind. She couldn't remember. Had it been there when she returned from her walk? Yes. She was almost certain of it.

"It was there around three o'clock. Maybe one of my neighbors saw it when they came home from work last night. I don't know the guy who parks in the one it's in now, but he lives in twenty-three D. He or someone else would certainly notice, because we each have our own space."

Conner nodded. "We'll ask them."

"In the meantime," Byers said, standing, "I'm going to have to ask you to come down to the station."

The blood left Jackie's face. She felt faint. "The station?"

She cast a desperate look at Dennis. She detected a hint of compassion in his expression, but he remained mute. At least he had the grace to look awkward.

Instead, comfort came from an unexpected source. Conner stood and crossed the room to stand in front of her. He did not smile, but his eyes held a measure of reassurance as he looked down into hers.

"You are not being charged with a crime, Miss Hoffner. We simply need your statement. You'll be there an hour or two at the most."

Fighting to breathe past a sudden painful lump in her throat, she nodded. "Can I comb my hair and get some shoes on?"

"Of course. Take as long as you like. We'll wait."

Jackie managed to contain her tears until she closed the bedroom door behind her.

* * *

Dennis felt like a heel. The look on Jackie's face when Byers opened the door to put her in the rear seat of his cruiser would haunt him for days. Like she was being led to the gas chamber. He could see the back of her damp head through the rear window now as he rolled to a stop behind Byers at a traffic light.

He'd felt the oddest sensation in her apartment, as if he should come to her rescue or something. But what could he do? He wasn't there as her friend. As a state trooper assigned to an investigation, his job was to take notes, period, no matter what he thought personally about the suspect.

And he held a definite opinion about Jackie as a suspect. No way had she run that girl down last night. He would stake his career on that. But facts couldn't be denied. A witness had seen a gray Toyota speeding away from the scene. Byers had notified the state police when he discovered the teenager was a member of the same church as their murder victim, and Conner tipped him that Jackie drove a car matching that description. Sure enough, blood had been found on the bumper of her car. The girl's blood, presumably.

No, Jackie was not a murderer. But she was somehow entangled in whatever was going on with the members of that church. First the murderer had used her casserole to administer poisonous mushrooms, and then he or she used her car to run down a teenager.

He looked at Conner in the passenger seat. The detective would be furious when he discovered where some of his tips came from. It had seemed like a good idea at the time, and not a big deal to just listen to information Jackie so obviously wanted to pass along. But now he wasn't so sure.

Better to confess than have Conner discover it from someone else.

"I need to tell you something." Conner turned his head. "That tip about Richard Watson having an affair? It came from Miss Hoffner. And the stuff I told you yesterday, about Mrs. Farmer suspecting him of embezzlement—that came from her, too."

The detective closed his eyes. "I was afraid of that. Not smart, Walsh. Not smart at all."

Dennis flinched. "But Mrs. Dorsey verified the second part when we talked to her last night. So that turned out to be true at least."

Conner opened his eyes. "Have you given Hoffner any information in return?"

The traffic light changed, and Dennis accelerated, glad for an excuse to look away from the detective's piercing glance.

"I told her about the toxicology report. But," he added defensively, "that's a matter of public record. And you have to admit, she's provided a couple of important leads, with the victim's letter-writing habit and the embezzlement suspicion. A good detective should cultivate all kinds of sources, shouldn't he?"

Conner remained silent for the rest of the trip, leaving Dennis to wonder if he would be removed from the case.

They followed Byers's cruiser into the parking lot outside the sheriff's office. When Dennis put the car in Park and turned off the engine, Conner made no move to open the door. An uncomfortable silence stretched between them.

Finally, the detective turned in his seat. "Yeah, a detective needs sources. But this girl is smack dab in the middle of a dangerous situation. I mean, she's marinating in it."

"I don't think she's guilty of anything," Dennis argued, but Conner held up a hand.

"I'm inclined to agree with you. But either someone has it out for her, or she is the most convenient dupe I've ever run into. Either way, it is entirely inappropriate for you to talk to her about the case."

"But she's a source. If she can give us—"

"You don't understand my point. It's not only inappropriate, Walsh, it could be dangerous for her. Have you thought of that? This killer is obviously someone she knows. When he decides he hasn't been successful in framing her, he might come after her. The less she knows, the less danger she poses."

Alarm shot through Dennis. He'd been so focused on trying to solve the case, and, actually, on enjoying Jackie's gung-ho enthusiasm in trying to weasel information from a bunch of old church ladies, he'd never considered that she might really be in danger. But this latest development—someone taking her car to run down a kid... That put a whole new spotlight on Jackie's position in this case.

She lived alone in that apartment with a cat and nobody to protect her. What if...

He rounded in his seat. "Should we assign her a twenty-four-hour guard? I can do that, sir. I'll be happy to protect her."

Conner's eyes narrowed, the shadow of a smile playing around his mouth. "I don't think we need to go that far, but we do need to keep an eye on her. And we need to make sure she stays out of this investigation." He caught Dennis with a meaningful glance. "You seem to be in a pretty good position to do that."

Was Conner saying his relationship with Jackie had crossed the line from professional to personal? She sure was on his mind a lot lately. But even if he admitted to himself that he found her attractive, he could still keep things at a professional distance.

He met the detective's eye and nodded. "I'll try, sir."

"Just remember what I said, Walsh." Conner reached for the door handle. "NBT. Trouble can take a man unawares."

Dennis ignored the implication and followed Conner out of the car, hurrying to catch up with Byers as he led Jackie inside with a hand on her elbow. Relief that he didn't have to stop talking to Jackie kept Dennis's step light. The thought of Jackie in danger was frightening, but whoever was behind these terrible crimes would have to get past him first.

SEVENTEEN

Jackie heaved a sigh of relief when she walked out the doors of the sheriff's office into the bright spring sunshine. The past two hours had been the most frustrating of her life. First they'd put her in a room more sterile than a hospital, and then left her sitting alone for forty minutes. When Byers and Conner finally showed up, they asked the same questions she had already answered at home. Over and over again, as if they were trying to trip her up.

The shock of having her car stolen and used to run over Samantha Carlson was starting to wear off. Instead, she boiled with anger and humiliation. The police were treating her like a criminal, as if they considered her capable of committing such a terrible act. To make matters worse, did they really think her stupid enough to drive her car home and leave it in the parking lot without even bothering to wash the blood off the bumper?

Jackie stood at the edge of the sidewalk, uncertain what to do. Her car had been impounded as evidence and no one could give her an idea of how long before she got it back. She should make some phone calls to find a rental for a few days. On Monday morning, she'd need a car to drive to work.

Behind her, the door to the sheriff's building opened.

When she saw Dennis striding down the sidewalk toward her, she took off down the street at a fast walk.

"Jackie, wait up. I'll give you a ride."

She increased her pace. Dennis was the last person she wanted to talk to right now.

"Hey, slow down a minute." He jogged up beside her and reached out to tug at her elbow.

Whirling, she jerked her arm out of his grip and allowed every ounce of fury she had suppressed over the past two hours to show in her eyes.

He took a step backward. "Whoa, what's got you so riled up?"

"Oh, not much," she spat. "I always enjoy spending Saturday morning being fed to the wolves by someone I trust."

"What are you talking about? I didn't feed you to the wolves."

"Well, you certainly didn't come to my rescue, either."

He folded his arms across his chest. "And what was I supposed to do? Provide an alibi for you? Tell them you were with me last night? I'm not going to lie for you or anyone else."

"I didn't ask you to lie, but you could have said something in my defense. Like you don't think I ran over Samantha Carlson."

"I did say that. I said it to both Byers and Conner when they called me early this morning, and again to Conner when we left your place."

She sniffed. "Well, you didn't say it in front of me." Tears pricked her eyes, and she blinked them back. "You just sat there like a statue and let them rake me over the coals."

"Believe me, they did not rake you over the coals. In

fact, they went pretty easy on you, considering your car ran somebody over last night." His voice softened. "Look, Jackie, nobody thinks you hurt that girl. But under the circumstances, those questions had to be asked. Surely you understand that."

Jackie looked away. What did she want from him? An apology? For what? For doing his job? Or for not jumping to her defense like…like a boyfriend would.

"Come on, get in the car."

She sniffed again. "I don't think so. I'll just walk home."

"It's almost five miles to your apartment. Those don't exactly look like comfortable walking shoes."

Her toes peeked from the sandals she had slipped on this morning. He was right about that. Her feet would be blistered by the time she got home. But when she looked up into his eyes, she caught a glimpse of amusement in those gray depths. Did he think this was funny? How dare he laugh at her!

"I'll manage, thank you."

She walked away, her head held high. Behind her, he heaved a sigh.

"Have it your way, then."

Proud of herself for her show of independence, Jackie marched down the street without looking back, even when she heard his footsteps receding in the opposite direction. As she walked, her anger simmered. No, of course she hadn't expected him to lie for her, but would it have been so hard to give one little smile of encouragement while his police buddies hounded her?

Obviously, Margaret was wrong. Dennis Walsh did not have any feelings for her. Well, that was just fine with her.

A traitorous tear slipped down her cheek as she walked in search of a pay phone to call a taxi.

At three o'clock that afternoon, Jackie got out of a taxicab under the awning at the Lexington airport. She leaned in the window to pay her second cab fare of the day, this one significantly higher than the first. Could expenses like this be turned in to the sheriff's office, since they had her car? She just might try it.

The row of rental-car counters lined the wall facing the two baggage carousels. Jackie had never flown in her life, but the Lexington airport was small enough not to be intimidating. Five minutes later, she crossed the street to find her car in the rental lot.

Central Baptist Hospital was huge compared to the one in Versailles. Jackie stopped at the main building's reception desk for directions and then proceeded to Medical ICU on the fourth floor. When she stepped off the elevator, she found the waiting room on her left.

The place was packed. A television mounted high in one corner played CNN, the volume low. Standing in the entrance, Jackie took a moment to scan the people sitting in the chairs that lined the walls. She knew many of them from church.

"Jackie," said Vince Carlson, rising from his seat to cross the room and take her hand.

Vince looked terrible, as well he might with his granddaughter lying critically injured in ICU. Dark circles tugged at the sagging skin beneath his reddened eyes, and his shoulders stooped as though they carried a weight too heavy to bear.

"Mr. Carlson, I'm so sorry. If there's anything I can do…"

He shook his head. "Coming to show your support is enough. That, and prayer." He looked deeply into Jackie's eyes. "Prayer is what Samantha needs most right now."

Several other people came to stand beside them, forming a long-faced cluster of Heritage Community Church members. Pastor Palmer, Julie McCoy, Beverly Sanders, Mr. and Mrs. Pearson.

Pastor Palmer took Jackie's hand when Vince released it. "Jackie, it was so good of you to come. Margaret will be sorry she missed you. She went home a little while ago with Esther to get some rest."

After yesterday, Jackie very much doubted Margaret would be sorry to miss her. She looked into Pastor Palmer's kind face and saw that he knew what had transpired between them. His grip on her hand tightened, and he gave an encouraging nod. "She'll be glad to hear you came by."

"It's the least I can do, after…"

They all stared at her, waiting for her to finish. Had the police told them whose car hit Samantha? She scanned the room. If they'd told anyone, it would be Samantha's parents.

"Is Sharon here?"

Vince gestured down the hallway. "They only allow two visitors at a time in ICU for fifteen minutes every few hours. She and Nick have been back there almost that long now."

At that moment, a set of electronic doors a few yards down the corridor opened. Sharon and a man Jackie had never seen stepped through. Nick, Sharon's husband. His resemblance to his father was striking. He had an arm around Sharon's waist, and she leaned on him for support, a tissue covering her weeping eyes.

Vince rushed toward them. "Is she worse?"

"No, Pop, nothing like that." The younger man turned

a tired smile on his father. "Actually, it's good news. She's starting to regain consciousness."

"Praise the Lord," said Beverly, and the others nodded.

Sharon blotted at her eyes. "It's just so hard to see her lying there, all bandaged up like that."

Vince enfolded the blond woman in his arms and squeezed. "She's going to be fine. I know it. So many people are praying."

Sharon's response went unsaid, for at that moment she noticed Jackie standing with the others. Her lips twisted. "What is she doing here?"

Jackie wanted to slink away at the venom in her voice.

Vince turned to look at her with surprise, then spoke to Sharon. "She goes to our church. She's here to offer support."

She glared at Jackie. "Just what we need. Another do-gooder hanging around."

"Sharon," said Nick, his tone low. "Be nice."

"I don't have to be nice." A sob escaped her lips. "My baby is lying in that hospital room covered in bandages and tubes."

"That isn't Jackie's fault," Vince said with an awkward glance in her direction.

"Actually," Jackie said, gulping miserably, "it sort of might be."

Every head swiveled her way. She found she could not look at Vince's rounded eyes, nor the shock on Pastor Palmer's face. Aware that everyone was watching, she took a step toward Sharon.

"Have the police told you they found the car that hit Samantha?"

Nick shook his head, but Sharon held her gaze without moving. Jackie took a shuddering breath.

"It was mine."

Exclamations sounded from those in the room.

"What?"

"Oh, Jackie, no!"

"My word!"

Jackie saw question lines appear on Sharon's forehead.

"Go on," the other woman said.

Jackie swallowed. "The police showed up at my apartment this morning. They say a witness saw the car that hit Samantha, and it was a gray Toyota. That's what I drive. They looked at my car, and found…" She hesitated, afraid of what she would see in Sharon's eyes when she continued. "They found blood on the front bumper."

Beside her, Beverly and Julie gasped. Jackie rushed on, willing Sharon to believe her.

"The car had been moved during the night. Someone took it, but when they brought it back they parked in the wrong parking space." She took another step toward Sharon. "Please, you've got to believe me. I would never hurt Samantha, not for anything in the world."

"Of course we believe you," Vince said, coming to put an arm around her.

Nick looked from Jackie to his father to his wife, uncertainty etched on his face. Sharon, frozen, seemed to stare inside Jackie's soul. Jackie returned her stare and did not flinch.

Sharon's shoulders slumped. "Yeah, I believe you."

The onlookers expelled a collective sigh, and Jackie's head went light with relief. "Thank you."

Sharon glanced at Nick, then stepped toward Jackie. "Could we talk privately a minute?"

Startled, Jackie shot a look at Pastor Palmer and then nodded. "Sure."

"Let's take a walk."

Jackie fell into step beside the blonde. They entered the elevator, and the voices of the others pressing Nick for details on Samantha's condition died away.

Side by side, they watched the display change from four, to three, to two, and finally to one. Neither spoke. Jackie's thoughts whirled. What did Sharon want to talk about? Maybe she didn't really believe Jackie after all, but wanted to get her away from the other members of Heritage Community Church before blasting her. Jackie swallowed, her throat dry. If that was the case, then so be it. She would take it without a word. Maybe it would help Sharon to have someone to blame.

They walked out the hospital's front door, and Sharon stopped. She tilted her face toward the sun and inhaled.

"I haven't been outside all day."

Jackie looked around. Across the front parking lot was a small grassy area with a stone bench. "Want to sit over there?"

Sharon shrugged. "Sure."

They weaved between parked cars until they reached the bench, then sat side by side. Sharon remained silent for a moment while Jackie cast about in her mind for something to say.

Finally, Sharon turned and propped one foot up on the bench. "That took guts in there."

Jackie flushed. "It wasn't the easiest thing I've ever done," she admitted. "And especially after I was so…rude the other day. I'm sorry about that."

Sharon said, "Don't worry about it. If either of us was rude, it was probably me. I tend to get my feathers ruffled whenever people who call themselves Christians want to talk to me."

"You know, Sharon, not all Christians are like Mrs. Farmer." Jackie looked away. "Or me."

Sharon looked toward the windows on the fourth floor of the hospital. "Yeah, I'm beginning to see that."

She fell silent again. She didn't seem to want to talk. Maybe she really just wanted someone to walk outside with her. Then Jackie noticed a tear slide down Sharon's cheek, followed quickly by another one. She reached up to blot them away with the tissue she still held in one hand.

"You want to know why I'm sure what happened to Samantha isn't your fault?"

Jackie nodded.

"Because I'm afraid…" She drew a shuddering breath. "I'm afraid it's my fault."

Jackie's jaw dropped. Sharon nodded, miserable. "I take a lot of nighttime walks. Nicky works the night shift, and I have trouble sleeping. A walk helps calm me down." She hesitated. "And that's not all. I used to smoke something every so often to help me relax, and I didn't want to do it in the house where Samantha might catch me. So I'd take a walk."

"You smoke pot?" Jackie tried to filter the shock out of her voice.

"Not anymore," Sharon shot back quickly. "But the people I used to buy it from aren't exactly the nicest sort. They've harassed me on the phone a couple of times, wanting me to buy more weed from them. I guess they miss the income."

"So you think these people were trying to run you down and got Samantha by mistake?"

Sharon nodded and sniffed. "We do look a lot alike, especially from behind. And in the dark she could easily be mistaken for me."

Her blue eyes filled again, and a river of tears poured down her cheeks unhampered. "Oh, Jackie, I stand in that intensive-care room looking down at my baby in that bed, and I can't handle the thought that something I've done may have hurt her."

Jackie scooted across the bench and wrapped her arms around the sobbing woman, her mind trying to process this new information. How awful, to think your own sins had hurt the child you loved more than anything.

Could it be true? Could these drug dealers have been aiming for Sharon and hit Samantha by mistake?

No. That scenario didn't make sense. Why would drug dealers take Jackie's car? No, this crime had to be related to Mrs. Farmer's death.

On the other hand, Versailles was a small town. Maybe the drug dealers and the murderer were somehow connected. Maybe... Maybe they had a customer in Heritage Community Church. Maybe that customer was a teenager. What was Samantha doing out that late at night, anyway? Perhaps she, too, was mixed up with these people, and her mother didn't know it.

Jackie couldn't very well suggest to a grieving mother that her daughter took drugs. She squeezed Sharon's arm and forced her to look her in the eye. "I don't think you're responsible at all. How in the world would these people pick my car out of all the cars in town? It makes far more sense that Samantha's accident is somehow related to Mrs. Farmer's death."

"Unless they heard about your casserole and decided to make the two look related."

The hair on Jackie's arm prickled. Was she being watched by murderous drug dealers? What if Mrs. Farmer had somehow found out Samantha was using drugs and had threatened to expose those drug dealers? They might decide to get the old woman out of the way, and then eliminate the only person who could tie them to the murder—Samantha.

"Listen, Sharon, you've got to tell this to the police."

Sharon sobered. She pulled away and turned a frightened look on Jackie. "Do you really think so?"

"I think it's critical," she urged. "Please?"

A wave of relief washed over her when Sharon nodded.

EIGHTEEN

Heritage Community Church had always been such a friendly place. That was one reason Jackie joined the church several months after moving to Versailles—because she'd felt right at home from the very first visit. But today people avoided her. She actually saw Mrs. Murphy look her way and whisper intently in Mrs. Watkins's ear. Jackie sat through the service, staring straight ahead at Pastor Palmer in the pulpit without hearing a word he said.

When the last hymn had been sung and the last prayer prayed, Jackie slipped into the aisle intending to leave quietly.

"Jackie! Oh, Jackie, wait a minute."

Jackie stopped as Kathy rushed up to her. The young mom looked much better today, her cheeks rosy and her eyes clear. She put an arm around Jackie's shoulders and hugged.

"Thank you so much for calling the police for me," she said with a quick glance to make sure they were not overheard. "When they came by the house Friday night, they acted totally different. Like they actually believed me. I was so relieved, and I told them everything."

Jackie warmed at the unexpected kindness in Kathy's voice. "I'm glad to help. It was the least I could do after what I put you through."

Kathy brushed that aside with a gesture. "What's done is done. Now let's just hope they catch the person responsible." She glanced behind her to where the Watsons stood talking to the Andersons. "I'd better get downstairs and pick up the boys. See you later."

With a final squeeze, she ran off in the direction of the basement. Jackie watched Richard Watson for a moment. Could he really be a killer? He seemed so…so civilized. But what about—

She stopped herself. Nope. She was off the case. She refused to even think about it.

At least she hadn't totally messed up her budding friendship with Kathy. Her mood brighter, Jackie headed for the exit. She had not taken two steps before she heard her name again.

"Jackie, over here."

She turned to see Margaret waving at her from the other side of a group of people. She watched as Margaret made her way through the crowd. She didn't look upset anymore. When she grabbed Jackie's hand and squeezed, Jackie almost cried.

"I am so sorry about your car," Margaret said without preamble. "I know how upsetting that must have been for you. You were so brave to go to the hospital yesterday."

"Thank you. Any word on Samantha today?"

"Actually, yes." Margaret's smile widened. "Vince told us this morning that she is now fully conscious, and she might even be moved out of ICU as early as tomorrow."

"That's great." Jackie looked at her shoes. "Margaret, I hope you can forgive me for Friday. I feel terrible."

Margaret's voice was soft. "Jackie, it's fine. We all make mistakes. And friends forgive each other."

She looked up, hopeful. "Are we friends?"

Margaret followed her nod with a big hug. "Of course we are."

"Thank you, Margaret."

Jackie's step had a definite spring as she left the church and headed toward her rental car.

"Jackie Hoffner, hold your horses. Where's the fire?"

Esther barreled down the sidewalk toward her, her considerable bulk jiggling with every step.

"I'm not as fast as I used to be," the older woman confessed, puffing for breath as she came to a halt beside Jackie.

"How are you, Mrs. Hodges?"

"Esther, remember? I'm fine, honey, but I wanted to ask you that same question." She lowered her voice and leaned forward. "I heard about that car business. Terrible." She shook her head. "Just terrible."

Jackie nodded. "Someone does seem determined to get me in trouble."

"Of course, everybody's talking about it." Jackie must have looked as startled as she felt at that admission, because Esther shook her head. "Not about you, honey. They're all wondering who'll be next. I even heard some say it's not safe to go to this church anymore, but I say that's hogwash."

"I don't know," Jackie said, feeling miserable again. "Maybe it's just me that shouldn't come anymore. Then maybe everyone here would be safe."

Esther drew herself up. "Don't you think that even for a minute. The police will find out who planted those mushrooms and stole your car."

A thought sneaked into Jackie's head. Without a doubt, someone had stolen her car. But how? Her key was still on the ring with her apartment key and the police had told her the spare was still in place inside the gasoline door. Of course, someone who knew where it was could have used it and then put it back, but she'd assured the police that nobody knew where she hid that key. She'd never told a soul, except for…

That day at Shaker Village, Esther had lost her spare key. And Jackie had mentioned the location of her own. She'd forgotten about that.

No, it was impossible. Dennis and Detective Conner had already questioned Esther and apparently cleared her of suspicion.

But others had been at Shaker Village, too. Julie, who'd dished up leftovers after the potluck. Margaret, who… No. She wouldn't even consider that. Her mind returned to the list in her notebook beneath Esther Hodges's name. Her throat constricted.

Esther peered at her. "Are you all right, honey? You look sorta pale all of a sudden."

Jackie forced a smile. "I'm fine. I've just remembered I forgot to feed my cat this morning. I need to go, or he'll get back at me by tearing the sofa to shreds."

The older woman guffawed. "I had a cat like that once. You'd better get home and feed that animal, honey."

Jackie nodded and hurried toward her car. Yes, she was through snooping. She had removed herself from the case. But if she remembered relevant information she was duty-bound to turn it over to the police.

Wasn't she?

"Detective Conner, please," Jackie said into the telephone twenty minutes later.

Though Dennis's home number lay scrawled across the back of the card he'd given her, the memory of that hint of laughter in his gray eyes yesterday made her angry all over again. She would not call him at home on Sunday afternoon. Nor would she call Deputy Byers, especially when she remembered his insulting manner during the questioning. Instead, she'd fished Detective Conner's card out of her purse and called his office. At least he had thawed enough to give her a kind word.

Predictably, the man who answered the phone informed her, "He's not in today. Can I help you with something?"

"Uh, no thanks. Does he have voice mail?"

"Sure does. Hang on, I'll put you through."

A moment later the detective's pleasant voice requested that Jackie leave a message, which he would return as soon as possible. *Beep.*

"Hi, this is Jackie Hoffner. I thought of something I didn't mention yesterday. I keep a spare key inside the gasoline door, in one of those box thingies. Several people knew about it, because I told them at lunch last week when Esther Hodges locked her keys in her car. Uh, that's all. Goodbye."

Her hand rested for a moment on the receiver after she replaced it. There. Her duty was done. Now she could forget about it.

A sense of failure nagged at her as she paged through a magazine, bored. An entire week's vacation time, wasted. She had nothing to show for it. The guys at work would want to know what she'd spent her week doing, and what would she say? Going to lunch. Talking to old ladies. Being questioned by the police.

It had all started with poisonous mushrooms in her casserole. The funny thing was she didn't even know what poisonous mushrooms looked like. Did they look like the regular kind?

She could search references to mushrooms, of course. But the thought of a frustrating session with her ancient computer and dial-up modem didn't sound appealing. Besides, she wanted to get a look at the real thing in person. If the mushrooms came from the woods behind Mrs. Farmer's house, there would be more. And the weather today was gorgeous, a perfect day for a walk.

She tossed the magazine aside and went to the bedroom to change into her sneakers. Linus watched from his perch on the pillow.

"It's not snooping," Jackie told the cat with a twinge of guilt. "I'm not prying into anybody's business or making anyone angry. I'm just going for a walk."

Linus did not look convinced. But what did he know?

As the rental car approached the turnoff to Mrs. Farmer's street, Jackie made a snap decision. The killer certainly wouldn't have parked in Mrs. Farmer's driveway, for fear of his car being spotted by a neighbor. He'd probably come through the wooded area behind the house. The next road lay not more than fifty yards past Mrs. Farmer's. Jackie turned there instead.

A few houses were scattered on both sides of the street the first half mile or so, followed by an empty field on the left and a wooded area on the right. Jackie drove around several twists and curves, trying to decide how far down the road Mrs. Farmer's house lay. When she figured she had driven an appropriate distance, she slowed the car and rolled off the pavement. A wide swath of grass lay between the asphalt and the first line of trees. The worn condition of the turf told of frequent use. People must park their cars here fairly often.

She got out and turned in a circle to examine the landscape. No houses in sight. No witnesses if someone pulled their car off the road for a stroll. In fact, the wood was sparse for about fifty feet or so. It wouldn't be difficult to park a car inside the cover of trees. A dark car at night would be hard to spot.

A canopy of leaves stretched overhead. The bright afternoon sun filtered through to cast green-tinted fingers of light onto the ground cover. The trunks were far enough apart to make walking between them easy, though Jackie did have to climb over the occasional dead log.

In a short time she came to the edge of the wood and peered into the backyard of an unfamiliar house. Not Mrs. Farmer's, but which way should she go? Taking a guess based on instinct, she turned left and followed the tree line past several yards.

Bingo. Not five minutes later she came upon the familiar-looking thicket of scrub bushes and unkempt trees that marked the border to Mrs. Farmer's yard. Though she had only seen the backyard through the kitchen window, she recognized the garbage cans on their rickety metal cart beside the concrete porch. This was the place.

Jackie turned her back on the yard. Wild mushrooms grew somewhere around here, she was sure of it. She paced slowly away from the house, heading into the trees, her gaze sweeping the ground.

Not twenty feet away from the tree line, a patch of white at the base of a nearby tree caught her eye. Mushrooms! She stooped to examine them. They had long stems and smooth white caps. Were these the agents of Mrs. Farmer's death?

When she stood, she caught sight of another cluster of mushrooms nearby. Those were also white, but bumpy.

And there were some fungus-looking things that weren't shaped at all like normal mushrooms, large brownish objects like flattened tulip bulbs poking up through a thick layer of dead leaves about ten feet away.

So many mushrooms! Jackie shook her head. How in the world had the killer known which ones were poisonous?

Research, obviously. You could find anything on the Internet. Or in books, if you didn't have a computer. And where could you find books *and* computers with reliable high-speed connections to the Internet? The library, of course.

The Woodford County Library on Main Street stayed open on Sunday until five o'clock. Jackie frequented the place. For a small-town library, the shelves held a surprisingly wide selection of exactly the sort of mystery novels she loved to read. She glanced at her watch. Three-ten. Plenty of time.

"Dennis, just a minute. I want you to meet someone."

Stepping through the church doorway and into the bright sunshine, Dennis looked down at his mother's two-handed grip on his right arm. Uh-oh. He recognized that determined look on her face. Maybe he could shake her loose and make a run for it.

"Mom," he warned, "I don't have time. I need to get back—"

"Nonsense." Mom scanned the crowd of churchgoers ahead of them on the sidewalk. "It'll only take a minute, and I've told her all about you. She'll be disappointed if you run off without saying hello."

He threw a desperate glance toward Dad, who shrugged a shoulder and jingled the change in his pants pocket. Great. The old man would be no help at all.

"There she is." Mom raised a hand and waved above her head. "Kelly Jean! Oh, Kelly Jean, over here."

A dozen heads turned their way. "Mom, do you have to be so loud?"

Ignoring his comment, Mom brushed a speck off his shirt as she gave him a quick inspection. "Here she comes. Now just keep an open mind, that's all I ask."

He swallowed a sigh as he was dragged forward on the sidewalk. A young woman strode toward them, fighting against the flow of traffic. Blond hair, trim figure, shy smile. She was okay-looking. Not pretty, but not ugly, either. She stopped several feet away, giving him a nervous look.

"Kelly Jean," Mom said, dropping Dennis's arm to latch on to the young woman and pull her closer, "I'd like you to meet my son, the police officer."

Dennis plastered a smile on his face and held out a hand. "Dennis Walsh. Nice to meet you."

She clasped his hand limply for a moment, then pulled hers away as though he'd burned her. "Nice to meet you, too," she mumbled, head down.

Mom's smile widened, as though trying to make up for the girl's lack of enthusiasm. "Kelly Jean is new to town. She works for the newspaper as a marketing analyst."

Dennis ducked his head, trying to catch the girl's eye. "That sounds interesting. What does a marketing analyst do?"

"Oh, you know." The girl risked a quick look up at him and then focused on the church's front lawn. "Marketing."

"I see." He glanced toward Mom, whose smile had begun to wilt. Behind her, Dad appeared to be having trouble hiding a grin.

Mom said to the Kelly Jean, "Dennis has a very important job with the state police. He's investigating a murder case."

Obviously murder investigations weren't high on Kelly Jean's list of things to be impressed about. She gave a slight nod but didn't comment.

Time to cut this interview short.

"Speaking of my investigation," Dennis said, "I've got to get going. Lots to do, you know. It was nice to meet you, Kelly Jean."

"You, too." She risked another quick smile in his direction. Dennis got the impression she was relieved to have the awkward introduction over. Not as relieved as he was.

Deep furrows appeared between Mom's eyebrows, but he ignored them and stepped forward to place a kiss on her cheek. "I'll call you tomorrow."

He headed toward his car as a huge rush of relief washed over him. What had his mother been thinking? That girl was so shy she couldn't even look at him. Not his type at all. He preferred a woman with a little spunk. Someone like—

Dennis shook his head. What was the matter with him? Jackie Hoffner was not his type at all. She was far too bullheaded.

"That was a close call," Dad said, falling in beside him. "Your mother was planning to invite you both to lunch. You got out just in time." His chest vibrated with a chuckle.

"I was afraid something like that was about to happen."

"Might still." Startled, Dennis cast a quick look at his dad, who shrugged. "When your mother gets her mind set on something, you have to pull her off it with a winch."

"Yet you've managed to live with her all these years," Dennis said, his thoughts whirling. Why had he never noticed how…determined Mom was? Dad was right. If she wanted to do something, she didn't let anything stand in her way. She'd always been that way.

Dad shrugged. "She keeps life interesting. Never a dull moment."

His smile said it all. That was the look Dennis had seen all through his boyhood, one that proclaimed, "This is real. This lasts. I love this woman."

Even if she was bullheaded.

"Hello, Jackie." Lucy McKinley, seated behind the library's front desk, looked at her over the top of a pair of half glasses. "Haven't seen you in a while."

"Yeah, I've been busy the past week or so," Jackie said with a smile of greeting.

"We got some new books in a few days ago, and there are a couple I think you'll like on the New Arrivals shelf."

"Great, thanks."

Jackie went to the row of computers and opened the on-line catalog. She typed in the word *mushroom* and clicked the search button. The computer returned a list of five titles. Three were fiction, but the last on the list looked like exactly what she needed: *The Mushroom Identifier, an Illustrated Encyclopedia*. The status was listed as available. A stack of scrap paper and a short pencil lay beside the computer, and Jackie jotted down the call number.

She made her way through the 500 aisle, scanning the numbers until she came to the right place. The book was not there. A quick search of the surrounding shelves turned up nothing.

Her pulse picked up speed as her mind ticked through reasons the book might be missing. Maybe Lucy or one of the other librarians had shelved it in the wrong place. Or maybe the computer was wrong, and someone had checked it out. But who?

She stopped. The murderer, that's who. More than likely, he'd just taken it. Of course, a killer wouldn't want a record of his research on file at the public library.

Her jog up to the front desk drew curious stares from a couple of patrons. She ignored them.

"Lucy, can you check something for me?"

Lucy looked up from her book. "Sure. What is it?"

"This." Jackie slid the paper across the desk. "The computer says it's available but I can't find it."

"Well, let's see." Bright pink fingernails flew across the keyboard. Lucy's brow puckered. "Mushrooms, huh? The police called earlier in the week to ask about books on mushrooms. I checked the catalog then and told the officer this book was available. It should be there. Are you sure it isn't?"

"I'm sure." Jackie tried to sound casual. "Maybe someone has it. Can you see the last time it was checked out?"

Lucy's mouse clicked. "That book hasn't been checked out in over five years, nor have any other books about mushrooms. I told the police that, too." Her brow creased. "I don't understand. The book should be on the shelf."

"Has someone asked for it recently? Maybe they walked out with it by accident."

"No." Lucy shook her head. "I don't remember anyone asking about mushrooms except that police officer. It has to be there. I'm sure you just missed it."

She rose, and Jackie followed her back to the 500 aisle where they both conducted a thorough search.

The mushroom encyclopedia was nowhere to be found.

The moment she got home, Jackie ran for the phone. Her fingers shook as she punched in Dennis's number. This information was too important to leave on voice mail.

"Hello, Hoffner J," he said when he picked up the phone on the third ring. "What are you up to this beautiful Sunday afternoon?"

It always threw Jackie when someone knew her name before she identified herself. She did not have caller ID, but everyone else in the world seemed to.

"You're not going to believe what I found out," she blurted.

She told him about her trek through the woods and her visit to the library.

"You went wandering in those woods alone?" Dennis sounded angry. "That was stupid, Jackie."

Sudden heat made her go damp under the collar of her T-shirt. "Did you just call me stupid?"

He ignored her question. "What were you thinking? There's a killer running around town, and apparently he knows you because he's trying to frame you for his crimes. You know he's familiar with those woods. What if he followed you? He could make short work of you back there without a single witness."

Fuming, Jackie drew herself up. "Well, excuse me, Trooper Walsh. I thought you might be interested in what I found."

"So a book's missing. So what? Unless someone saw who stole it, that doesn't do us any good."

Did she have to spell it out for him? "You could search people's houses. If you find the book, you'll have proof."

"And whose house would you suggest we search?"

"Esther Hodges," Jackie shot back. She told him about the message she'd left earlier for Detective Conner. Dennis did not sound impressed.

"That woman is not a killer anymore than you are. And

besides, that's a really common place to hide a spare key. Anyone could have found it there."

She twisted a stray lock of hair. Was it? She thought she'd been clever to think of it. "Then what about searching Richard's house?"

"For your information, your friend Richard Watson has an airtight alibi for both crimes. His and the bank's security records verify his claim that he worked late and went straight home the night the mushrooms were planted. And he registered at a hotel in Paducah Friday night."

Jackie chewed furiously on a nail. "Maybe he checked into the hotel and then came back here. Or maybe someone checked in for him, did you think of that?"

"Actually—" Dennis's voice sounded condescending "—we did. We faxed a photo for the desk clerk to verify. Mr. Watson checked in late, at ten-thirty Friday night. And it's a four-hour drive from Versailles to Paducah. There was no time for him to get back here. Besides, the clerk on duty said no one could get in or out of the hotel in the middle of the night without being seen." He paused. "We know how to do our jobs, Jackie. We don't need a civilian to tell us how to search for clues. You need to just back away from this and leave the investigating to us."

His tone sent shivers of anger down her spine. So patronizing, so…paternal. Apparently, he had been taking lessons from Detective Conner in how to make people feel insignificant.

"I see. Well, I'm sorry to have bothered you. Goodbye."

"Jack—"

She slammed the phone down. If that's the way he wanted to be, fine. Jackie didn't need him. That was the last time she would call Dennis Walsh for anything. Ever.

NINETEEN

Dennis stared at the telephone in his hand, his stomach churning. The conversation hadn't gone the way he hoped. That girl was infuriating! Here he was, halfway considering asking Jackie out on a date after this case was over, and what did she do? She pushed her nose in even further.

Her discovery of the missing library book was a development, no doubt about it. But it would only encourage her to continue meddling. Conner's warning echoed in his mind. Nothing But Trouble. A more apt description of Jackie could not be found. That girl seemed determined to find a new method of throwing herself in harm's way every day.

Still, he shouldn't have called her trip to the woods stupid. Bad word choice. He didn't blame her for being upset. He pressed the talk button, then let his finger hover over the numbers before finally hanging up again. In five minutes he needed to leave the house, and a conversation to appease an angry Jackie would take more time than he could spare. He'd have to call her tomorrow. Maybe she would have calmed down by then.

He went to the bedroom to finish dressing. His Kevlar vest was standard police issue, and he hated wearing the thing. But the instructors who had taught his police academy class harped on the importance of wearing some form of protection—so much that he'd developed a healthy respect for body armor. Even in a sleepy town like Versailles, a bulletproof vest might save a life.

Especially tonight. Dennis felt his pulse quicken. Tonight he and Conner had been invited to participate in a drug raid. The invitation had been reluctant, but Conner's call to Colonel Smith in Frankfort had resulted in a second call to the captain of the narcotic enforcement unit investigating a drug ring in Woodford County. The same drug ring, it turned out, who used to sell marijuana to Sharon Carlson.

In Dennis's opinion, a connection between these drug dealers and the teenager's hit-and-run accident was unlikely, but the timing of the tip was incredibly good. The narcotics team planned to send in an undercover officer to buy drugs tonight, in search of enough evidence to convict the dealers. Mrs. Carlson's phone call to Conner yesterday had given Dennis the opportunity to get involved in yet another aspect of police work with which he had no experience. As far as he was concerned, the more times his name came up in front of the bigwigs in Frankfort, the better.

He buttoned the shirt of his gray uniform over his vest. Back in the other room, he looked at the telephone. Yeah, that's what he'd do. He'd call Jackie tomorrow and apologize for upsetting her. And he'd tell her in no uncertain terms that she needed to stay out of their case. For her own safety.

That decided, he strapped on his belt and pulled the door closed behind him as he left.

"This should be pretty cut-and-dried, boys." Sergeant Felter sat behind the wheel of an unmarked car, eyeing Dennis in the backseat through the rearview mirror. "We've been working on this for months. The supplier over in Louisville's getting nailed at the same time, so that's one drug gang shut down in Kentucky."

Dennis nodded. "Good job. I'm glad we're getting in on the bust."

Felter caught his eyes in the mirror. "Just remember. You're here as observers."

Beside Dennis, Conner answered, "Don't worry, Felter. We'll stay out of your way. We just want to watch, and maybe ask a question or two."

"You coulda met us down at the station to ask your questions," Felter muttered.

Apparently not in a mood to rise to Felter's bait, Conner chose to ignore the comment and looked out the window.

On both sides of the deserted two-lane country road grew tall trees crowded with leafy underbrush. Twilight darkened the interior beyond the first few trees. The undercover officer, a guy named Ben Holmes, had disappeared around a wide curve ahead to make the final deal. Behind him, Dennis saw three state police cruisers, each with a pair of state troopers waiting for the word to move in. A glance at his watch told him Holmes had been gone almost twenty minutes. It seemed like hours. How long did it take to buy drugs, anyway?

Apparently, about twenty minutes. A car rounded the bend heading toward them. Holmes.

He executed a U-turn and rolled to a stop directly ahead of them. His hand stuck through the window, waving a thumbs-up.

"Here we go, boys," said Felter, and he started his engine.

He pulled out behind Holmes, and the convoy of cruisers fell in behind him. Dennis glanced toward Conner. A casual observer would think him as calm as ever, but a twitch in his jaw told Dennis the detective's teeth were clenched tightly together.

On the far side of a deep S-curve, Dennis saw their target—a single-wide trailer, its tin roof crusted with rust. Cardboard and masking tape covered one window. Three cars were parked on the grass in front of the trailer, and a rickety set of metal stairs led up to the front door.

Felter pulled across the dirt driveway behind Holmes to block any attempted escape. The cruisers rolled off the road onto the grass behind him. Doors opened and everyone got out, taking care to move through the yard toward the trailer as silently as possible. No one closed a door. If the occupants hadn't heard the engines, there was no sense in alerting them to their presence before they were ready.

Heart pounding, his senses on high alert, Dennis stepped from the car onto the hard-packed soil. The troopers converged and moved toward the front door, weapons drawn. Silently, Felter nodded at two of them and jerked his head toward the far corner of the trailer. The two troopers crept quietly around to guard the rear exit.

Felter waited a moment to allow his team to get in place. Dennis saw the man's shoulders rise as he drew in a breath, and then with a glance toward Holmes, he mounted the metal stairs and pounded on the door.

This was the most dangerous time of the raid. The sight of uniformed police officers outside their trailer might cause the dealers to panic. If they were desperate enough, they might open fire. Dennis whispered a prayer. Never had he felt as much need for the Lord's protection as now. He unsnapped his holster strap. Observer or not, he wanted to be ready in case he needed to retrieve his weapon quickly.

The door opened. From where he stood Dennis couldn't see inside, but he watched as Felter held up his badge.

"Kentucky State Police. Do you mind if we come in?"

Dennis heard the response, an insolent snarl. "Not unless you have a warrant, dude. I know my rights."

Without turning his head, Felter extended a hand out behind him. A trooper stepped forward and slapped a paper into it. Felter held it toward the man inside the trailer.

"As a matter of fact, we do."

Forty minutes later, after three male Caucasian suspects in their late thirties had been led away in handcuffs, Dennis and Conner stood in the crowded living room while Felter's team bagged crack and marijuana. It was enough to put the dealers away for a long time.

"I guess you were wrong about these guys being involved in your hit-and-run." Felter's mouth twisted into what had to have passed as a smile for him.

Conner shrugged. "We'll question them in more detail back at the station."

Felter snorted. "Don't know why you'd bother. You saw the reaction when you mentioned the Carlson chick. Nothing. Those faces were as empty as my wife's bank account."

Conner turned toward Dennis. "Did you search the kitchen?"

"Yeah." Dennis shook his head, trying to hide his disappointment. "No knives resembling the one we found."

Conner chewed the corner of his mustache. "Well, it was a tip. We had to check it out."

"Yeah, tough luck," Felter said. "But keep at it. I'm sure you'll crack that case sooner or later."

Before they left, Dennis made one last search through

the tiny trailer. He didn't really expect to find anything, but the intensity of Jackie's voice on the phone this afternoon forced him to at least look for the mushroom book.

As he expected, it was not there.

TWENTY

Why did Mondays always seem like the longest day of the week? Especially the Monday after vacation? Jackie spent the entire morning plodding through a gigantic stack of mail before her client meetings started after lunch. Had no one bothered to cover her desk the whole week?

Actually, that wasn't fair. Her coworkers had pitched in to take care of every single client appointment on her schedule last week. And none of them seemed angry at the short notice, either. She responded to their questions about her vacation with vague answers about desperately needing a rest, and since child-support caseworkers were an overworked bunch, no one found that hard to believe.

When four-thirty finally arrived, Jackie breathed a sigh of relief as she swept the piles of sorted mail into her drawer and locked it. She was ready for this day to be over.

The twenty-minute drive from Frankfort to Versailles restored her sense of peace. Acres and acres of beautiful horse farms stretched along both sides of U.S. 60, the softly rolling hills divided by long double rows of black plank fencing. Thoroughbreds grazed in vivid green fields, their graceful bodies gleaming in the late afternoon sun.

This drive, in her opinion the most beautiful in all of central Kentucky, never failed to put a smile on her face.

At home, Linus meowed his greeting with volume that belied his small stature. Honestly, you'd think the creature had been starved for days.

"Calm down, fuzz face," she scolded. "Supper's on the way. Just give me a minute."

The light on the answering machine blinked at her, and she pressed the play button on her way into the kitchen.

"Jackie, it's Margaret. Good news! Samantha is out of intensive care. She's being moved to a regular room this afternoon. I thought you'd like to know. Earl and I are going to visit this evening, so call me tomorrow and I'll give you an update. I hope you had a nice day at work. Goodbye."

What a relief. Sharon and Nick must be ecstatic.

The machine whirred on to the next message while Jackie opened the cabinet and surveyed Linus's menu choices for the evening. He hadn't eaten turkey in a while. At the sound of the second voice, she slammed the cabinet closed and ran back into the living room, staring at the machine in disbelief as it filled the room with sound.

"Hey, it's Dennis. Listen, I know you were mad at me yesterday. And that *stupid* crack—uh, I'm sorry for that. I shouldn't have said it." He paused before going on in a harder voice. "Even though you had no business running around in those woods alone. Anyway, I'd like to talk to you. I'm off this afternoon so give me a call at home when you get this. Later."

Stunned, Jackie pressed Reverse and collapsed onto the couch as she listened to the message again.

He'd called. Dennis Walsh had actually called her

house. And his apology sounded sincere. He was sorry he had made her mad. Did this mean he might…

No. Jackie shook her head, rejecting the flicker of hope that threatened to warm her insides. If she'd learned one thing in the past week, it was that Dennis Walsh was only interested in her for one reason: he wanted any information she could give him about the murder. Nothing else.

With a sigh, she heaved herself off the couch. Dennis could wait by his phone all night, as far as she was concerned. She would not call.

A third message had begun. She hit Reverse again and took a step toward the kitchen.

"Hello, Jackie? This is Lucy McKinley at the Woodford County Library. Remember that book we looked for yesterday? I found it. It was misshelved. Someone put it in Fiction, in the *C*'s. I can't imagine how that happened, because the author's name starts with an *F,* not a *C,* and obviously an encyclopedia isn't fiction. Anyway, I've put it on hold for you, if you want to come by and pick it up. Thanks. Bye."

Wow. This was big, really big. No matter what Lucy thought, no library worker would make such a mistake. Possibly a lazy patron would drop a book on the wrong shelf, but Jackie didn't think that's what had happened.

Her resolve flew out the window as she grabbed the telephone and dialed Dennis' home number.

His voice held a note of warmth. "Hi, Jackie. I was hoping—"

She cut him off. "Meet me at the library. It's important."

She slammed the receiver back into its cradle and whirled to grab her purse off the dinette table. Linus, sensing her impending departure, launched himself at her legs, yowling loudly. Though her head buzzed with urgency, responsibility stabbed at her.

"Oh all right, pest. Come on. I'll feed you first."

Twenty minutes later, Jackie catapulted through the library door at something just short of a run to find Dennis waiting for her. He stood leaning against Lucy's desk, dressed in jeans and a blue U.K. T-shirt.

"Odd place for a meeting," he said with a grin.

Her tongue struck by a momentary bout of paralysis, Jackie stopped dead in the middle of the floor. For a few heartbeats she was unaware of anything except the depths of the gray eyes that held hers captive.

Lucy broke into the moment by standing from her chair behind the desk.

"Jackie, I see you got my message. I put your book right over here on the Hold shelf."

Jackie tore her gaze away from Dennis. "Don't touch it!"

The librarian turned a surprised expression Jackie's way, her hand hovering above the book. "Why not?"

"Yes, Miss Hoffner," said an arrogant voice behind her. "Why don't you tell us all?"

Jackie whirled to see Detective Conner striding through the door, his ever-present smile plastered on his face. She looked back to give Dennis a quick eye roll. Couldn't the guy make a move without his keeper?

At least the detective could make things happen. Jackie took two steps toward the man and grabbed his arm.

"Detective Conner, we found the book the killer used to identify the poisonous mushrooms."

Conner's attention shifted from Jackie to Dennis, then back again. "Walsh told me about the book. Since it turned up here at the library and not in the killer's possession, how can that help us find the killer?"

"This book is a mushroom encyclopedia with pictures. The killer came here to find pictures of poisonous mushrooms. He got the book, found the pictures, and then hid it in the fiction section before anyone saw him reading it."

Detective Conner nodded slowly. "That is a plausible explanation, but how does that help us apprehend the murderer?"

"Don't you see?" Jackie stomped her foot. "Fingerprints! Dust the book for fingerprints. That's what *CSI* would do."

"*CSI* has Grissom, Miss Hoffner. We do not."

"Are you saying you can't dust for fingerprints?"

"Of course we can dust for fingerprints. And we collected a good set of prints from the inside of the rubber gloves the killer wore while picking the deadly mushrooms. But AFIS didn't have a match."

Dennis explained. "In order to identify an individual using their fingerprints, they must be on file with the criminal justice system database that stores the prints of—"

Jackie cut him off. "I know what AFIS is."

"Ah, yes." Conner awarded her a long-suffering smile. "*CSI* again."

She wanted to scream. Why wouldn't they listen to her? "At least you could try! If nothing else, you might be able to match some prints on the book with the ones you got inside the gloves."

Her breath lodged in her chest, she stared up into Conner's face, silently begging him to act. Finally, he gave a tiny nod.

"All right. Anything that can help us piece together the killer's steps leading up to the crime will help." He looked up. "Walsh, bag the book."

Jackie's lungs deflated. Thank goodness.

Dennis retrieved an evidence kit from his police car and placed the book in a big zipper bag. Jackie saw that it was an oversize paperback with, thankfully, a coated cover that would hopefully yield a good set of prints.

"Hey," said Lucy as they turned to leave. "You can't take that book without checking it out. Library policy."

They all froze. Dennis and Conner exchanged glances, momentarily stumped.

"I guess we could call the judge at home and get a warrant," Dennis suggested.

Honestly, men could be so simple-minded at times. Shaking her head in their direction, Jackie reached into her purse for her library card. "Here you go, Lucy. I'll be responsible for the book."

Samantha's hospital room looked like a florist shop when Jackie stepped through the door holding the spring bouquet she'd bought on the way. Bright spots of color covered every available surface, and a big bouquet of Mylar balloons hovered above the teen's bed. Probably a good thing she had the room to herself. Another patient wouldn't fit.

Samantha looked pretty grim. Her nose, lips and cheeks were swollen grotesquely to twice their normal size. A bandage covered her head and half her face, and tubes protruded from her arm. The unbandaged eye was closed. Jackie caught sight of a nasty bruise spreading from beneath the bandage to cover most of her jaw, lips and nose.

Margaret and Pastor Palmer stood at the foot of the bed talking quietly with Nick. When she stepped through the door, Sharon rose from a chair on the far side of the bed and rushed toward her. She threw her arms around Jackie and delivered a bear hug that sent a lump to her throat.

"Isn't it wonderful?" Sharon pulled back to look at her. "She's going to be okay." Her voice lowered. "And police say there was no connection to…you know."

"That is wonderful." Jackie squeezed her in return. "I'm so glad, Sharon."

"Hello, everyone," boomed a voice behind Jackie.

They all turned to find Esther standing in the doorway, her arms wrapped around a huge picnic basket covered with a bright yellow cloth. On the bed, Samantha's eye opened.

"Hello, Mrs. Hodges. Hello, Jackie."

Her lips barely moved as she spoke, and she sounded so weary Jackie wanted to weep. So young to be hurt so terribly.

Esther's voice softened as she thrust the picnic basket into Margaret's arms and stepped to the teenager's bedside.

"Hello, honey. How you doing under all that gauze?"

"Okay, I guess."

Sharon pulled Jackie forward to stand beside Esther. Jackie smiled at the teen, hoping her face didn't register the horror she felt at the disfiguring results of the attack.

"Well, don't you worry, baby," Esther soothed. "You're gonna be just fine. You've got the whole church praying for you, and the Lord Himself is watching over every breath you take. You just remember that."

The corners of the girl's swollen lips lifted. "I will."

Jackie couldn't help but stare at Esther's tender expression. If love for a fellow human being could be seen in a face, Jackie was seeing it now. Guilt rose from deep inside to warm her cheeks. How could she have thought this woman capable of harming anyone?

Lord, I need to learn how to love like that.

Esther turned from the bedside and reached for the basket.

"I don't know what you have in this thing," Margaret commented as she handed it over, "but it smells heavenly."

It did. The savory odors of garlic and sage filled the hospital room, chasing away the less appetizing smell of antiseptic and rubbing alcohol.

"Chicken and dumplings, with Caesar salad and fresh green beans. But don't get excited, Margaret." She turned a wide smile on Sharon. "They're for Sharon and Nick."

Sharon's mouth opened in surprise, and Nick said, "Mrs. Hodges, you didn't have to do that."

The stout woman dismissed that with a wave. "Call me Esther. Everybody does. And of course I didn't have to. I wanted to. There's plates and silverware in here, too, and it's a beautiful evening. I bet you haven't been outside all day, have you?"

Sharon and Nick shook their heads.

"Thought so. I saw a picnic table around the side of this building, and I'm gonna take you out there and serve you myself while there's still some sunlight to enjoy."

Sharon's attention flew to the bed. "Oh, thank you, that's very kind. But we couldn't leave Samantha."

"Nonsense. Margaret can watch her for a few minutes."

"Go on, Mom," Samantha managed. "It's fine."

"Well…"

Esther took charge. She thrust the basket into Nick's arms and locked her elbow through Sharon's. "C'mon. We'll be back before you know it. This dumpling recipe is an old family secret, handed down from my grandmother's…"

She deftly guided Samantha's parents out the door, her voice growing dim as she steered them down the hallway toward the elevator.

"Actually," Pastor Palmer said, "I was just about ready to leave myself. Jackie, would you mind bringing Margaret home when you come?"

"No problem."

He went to the bedside and laid a hand gently on the teenager's. "Do you mind if I pray for you before I leave?"

"Please."

Jackie and Margaret bowed their heads, as well.

"Father, I know Your heart grieves for the pain Samantha is suffering. Thank You for the marvelous job You've done in her recovery so far. We trust You to finish the good work You've begun in her body and in her life. In Jesus' Name, Amen."

"Amen," Jackie chorused along with Margaret.

Samantha managed a feeble smile. "Thank you."

He kissed Margaret's cheek and smiled at Jackie as he left the room. "See you later."

"Bye."

Margaret leaned over the bed. "Samantha, why don't you try to sleep? We'll sit here and be quiet and try not to disturb you."

"Okay."

The blue eye closed. Margaret dragged the visitor chair from her bedside to the doorway, next to the other one. She sat and patted the other seat with a smile at Jackie.

"How was your first day back at work?" she whispered.

"Busy," Jackie replied, matching her volume. "But I had some excitement when I got home tonight."

Jackie described her visit to the library yesterday and Lucy's message tonight, and her conversation with Dennis and Detective Conner. By the time Jackie finished her tale, Margaret's eyes were round.

"Jackie," she rasped, breathless. "You're not going to believe this. I think I know who had that book!"

Jackie's breath caught in her throat. "Who?"

"Just a minute."

Margaret went to the bedside. Jackie joined her.

"Samantha," she whispered. "Samantha, are you awake?"

Samantha looked up at them, her eye glazed with drug-induced sleep.

"Listen, honey, I'm sorry to bother you, but this might be important. Do you remember telling me you saw someone from church at the library a few weeks ago?" Samantha stared at her, blank. "You were there doing research about your friend, remember?"

Her head dipped a fraction. Jackie's pulse took off like a thoroughbred out of the starting gate.

"Who was it, dear? Who did you see?"

The girl's throat convulsed as she swallowed. When she spoke, her lips barely moved.

"Mrs. Watson."

Jackie jerked back. Laura Watson? No! It couldn't be. Not sweet, elegant, beautiful Laura Watson.

Margaret's eyes locked with hers, and Jackie saw her own shock mirrored there. The older woman leaned over the bed again.

"You're sure, dear? You aren't mistaken?"

Again, Samantha gave a tiny nod. "I'm sure. Why?"

"Nothing. Don't worry about it. Go back to sleep."

Jackie rushed toward the hall, Margaret close on her heels. They stood just outside the doorway so their voices wouldn't disturb the teenager.

"I don't believe it," Jackie murmured. "Laura is so… so gracious!"

"Let's not jump to conclusions," Margaret cautioned, but uncertainty saturated her tone.

"Don't you see?" Jackie insisted. "It fits. Dennis told me the security records proved Richard worked late the night of the potluck, and all day the next day. That means Laura wasn't with him. She was probably home alone."

"Without an alibi," Margaret said.

"Exactly. And the night Samantha was run down, Richard was out of town. Again, Laura was alone. Oh!" Jackie slapped her hand on the top of her head as another clue fell into place. "The gloves. Laura goes to the dentist every month—she told us so at lunch that day. Dentists have boxes of rubber gloves in their examining rooms, don't they?"

Margaret's brow creased. "Mine does."

"So does mine."

They stared at each other. Then Margaret shook her head.

"I can't believe Laura would go so far as to steal your car and try to kill Samantha just because she saw her at the library."

Jackie sucked in a breath. "That might be another clue, Margaret. Was Laura standing nearby when I told Esther where I hide my spare key?"

"I don't remember."

"Well, I can find out pretty quick."

Jackie raced into the hospital room and grabbed her purse off the empty bed. Samantha still slept. Her chest rose and fell in an even rhythm.

Back in the hallway, Jackie rummaged in her purse. "I haven't erased any of the recordings yet, so it should still be on there. Maybe we can tell who was standing around."

Jackie pulled out the recorder. She hadn't used it in days, but thank goodness she hadn't bothered to take it out of her purse yet. She adjusted the volume so they could hear it, but low enough to not disturb Samantha in the room behind them.

"Let's see, I talked to several people before that lunch. The nursing home people, and then Sharon, so it won't be all the way at the beginning."

She pressed Reverse and Play several times until they heard a snatch of conversation from the lunch at Shaker Village, then she reversed again. The voices from the internal speaker sounded like chipmunks on amphetamines.

"There," said Margaret. "That sounds right."

Esther's voice spoke to them from the recorder.

"*—all my fault. Locked my keys in the car, so Julie had to come get me.*"

"*Oh, no. Not again.*" Margaret's voice.

Jackie and Margaret exchanged a glance.

"*Yep. Third time this month. And that hide-a-key thing Jim put under the back bumper musta fell off, because I couldn't find it. And he's out of town again, doggone him, and has my spare on his key ring.*"

"*What will you do?*"

"Sylvia," said Jackie.

Margaret nodded.

"*Oh, not to worry. I'll call Triple A when I get home. They're getting so they know my voice.*"

"*You need to get another spare made immediately. This time, put it someplace where it won't fall off.*"

"That's her," said Margaret. "That's Laura."

Then Jackie's own voice sounded in her ears, giving the critical information that would aid a killer in inflicting terrible injury on the teenager in the room behind them.

"*I keep a spare key inside the gasoline door. The little box fits right in there, and it can't fall off with the door closed.*"

"Hey, that's a good idea. Never thought of that."

Jackie pressed the off button. The blood drained away from her face, leaving her shivering with cold.

"She was standing right there. She knew where I hid my key."

Margaret looked as sick as Jackie felt. "I think you'd better call the police. Now."

TWENTY-ONE

At eleven-twenty on Tuesday afternoon, Jackie parallel parked the rental car on Main Street a block from Kessler's Deli. Her boss had not been happy when she had asked for a couple of hours for lunch that day. She'd sweet-talked him by promising to work overtime the rest of the week. No way was she going to miss this all-important Tuesday lunch with the church ladies.

She hurried down the street toward the restaurant. She was ten minutes early, and hopefully Margaret would be here soon. Or Esther, or Julie, or somebody. Jackie's stomach twisted tighter than a rope at the thought of facing Laura Watson alone.

"Psst. Jackie."

Jackie's step slowed as she approached the corner of the stone building that housed the deli. She surveyed the small parking lot, but she didn't see anyone.

"Over here."

From inside a dark blue sedan, Dennis gestured for her to approach. When she drew near, Jackie leaned down to look through the open window and saw Detective Conner in the driver's seat. He did not wear a smile today. In fact, he was glaring at her.

"What are you doing here, Miss Hoffner?" he demanded. "You're supposed to be at work."

"I know." Jackie looked around with a quick glance. If someone saw her talking to the cops, her cover would be blown for sure. "I couldn't stand it. Margaret might need my help."

"Help with what?" Dennis asked. "She looks perfectly capable of eating lunch without assistance."

Jackie rolled her eyes. "You know what I mean."

"No, I don't. Mrs. Palmer is going to have lunch, period. She's not going to ask any questions. She's not going to do anything except eat a sandwich. You know that."

Yes, Jackie knew the plan they'd hatched last night in Samantha's hospital room. Though they had enough evidence to pick Laura up for questioning, everyone agreed that was sure to cause a media extravaganza. Better to avoid that until they had solid proof. So Dennis and the detective were to wait until today's lunch was nearly over and then they would enter Kessler's through the delivery door in the rear and ask the server to retrieve Laura's water glass as unobtrusively as possible. They'd decided to wait until the meal was nearly over so as not to cause undue stress to the server, who might give away the scheme with nervous behavior.

Then they would take Laura's fingerprints from the glass. With luck the prints would match the ones they lifted from the rubber gloves and hoped to lift from the mushroom encyclopedia. Then they would have enough evidence to arrest her.

All morning Jackie had been unable to concentrate on her paperwork. She'd put forth so much effort on this case. After all, her casserole and her car were used to commit the crimes. It wasn't fair that Margaret got to be there for the grand finale, while she sat stuck behind a desk, going through week-old mail.

She nudged her lower lip out a tiny bit and looked from Dennis to Detective Conner with wide, hopefully innocent looking eyes. "I just want to be there. I can eat a sandwich as well as Margaret. I promise I won't say anything."

Conner heaved a resigned sigh. "See that you don't."

Dennis watched Jackie disappear around the corner of the building, a feeling of unease churning deep in the pit of his stomach. That girl was too nosy for her own good. Yes, she had led them to the person he firmly believed was the murderer. But Mrs. Watson had killed once and attempted to kill a second time. What if she tried a third time, with Jackie as her target?

"I don't like it," he said, staring at the edge of the building.

Conner sighed. "I don't, either. But short of handcuffing her in the backseat, I don't see how we could have stopped her."

Esther and Julie had already arrived and selected a round table near the big picture window to the left of the front door when Jackie entered the restaurant.

"Why, Jackie," Esther exclaimed when she stepped inside, "I didn't know you planned to join us today."

Jackie forced a smile and tried to look normal. The police had arrived after Esther's departure last night. The older woman knew nothing of the importance of today's lunch, and Jackie wasn't about to spill the beans.

"I had such a good time last week I decided to come today, too."

Julie waved to the server and called across the small room, "Can we pull up another chair? There's plenty of room."

At that moment Sylvia came through the door with Audrey Coates. They proclaimed themselves delighted over Jackie's presence. Just as they were about to be seated, the door opened again.

Laura Watson, wearing an elegant dark blue suit with an immaculate white silk blouse, stepped into the restaurant. Jackie's heart skipped a beat as she willed her breathing to remain steady.

"Laura, sit here," she said, indicating the seat beside her. Her voice came out sharper than she intended. The ladies' heads turned to give her an odd look. "I've been…saving it for you," she finished with a lame smile.

"Why, thank you, Jackie. That's so sweet of you."

As Laura hung her handbag over the chair back, Margaret came through the door. She looked nervous. A smile flashed onto her face and disappeared just as quickly. Her eyes darted around the table, stopping when they came to Jackie.

"I thought you were working today."

Jackie shrugged. "I've wanted to try this place. What better way than with a group of friends from church?"

She avoided Margaret's eyes, aware that the older woman looked as if she wanted to snatch Jackie by the hair and march her out of the restaurant. The others watched the two of them with varying expressions of curiosity.

Jackie picked up a menu and allowed her smile to sweep around the table. "What's good here?"

"The pork tenderloin sandwich is to die for," Esther said, peering at her own menu.

"And their coleslaw is the best," added Laura. "It's homemade."

"Turkey and avocado for me." Julie slapped her menu closed.

The server approached to take their orders, pen poised over a small notepad.

"We need water," Jackie demanded.

Heads swiveled toward her. Had her voice been a little too loud? She felt jumpy, her nerves stretched to the limit. She took a breath. If she didn't calm down, she would blow the whole thing.

"I'm parched," she explained with an apologetic shrug.

They placed their orders, and the server left. Jackie turned in her chair to stare after the woman. She seemed distracted but not necessarily nervous. Obviously Dennis and Conner hadn't enlisted her help yet.

Within minutes, she returned and set a glass of ice water in front of each of them. They all watched as Jackie picked hers up and drank noisily. She eyed Laura's glass. The smooth surface would hold a fingerprint perfectly. Good.

"Any word on poor Samantha?" asked Laura.

Jackie's head jerked toward the elegantly dressed woman. What nerve, running over the girl and then asking about her in that oh so concerned voice. And why wasn't she drinking her water?

"She's out of intensive care," Esther announced. "Looks terrible, but that's to be expected."

"She's barely conscious," Margaret added quickly. "You can hardly understand a word she says, because she's drugged."

Jackie stopped herself in the act of disagreeing when Margaret glanced nervously toward Laura. Of course. Margaret didn't want Laura to think Samantha was conscious and talking coherently.

Esther, however, was not in on their scheme. She frowned at the pastor's wife. "I understood her perfectly well."

"Oh, no," Jackie insisted. "She's definitely still foggy. And doesn't remember a thing before the accident." She cast a glance sideways. "For weeks and weeks before."

Margaret caught her eye and gave a nearly imperceptible shake of her head.

What? Jackie was only trying to protect the girl from a vicious killer.

One who still had not touched her water glass. Jackie picked up her own glass again. Maybe seeing someone else drink would make Laura thirsty. Her hand shook with nerves as she held the rim to her lips.

"Her poor parents," said Julie.

"And Vince," added Audrey. "I've never seen him looking so tired. I'm afraid he might make himself sick with worry."

Jackie drained her glass. Everyone else had at least taken a sip or two, but still Laura made no move to drink her water. What was the woman, a camel?

"My goodness, Jackie," Laura exclaimed. "You are thirsty."

She turned, her hand partially raised to signal the server to refill Jackie's glass. But the server had left the dining room, probably to turn in their orders.

"Here," Laura said, a gracious smile on her tastefully colored lips, "have mine."

Time seemed to stumble. As if watching a slow-mo replay on television, Jackie saw Laura's arm extend. She opened her mouth to protest, but Laura's hand grasped the glass, all five fingers touching its smooth sides. She picked it up and set it down in front of Jackie.

"I drank a bottle of water in the car on the way here, so I'm not thirsty."

A tornado spun in her mind. Laura not thirsty? That meant she wouldn't request another glass of water. And when Detective Conner and Dennis asked for her glass, the server wouldn't know to give them the one row in front of Jackie.

The one with Laura's fingerprints on it.

She looked up to see Margaret staring at her across the table through eyes the size of grapefruits. Their plan lay before Jackie in shreds. She had to do something. Something drastic.

She turned a smile on Laura. "Thank you."

Judging by the sudden creases between Laura's eyebrows, Jackie failed to make her smile look natural. No time to think about that now. Blood surged in her ears in rhythm to an urgent voice whispering *Hurry, hurry, hurry* in her mind.

Jackie made a show of reaching for her own glass, to move it out of the way. In the process, she bumped the full one hard enough to knock it over. Water sloshed across the table like a tidal wave. Margaret leaped to her feet, and Julie and Esther jerked their chairs backward to avoid being drenched.

"Here," commanded Esther, taking charge, "give me your napkins."

Grabbing the cloth napkin draped across her lap, Jackie leaped to her feet. Her chair tumbled backward and crashed to the floor.

"I'll get more napkins," she shouted, cringing at the unintended volume.

But instead of tossing her napkin onto the quickly spreading puddle, she covered the now-empty water glass and snatched it up.

"Uh, and more water."

She whirled and ran in the direction of the kitchen, aware that she had drawn the openmouthed stares of everyone in the restaurant. As she burst through the swinging door that led to the kitchen, she heard Audrey say, "My goodness, she's an odd girl, isn't she?"

Equipment and people crowded the small kitchen. Jackie ignored their surprised exclamations as she dashed toward the far wall and the door she spied there, carrying the all-important water glass, its evidence safe beneath her napkin.

Outside in the sunshine, she came to a sudden stop, casting her eyes wildly around the back alley. Deserted. Where were Dennis and Conner?

She took off down the alley at a jog. When she reached the corner of the brick building, her eyes were drawn to the detectives' car and two figures in the front seat. Yes, there they sat, their heads turned away from her, waiting for the right time to approach the restaurant.

At that moment a voice froze her blood.

Laura's voice.

"Jackie, where in the world are you going?"

"What does she think she's doing?"

Dennis followed Conner's gaze to the back of the parking lot in time to see Jackie screech to a halt on the loose gravel covering the pavement.

"No clue," he answered. "But what's that in her hand?"

Conner's jaw tightened. "Looks like a glass."

Jackie whirled. Laura had followed her through the restaurant's back door. Her purse clutched in manicured fingers, the elegant killer advanced at a fast walk.

"Uh, nowhere," Jackie stammered. "I, uh, just needed some air. It was really hot in there."

"No, it wasn't."

Jackie took a couple of steps backward as Laura drew near.

"Stuffy, then," she corrected. "I needed to take a walk."

"You're acting strangely, Jackie. And what are you doing with my glass?"

Jackie's mouth dried in an instant. Laura still stood in the shelter of the building. If she could just get her to take another step or two, Dennis and Detective Conner would be able to see her. She edged backward.

"Glass? What do you mean?"

Dennis heaved a frustrated breath. Didn't that girl understand the concept of a plan?

He reached for the door handle. "I'll get it from her."

"No, wait!" The urgency's in Conner's whisper stopped him the second before he opened the door. "She's talking to someone."

Laura took another step. Jackie faced forward, desperately wanting to look in the direction of the detectives' car but terrified to do so. What if Laura followed her glance and saw the police waiting in the parking lot? What would she do?

"You figured it out, didn't you?"

Jackie's heart leaped into her throat. "Figured what out?"

Laura shook her head slowly, her eyes boring into Jackie's. "I'm guessing everything. Mrs. Farmer, the teenager, the casserole, the car. Samantha talked, didn't she? She told you about seeing me at the library."

One more step. Just one more. Blood roared in Jackie's ears as she edged backward once again.

"Get down," Conner muttered.

Dennis mimicked the detective and sank down in the seat. He peeked over the door panel and saw Jackie take a backward step. Her body was so tense she looked as if she might shatter into a million pieces any minute. Her hand trembled violently as it clutched the napkin-draped glass.

An unfamiliar emotion rose up inside him. Jackie looked terrified. And extremely vulnerable.

A woman moved into view, her eyes fixed on Jackie as she took a determined step forward.

His lungs emptied as he watched the killer advance toward Jackie.

"You admit you killed Mrs. Farmer?"

Her eyes still locked on Laura's, Jackie spoke as loudly as she dared. Was Conner's window down? Was Dennis listening?

"She was a meddling old woman. She would have gotten Richard sent to prison."

"You mean because she caught him stealing from the bank?"

Laura took another step. "The bank never missed the money. It's not like he stole from a person or anything."

The glass in Jackie's hand quivered like a hula doll. "Stealing is wrong no matter who it comes from."

Laura's laugh came out in a short blast. "You don' understand. Mrs. Farmer didn't understand, either. I tried to talk to her, tried to explain that we give a lot to charity. We've built houses for poor people in Appalachia, peopl who would live in horrible poverty if not for Richard. I gave her a chance before I put those mushrooms in her food, but she refused to listen to me."

"And Samantha? You tried to kill an innocent teenager to cover up your crime."

Laura shrugged. "Samantha's no dummy. She would have figured it out sooner or later."

"And what about me?" Jackie's throat convulsed as she forced the question out. "Were you trying to frame me?"

"Oh, Jackie, don't be so dramatic. Your casserole happened to be on the top shelf of Mrs. Farmer's refrigerator. And I really didn't plan to use your car at all. I parked outside the Carlsons' house late Friday night, just looking at the place and trying to figure out what to do about Samantha. That's when I saw her sneak out through a window." She shook her head. "Teenagers. She gave me the perfect opportunity, but of course I couldn't do it with my own car. I knew she'd have to come home eventually, and that's when I remembered where you hid your spare key. So it really was just convenient timing. Nothing personal."

"Nothing personal?" Anger flared, and Jackie felt a drop of sweat trickle between her shoulder blades.

"I just couldn't let anyone discover Richard's secret. If anything happens to him, I'll be left with nothing." Laura looked down at her feet. When she raised her face, her eyes were hard. "I grew up in the mountains of eastern Kentucky, number eight of twelve children. Do you know what it's like to never have enough? To wear clothes worn by your older sisters before you got them? To live in a run-down shack you're embarrassed of?"

Laura paused to draw a shuddering breath. "I can't go

back there, Jackie. I won't. Richard took me away from that, and I'll never go back."

Her right hand moved slowly toward her left side, where her purse dangled from her shoulder.

What was she doing? Jackie's heart threatened to pound through her chest. Did Laura have a gun in her purse?

"She's going for a weapon!"

Jackie was in danger! Dennis reacted blindly. Pulse racing, he jerked upright in the seat and threw open the door. As he tumbled out of the car, he unsnapped his holster and drew the weapon in one smooth motion. When his feet hit the pavement, he dashed around the rear of the sedan, elbows locked, both hands clutching the grips straight in front of him.

Dimly aware of Conner close on his heels, he ran toward the two women, shouting.

"Police! Move an inch and you're dead!"

Relief wilted Jackie's muscles as Dennis dashed forward and thrust himself between her and Laura. She stared at his uniformed back, her heart pounding in her ears. He had come to her rescue. Dennis put himself between her and a murderer to protect her.

Stunned, Laura's hand froze halfway out of her purse, holding…

A tissue.

"Both hands up, ma'am," said Detective Conner. His level tone restored a sense of calm to the situation. "I'll take the purse."

Laura calmly blotted a bead of sweat from her forehead before complying. As he lifted the purse strap over her raised arm, a sneer twisted her stylishly lipsticked mouth. "I guess the gossips at church will have plenty to talk about now."

Jackie's knees wobbled as Conner took the handcuffs from Dennis's belt and cuffed Laura's hands behind her back. Only when she had been secured did Dennis lower his gun and whirl to look at Jackie.

"Are you okay?"

Jackie looked up into his eyes and felt a fluttering tickle in her stomach. A smile tugged at her mouth. The emotion she saw in those gray depths told her that, yes, she was definitely going to be okay.

Before Conner led the handcuffed Laura toward his car, he peered first into Jackie's face and then into Dennis's. A knowing grin stole across his lips.

"I told you she was trouble, Walsh. You can't say I didn't warn you."

TWENTY-TWO

Clutching the back of the pew in front of her, Jackie kept her eyes squeezed shut as she shifted her weight from one foot to the other. Pastor Palmer's sermon had been as good as ever, but once again she couldn't seem to concentrate. She forced herself not to fidget as his prayer droned on and on. For goodness' sake, she would have to ask Margaret to speak to him about this habit of recapping the entire sermon during the closing prayer. Would he never say *Amen?*

Three pews ahead, she heard a loud sigh and a quickly repressed giggle. As though the noise reminded their devout pastor that an entire congregation was eager to get home to their Sunday dinners, he intoned the words she longed to hear.

"In the precious Name of our Lord Jesus Christ, Amen." She bit back a sigh of her own as his smile swept the congregation. "We are so happy to have Samantha Carlson back with us this morning. I know you'll all want to speak with her before you leave."

Jackie turned and looked across the aisle to the place two rows back, where Samantha stood propped on crutches. The swelling in her face was nearly gone, though the yellowish remnants of that nasty bruise still stained he youthful skin and her hair had not yet grown enough to cover the terrible scar on her scalp. Standing on one side of her was a dark-haired teenager, presumably a friend from school. And on the other side, Samantha's parents stood with clasped hands. Jackie caught Sharon's eye and they exchanged a grin.

At the front of the sanctuary, Pastor Palmer raised his hand, palm toward the congregation as he delivered the morning's benediction. The center aisle filled immediately. Thank goodness they sat near the rear of the church, so they could get out quickly. She'd skipped breakfast, and she was starving.

As she pushed her way into the press of worshippers to carve an exit path toward the back door, she heard a shout carry over the noise of the crowd.

"Jackie! Jackie Hoffner, hold up a minute!"

With a grin, she stepped into the narthex to wait for Margaret. Of course her nosy friend would want to speak with her before she left. Especially today. Jackie had brought something much better than a casserole to church. She glanced up at the handsome man standing beside her, her stomach giving a giddy flip-flop when he smiled down at her. If only Aunt Betty had lived to see this day!

Moments later, when Margaret finally managed to dart through the horde, she rushed up to them as though afraid they might have left without speaking to her. Not a chance of that happening. Empty stomach or not, Jackie would stand here all morning to let everyone get a gander at the man on her arm.

"Trooper Walsh," Margaret gushed, "we're so glad to have you with us today."

Jackie rolled her eyes toward the ceiling. Margaret was

staring at Dennis with such a wide grin it was embarrassing. As though she was personally responsible for his presence here today.

"Thank you, Mrs. Palmer. Please call me Dennis. I've meant to visit before, but this is the first Sunday I've had off in weeks."

"I'm sure you've been busy wrapping up all the loose ends of the murder case."

"And other cases besides." Jackie beamed with pride. "Detective Conner was so impressed with his handling of the murder investigation, he requested Dennis as his permanent partner."

Dennis laughed. "I don't know how impressed he was. He said he'd rather have me close by, so he can keep an eye on me."

"Congratulations!" Margaret grew serious. "I saw in the paper that charges have been filed against Richard for embezzlement. Have you worked on that, as well?"

"Yes, ma'am. Turns out Mr. Watson and a partner in the bank's loan audit department have been stealing money in increasing amounts for several years and hiding them as bad loans. Since Mrs. Farmer was a stockholder, she noticed the increase in the amount of bad debt on the bank's annual report."

A questioning look marred Margaret's forehead. "Wouldn't someone else have noticed it, too?"

"Oh, they did," Jackie said. "Dennis found out that a federal investigation has been quietly underway for months now."

Dennis nodded. "We've been working with the feds to piece everything together."

Margaret shook her head. "Poor Laura. She committed murder to protect someone who would have been caught anyway."

"Poor Laura? How can you say that? She's a vicious killer." Jackie shook her head. "I just don't understand how a Christian could commit such a terrible crime."

Margaret laid a warm hand on Jackie's arm. "She's a member of the church. Unfortunately, that doesn't necessarily mean she's a Christian, Jackie. Being a Christian is all about having a relationship with a personal Savior, not a membership card."

"That's right," Dennis agreed. "We need to pray for her. Maybe the Lord will be able to use this to bring her to her knees and draw her to Him."

Jackie looked up at Dennis, her heart full. Was she blessed to have such a guy, or what?

Clearly impressed, Margaret eyed the young man with delight. At that moment, a pair of young women came through the sanctuary door. One spoke to Jackie as they headed toward the exit.

"See you tomorrow night?"

Jackie nodded. "You bet. Seven o'clock. I'll bring the Dr Pepper." Jackie answered the question in Margaret's face as the girls disappeared through the exit. "Some of us are going over to her place to see who gets voted off this week."

"I didn't know you watched that show."

Jackie shrugged a shoulder. She still thought reality shows were stupid, but when she'd been invited to join them last week, she'd jumped at the chance. And actually, she could sort of see what the craze was about. Besides, it gave her something to talk about in the break room on Tuesdays.

"So what are you two young people up to this afternoon?" Margaret gestured toward the sunlight streaming through the glass doors. "It's a beautiful day out there."

Jackie smiled shyly at Dennis. "Dennis is taking me home to meet his parents."

His arm stole around her waist as he looked down at her. "They're going to love her."

Her face warm, Jackie returned his grin. Was that really love she saw shining in those gray eyes? *Thank You, Lord!*

"But first," Dennis said, "I'm taking her to my favorite pizza restaurant for lunch. You and Pastor Palmer are welcome to join us, if you're free."

"But only if you like my kind of pizza," Jackie added. "I'm quite particular, you know."

"Oh, really?" Margaret asked. "What toppings do you like on your pizza, Jackie?"

She turned a mischievous grin on her friend. "Mushrooms, of course!"

Dear Reader,

I love Potluck Sunday at my church. At the close of the service the entire congregation files downstairs to fill the kitchen with chatter, laughter and delicious smells. What fun to taste so many foods that I don't normally cook myself. And the desserts! Like Margaret, I always end up eating far more than I should, and enjoying every bite.

At a recent potluck, I mentioned that I had a new book coming out. Someone at the table asked what the book was about. When I announced that the victim in the story is poisoned with food from a church potluck, every fork froze midair. Eyes grew round and an uncomfortable silence descended. Finally, one man asked hesitantly, "Uh, which dish did you bring today?"

I had fun creating the characters of Heritage Community Church—and, no, I didn't model them after any real people! They make mistakes, but what Christian doesn't? We gossip. We treat others carelessly, sometimes callously. We hurt each other, and are hurt in return. What a comfort to know that we serve a God who forgives us, who justifies us by His grace and who loves us so much that He sacrificed His Son to save us.

As Jackie learns in this book, Christians aren't perfect. But occasionally we get a glimpse of His love in the actions of His children. May we all strive to exhibit His love to one another. After all, isn't that what being in God's family is all about?

Virginia Smith

QUESTIONS FOR DISCUSSION

1. As a child, Jackie felt awkward and isolated from others her age. She responded by associating primarily with older people, by whom she felt accepted. Have you found yourself in a situation where you felt isolated from your peers? How did you respond?

2. Some of the members of Heritage Community Church behave in ways that are decidedly un-Christlike. Identify some of these actions and attitudes. How should we respond when we see these behaviors in Christians with whom we are associated?

3. An often-quoted paraphrase of Proverbs 16:18 is *Pride goeth before a fall*. How does Jackie's behavior exemplify this saying at the beginning of the book? Have you ever succumbed to prideful behavior only to find yourself embarrassingly fallen?

4. Have you ever been unjustly accused of wrongdoing? How did you feel? How did you respond?

5. Detective Conner's arrogance is legendary and extremely irritating to everyone. Yet he is undoubtedly the best in his field. Does his competence excuse his sometimes rude behavior? Why or why not?

6. Dennis has a firm idea of what he wants from a permanent relationship, and he doesn't think Jackie fits the bill. What changes his mind? Have you ever been

surprised to discover that the thing you desired was packaged differently than you imagined?

7. In her zeal to discover the murderer, Jackie offends and even injures Sharon Carlson. Have you ever unjustly accused another person? How did you rectify the situation?

8. Samantha Carlson experiences a painful lesson in integrity when she inadvertently encourages her non-Christian friend to enter into dangerous and addictive behavior. Have you made similar mistakes? If you were in Margaret's position, how would you advise Samantha?

9. Esther Hodges shows her Christian love in a very practical way when she arrives at the hospital with dinner for Samantha's stressed parents. What acts of true Christian charity have you observed by people with whom you are acquainted?

10. The murderer's painful past is an all-too-real situation in today's world. But obviously not all victims of extreme poverty develop murderous tendencies. What makes the difference? How can we, as Christians, help those suffering in such needy environments?

REQUEST YOUR FREE BOOKS!
2 FREE RIVETING INSPIRATIONAL NOVELS
PLUS 2 FREE MYSTERY GIFTS

Love Inspired®
SUSPENSE

YES! Please send me 2 FREE Love Inspired® Suspense novels and my 2 FREE mystery gifts. After receiving them, if I don't wish to receive any more books, I can return the shipping statement marked "cancel." If I don't cancel, I will receive 4 brand-new novels every month and be billed just $3.99 per book in the U.S. or $4.74 per book in Canada, plus 25¢ shipping and handling per book and applicable taxes, if any*. That's a savings of 20% off the cover price! I understand that accepting the 2 free books and gifts places me under no obligation to buy anything. I can always return a shipment and cancel at any time. Even if I never buy another book from Steeple Hill, the two free books and gifts are mine to keep forever.

123 IDN EL5H   323 IDN ELQH

Name	(PLEASE PRINT)	
Address		Apt. #
City	State/Prov.	Zip/Postal Code

Signature (if under 18, a parent or guardian must sign)

Order online at www.LoveInspiredSuspense.com

Or mail to Steeple Hill Reader Service™:

IN U.S.A.: P.O. Box 1867, Buffalo, NY 14240-1867
IN CANADA: P.O. Box 609, Fort Erie, Ontario L2A 5X3

Not valid to current Love Inspired Suspense subscribers.

Want to try two free books from another series?
Call 1-800-873-8635 or visit www.morefreebooks.com

* Terms and prices subject to change without notice. NY residents add applicable sales tax. Canadian residents will be charged applicable provincial taxes and GST. This offer is limited to one order per household. All orders subject to approval. Credit or debit balances in a customer's account(s) may be offset by any other outstanding balance owed by or to the customer. Please allow 4 to 6 weeks for delivery.

Your Privacy: Steeple Hill is committed to protecting your privacy. Our Privacy Policy is available online at www.eHarlequin.com or upon request from the Reader Service. From time to time we make our lists of customers available to reputable firms who may have a product or service of interest to you. If you would prefer we not share your name and address, please check here. ☐

LISUS07

Love Inspired

Celebrate Love Inspired's 10th anniversary with top authors and great stories all year long!

A Mommy in Mind
by Arlene Jones

A Tiny Blessings Tale

Reporter Lori Sumner's adoption of a little girl was nearly complete when the baby's teenage mother changed her mind. And even if it meant being pitted against handsome attorney Ramon Estes, Lori was determined to fight for her child!

Steeple Hill®

Available September wherever you buy books.

Love Inspired®
SUSPENSE

TITLES AVAILABLE NEXT MONTH

Don't miss these four stories in September